Paradise Revisited

By

Shane Joseph

Paradise Revisited
Copyright © 2013 Shane Joseph
All rights reserved
Published by Blue Denim Press Inc.
First Edition
ISBN 978-0-9881478-8-1

No part of this book may be used or reproduced in any manner whatsoever without written permission, except in the case of brief quotations embodied in critical articles or reviews.

This is a work of fiction. Resemblances to persons living or dead are unintended and purely co-incidental.

The story "Nombera Eka" was previously published in ***Forever Travels*** (Mandinam Press) in 2010, and the story "Uphill or Down?" was previously published in ***Abandoned Towers*** magazine in 2010.

Cover Design—Joanna Joseph/Typeset in Cambria and Garamond

Library and Archives Canada Cataloguing in Publication

Joseph, Shane, 1955-, author
        Paradise revisited / Shane Joseph. -- First edition.

Issued in print and electronic formats.
ISBN 978-0-9881478-8-1 (pbk.).--ISBN 978-0-9881478-9-8 (epub).--
ISBN 978-1-927882-00-9 (kindle)

        I. Title.

PS8619.O846P37 2013   C813'.6   C2013-904464-7   C2013-904465-5

To Sarah

Other books by Shane Joseph

<u>Novels</u>

Redemption in Paradise
After the Flood
The Ulysses Man

<u>Short Stories</u>

Fringe Dwellers

Contents

Nombera Eka (Number One)

Bandu sits on the terrace of the hotel on the beach at Mt. Lavinia and sips a Coke. The sun is turning hot and soon the tourists will be out. A Scandinavian woman is already sprawled on a deckchair, her body glistening with suntan lotion. Bandu surveys her: blonde hair, eyes behind orange sunglasses, a flimsy bikini stretched to bursting, pubic hair threatening to emerge from all corners of her G-string, body yielding to the sun as if to a lover.

The woman removes the bikini top and her white breasts flop out and level against the rest of her tanned skin; nudism is against the law but tourists are brazen and no one objects. These are the late '70s and casual sex is de rigueur; the woman looks like she is putting herself out like bait for stalking gigolos who roam freely through the hotel. She suddenly sickens Bandu and he turns his gaze away, only to encounter the waiter eyeing him and his empty Coke glass.

The waiter, in his early twenties and a few years older than Bandu, is one of his own kind. He must have studied and made it through hotel school to land this job; and his parents must be proud of their son, who, after all those years of hard work and earning a diploma, is serving drinks to blue-collar Europeans that choose Sri Lanka for a vacation. Bandu glares at his fellow countryman.

"Yes?"

"Is there anything else you want?" The waiter speaks in Sinhala, and is not hiding his contempt. Bandu laughs; serving a fellow countryman, and a tout at that, had not been on the waiter's curriculum at hotel school.

"What?" Bandu barks, his eyes narrowing in cruel delight as he remembers his last complaint to the food and beverage manager about the poor service. "Do you want me to speak to Mr. Perera about your attitude?"

The waiter gulps. "Is there anything else you want—sir?"

Bandu laughs louder. "Bring me another Coca Cola."

"Yes sir."

On the street one of these days, out of uniform, the waiter will get even by pulling in neighbourhood thugs to do the work for him, Bandu is sure of that. But right now that doesn't matter, Bandu is a guest and companion of a foreign tourist, and the waiter is there to serve. Bandu is *Nombera Eka* or *Numero Uno* as his Italian tourist clients would say.

Bandu glances at the used newspaper spread carelessly on the table before him. More bad news: *Tamils Arming in the North*. Why do they leave these banners of doom for tourists to read? He crumples the newspaper and tosses it into a nearby trash can.

Hoffman comes out on the terrace and smiles sadly when he sees Bandu. He makes his way over.

"Ach, Bandu—so it is my last day." Hoffman sits down.

Bandu switches on his practised smile. He holds his hand out and Hoffman takes it greedily, fondling. The German's knee touches Bandu's under the table, rubs and stays pressed.

"I hope you have had good holiday, Kurt." By now, they are even familiar with each other's broken English.

***

Kurt Hoffman, a balding man of 45, with missing teeth and bad breath. Bandu had met him two weeks ago when a tourist charter arrived at the hotel. It was easy to spot his type in the group: while the rest were couples, and the men who came without women had other male company, Hoffman was alone, hugging his shoulder bag and his garland of flowers, looking nervously at the male receptionist at the front desk.

Bandu was hanging around at the entrance at the time, chatting with the drivers at the taxi stand.

"Like to buy some devil masks, sir?" Bandu had asked, hoping Hoffman would understand English; most European tourists did, unless they were Russians.

"Ja," replied Hoffman, his eyes holding Bandu's. He took Bandu's proffered hand in his moist grip and exhaled; then he sighed. Their intentions connected immediately.

Bandu took Hoffman to a curio shop by the beach that evening. By arrangement, the owner paid Bandu a commission for sales from tourists introduced to the shop. Bandu also used a room at the back of the establishment to sleep the nights he was in Mt. Lavinia. Hoffman was pleased with the deals and the selection; they made the prices at the hotel's official tourist shop look like a rip-off.

Later, they had drinks on the terrace and watched the fiery sun sink below the horizon bathing them in a red glow. Bandu paid the bill. Hoffman started talking. He said that he worked in a diamond cutting factory in Munich, was single, and this was his first trip out to Asia.

"I can show you lots of nice places, Herr Hoffman. You like beach? Maybe you like to go Kandy or Anuradhapura? Or maybe, you like to buy some gem stones, ja?"

"Ja, ja…I would like very much to see…ah…all."

Hoffman had one problem however: all the places Bandu had mentioned were on the itinerary of the tour charter he was attached to.

"No problem," Bandu countered. "We can leave early, before Guide comes. Leave message at the reception." He was scared of the resident German guide. She was a muscular woman in her late thirties who detested local parasites that spirited away her tourists.

When they parted that night, Bandu shook hands with Hoffman once more and let his hand linger in the German's for a while. "Tomorrow morning, I meet you at eight o'clock. We go to Kandy, ha?"

They rented a car the next morning, which Hoffman paid for. The German loved Kandy—very few didn't. Bandu took his client to the Temple of the Tooth and the adjoining museum; later they walked around the lake. Bandu exercised his flair for dramatics by going into vivid descriptions of Kandyan kings, the wars with the British, the tooth relic reputed to be from the Buddha Himself. He'd never retained much from school, let alone history, and most of his stories were from movies he had seen, but Hoffman was enthralled with the graphic descriptions of bloodletting, treachery and intrigue in the Kandyan kingdom.

They got two single rooms at a guest house, but that night Bandu went into Hoffman's room. The German was tired after the day's travel and cultural absorption, and was slightly drunk. Bandu observed the half empty bottle of Schnapps on the table.

"I like you Bandu. I very much like you. Come here to me."

Bandu slept with Hoffman that night. The German was no different from the older boys in school; except where they had used force and threats, Hoffman cried and kept mumbling in his language. Afterwards, Hoffman held Bandu pressed against his breast and snored, his foul smelling breath keeping Bandu awake for most of the night.

They toured everywhere after that: going to the ancient kingdoms of Pollonaruwa and Anuradhapura, up northeast to the natural harbour of Trincomalee, down the east coast and up through Galle to the beach at Bentota. The German bought souvenirs from all the shops that Bandu took him to. In Ratnapura, the country's official gem capital, Hoffman bought emeralds and sapphires. "These stones have much value in my country," he said, proud of his purchase. Bandu realized that Hoffman had a lot of money on him; the gems were worth fifty thousand rupees, at least.

"In Germany, I work a lot of over hours, ja…how do you say…overtime?"

"Why do you work so hard?"

"Because there is nothing to do when I come home, except to look at the television."

In Bentota, they took long walks by the sea. Hoffman could not swim, so they sat on the beach until sunset passed and sand flies drove them indoors.

"Do you live with your family, Bandu?"

Bandu dreaded this question, but eventually all tourists got around to it. "No," he replied.

"My family—they are all dead. Two sisters, a brother, my father and mother—all dead. The big war, you know."

I wish mine were dead too. Mine live to disgrace me.

"I like to visit your family, Bandu. Please take me. Tomorrow, we go back, so maybe we have the time?"

"My family live far away. Is not possible."

"But you must!" Hoffman was pleading, his eyes were moist and the grip on Bandu's was urgent. "You promise?"

"All right. Maybe tomorrow." It wouldn't make any difference, Bandu thought. Besides he had to give his mother some money.

They checked out of the hotel the next morning; Hoffman paid the bill and had covered most of the expenses on this personalized tour. For his part, Bandu had collected fat commissions along the way, unknown to his client. They reached Mt. Lavinia in the afternoon. Hoffman returned the rental car and dropped off his bag at the hotel. They took the bus to Maharagama, a few miles away.

Magilin, Bandu's mother, lived in a tenement annex with her present live-in boyfriend Jamis. She was in her early forties, the vivacious looks fading and her frame turning squat; she had been having words with Jamis, ten years her junior, about his irregular hours in the house in recent times. Bandu knew of their rows and Jamis's heavy drinking. He pitied his mother and despised her at the same time; she always attracted losers.

Magilin's eyes opened wide when Bandu arrived with Hoffman. The annex had a trellised verandah and two rooms; one room doubled as a living room and bedroom, and the other was the kitchen. The furniture inside was broken and the curtains bore sooty trails. The German stood inside the narrow confines until Magilin pushed off a pile of saris, brassieres and underskirts to reveal a rattan chair that could take his bulk. Hoffman sat tentatively, looking around him and smiling whenever he caught Magilin looking askance at him.

Magilin could not speak English but did everything possible to make her guest feel welcome, plying him with oil cakes and crème biscuits that she dug out of various corners of her kitchen. She put the kettle to boil. With Bandu as translator, she asked Hoffman about Germany. Her guest was eager to comply, with long descriptions of the material goods available in the big shops in Munich, of the castles on the Rhine, and of the discipline and hard work of his countrymen.

Magilin became nervous when Hoffman finally rose to use the toilet. Hygiene facilities were shared with other residents at the communal lavatories and taps at the end of the garden. The latrines were squatters that smelt of urine. Magilin rushed to the taps to fill a basin with water and place it inside the lavatory, bowing and saying "please, please" to Hoffman who tiptoed gingerly after her.

As his client was navigating his way inside the lavatory, Bandu slipped his mother five hundred rupees back in the kitchen. "Keep this for the house expenses."

She looked disappointed. "Things are very expensive these days."

Why don't you get your man to provide for you? Bandu had heard that Magilin now made hoppers for the cafeteria in town, and escorted the doctor's little boy to and from school to earn a few extra bucks, while Jamis drank away their earnings.

"Have you met your old friends back in Kotte?" She was busying herself with the pot of tea, ensuring that Hoffman was served from the one good cup and saucer she saved for such propitious occasions.

"No. But I know how they are doing." Bandu replied. "They are well."

"I wish you had finished your studies at St. Bernard's."

He didn't reply. This was old ground. The silence hung around them like a big hurt.

They were spared further conversation when Hoffman returned, a big grin on his face. "Ja, I think I have mastered this squatting thing, Bandu."

Magilin served tea and gestured for Hoffman to have another oil cake from the plate on the table that was now attracting flies.

"Bandu has promised to come and live with me in Germany," Hoffman said, sipping his tea and politely ignoring the confectionery.

Bandu hesitated before translating.

"Is it true, *putha?*" There was a feigned sadness in her eyes.

Not that she cares, but where would the money come from now?

Hoffman felt the awkwardness between mother and son, and quickly added. "But we will send you money and anything else you want." Although Bandu made no attempt to translate this statement, Magilin's eyes lit up at the word "money."

"We will send you money. Ja, Bandu?" Bandu noticed that Hoffman and Magilin were beginning to connect, despite their lack of a common language. Money was a powerful glue.

When they were about to leave, Hoffman pulled out his purse, "Ach so, a small gift, before we leave, ja?"

Bandu tried to restrain Hoffman but his mother's hand was already outstretched with a big "*Stuthi*" forming on her lips. That's when Bandu couldn't take it any longer and burst out, "*Balli*—you will take money only from me," and stormed out of the house, running down the lane to the bus stop. Hoffman followed after a while, apologizing for the misunderstanding. But knowing his mother, Bandu knew that she had already relieved the German of his "gift."

***

The waiter places the second glass of Coca Cola in front of Bandu and breaks his reverie. Bandu holds out a fifty rupee note and dismisses the man.

Hoffman is still holding Bandu's hand and saying, "It is so sad to go back to Germany. You will come, will you not?" He takes silence for assent and continues repeating what Bandu has heard many times already, "I will send you a ticket in one month's time. I will find you a job in a factory—do not worry. You will live with me. We will be happy."

Bandu looks over at the Scandinavian tourist's breasts roasting out on the terrace, slowly turning the colour of the rest of her body. *So much flesh out there and they have to come here to pick on us.*

"It is time to go to the airport, Kurt. I will tell porter to bring bags down. Give me key."

Bandu leaves Hoffman to make his way over to the front desk and heads for the rooms. In passing, he notices the bus at the entrance, and members of Hoffman's tour party slowly making their way over. Bandu accosts one of the porters and asks him to come up to room 304 in five minutes. Then he takes the stairs, two at a time.

He lets himself into Hoffman's room and sees the locked suitcase on the bed, exactly where it had been when he had left the room earlier. He opens the lock with a set of duplicate keys he had made at a locksmith's while they were touring together and while Hoffman was busy shopping. The packet of gems slips easily into his pocket. He closes the suitcase, locks it, and leaves it by the door. He goes over to the window, looks down into the courtyard, and sees the German resident guide pacing in front of the bus, smoking. A knock, the bedroom door opens, and the porter takes the suitcase away on his luggage trolley. Bandu follows on the man's heels.

Hoffman is waiting anxiously in the lobby. "So, I am late. The bus is going now." He pauses; there are tears in his eyes. He embraces Bandu and kisses him. "But you will come to Germany, ja?"

"Ja."

The German resident guide is bellowing to Hoffman to get on board.

"Kurt, I will give key to reception for you. Now go soon."

"Ja. Many thanks. And…and…*auf wiedersehen!*"

The bus pulls away with Hoffman madly scrambling for a seat, peering through the window and waving, all at the same time.

Bandu walks out of the hotel and gets into a taxi, giving instructions to be taken to the curio shop along the beach. Tomorrow he will go down to Hikkaduwa, rest for a few days, and surf out on the reef. Maybe, next week he will pick up another tourist. He thinks about Hoffman and feels only revulsion. The German had been more sincere than the rest. In the hotel room, a little while ago, Bandu was surprised at not having that feeling of indecision when relieving the man of his valuables—a feeling that had been strong two years ago when he first got into this business.

Perhaps, one day, when he has saved enough tourist dollars, he too will go abroad, with one of those kind tourists who will pay for his room and board and shower him with gifts and help him lead the good life in exchange for feasting on his body at night. He will have no option, now that there are strong rumours that the Tamils are going to start an insurrection in the North.

He grins. He is a survivor. Looking after Number One is all that matters despite the shit going on in this place. And in Bandu's world, he is *Nombera Eka.*

Rebels of Lost Causes

The first time I met Sena, I recognized him as a shanty dweller from the other side of the paddy field. We rarely went over there other than when flying kites during the day. After sunset, the men—subsistence farmers, rickshaw coolies, bullock cart drivers and casual labourers—returned drunk to their cadjan-roofed shanties. Their women chewed betel and spat red streams into the sand outside the shacks while huddling over scraps of food cooking on wood-fuelled open-air fireplaces. They seemed afraid to go indoors to be ravaged by the men. Sex was the only entertainment inside those sooty candlelit hovels, further dulled by the effects of *kassippu* and toddy. Yells of lust and pain echoed across the paddies on clear nights when the mosquitoes weren't hissing and the wind blew in from the fields.

By contrast, our burgeoning housing estate was an oasis of peace and affluence in what had once been a rural community. Available land in the city of Colombo was running out, and so my father had decided to move back to his childhood home in Kotte, to the suburbs, at the dawn of the '70s. My grandfather had left Dad a piece of land that he built our house on. The area had received a boost 10 years later when the federal parliament moved out of Colombo into Kotte. Bank and Mercantile executives, the nouveau-riche who had made it in the new export industries, and returning petro-dollar workers from the Middle East were pouring their wealth into new brick houses with all the modern conveniences of running water, electricity, telephones and TV, while squeezing the rural folk into the margins of shanty-towns. Resentment by the locals hovered under the surface, but it was rarely expressed in those days.

One day, a huge fire broke out in the shanty town and its inmates ran out frantically; children screaming, women wailing, as meagre possessions were tossed out of cinder box houses that were flaming like overlarge kilns. Black smoke swirled over the paddy fields sending crows squawking into the heavens.

Our housing estate's denizens hunkered down. Opening our doors to these folk was to invite trouble—after all, they were riff-raff, and good middle-class people did not associate with them!

The fire brigade never arrived. A police jeep came by only the following day, and an inspector, aided by two constables, disembarked to walk amidst the smoking ruins and write his report. The few people who returned to their shacks began piling up whatever had been salvaged and the bolder ones had already started to rebuild their destroyed homes. They ignored the cops, as if handouts and help were things that they never expected in their lives. Shanty towns made their own rules and outsiders were not invited.

***

Sena was my age, sixteen, but a good head shorter and fifty pounds lighter; he was almost emaciated. A pencil moustache struggled to grow on his monkey-like face and he wore shorts, out of which shot ekel-thin legs. A nylon shirt with multiple sweat stains under the arms was his only other piece of visible clothing. His bare feet were coated in grime, and calloused. He showed up at our front door, two months after the fire.

"I want a job." he said in Sinhala.

"We don't have one." I was heading out for cricket practice at the school grounds and I did not want to be late.

When he grinned, his betel scarred teeth were uneven and crowded inside his mouth. "Tell your mummy, I cook and clean and cut grass and go to market and break coconuts. I good butler." He had switched to patois English, and there was a glint in his eye.

"Butler? What the heck are you talking about? This is not a Wodehouse novel." Then I realized that this guy would have no clue about P.G. Wodehouse, a colonial staple we city kids had been weaned on.

"Ah, Jeeves, *mahattaya?* Yes, I know. My father told. You tell your Daddy and Mummy that I am Somapala's son. Somapala look after your Daddy when he small."

I kept him standing at the door and went to fetch Mum. Dad was still at work.

My mother was harried in those days, as we had lost our last servant, and my grandmother was slipping into her dotage and giving Mum a lot of grief.

"Somapala's son? You look like his grandson?" Mum said, sniffing suspiciously and eyeing the newcomer.

Sena grinned impishly. "Somapala very fertile, *missie*—having eight children now. I'm last. Oldest is forty."

"Can you clean bedpans, wash clothes, pots and pans, and look after an old lady for a few hours a day?"

"Anything, *missie.* Simple to do. Can even cook hot chicken curry."

Mum's eyes widened. "I have to ask my husband. But come in." She virtually dragged him inside. Mum made him sit in the kitchen until Dad returned home so she could verify his credentials—no sense in losing a hot prospect for domestic servant-dom.

***

Sena took up residence with us and quickly proved his capabilities. He did all the things he boasted he could do, and more. Initially, he was up at six and did not stop working until late in the evenings. He even wheeled Grandma around the garden in the afternoons, and cursed her under his breath when she spat all over the place, "What this *Loku Nona* is doing? Spitting like snail, no?" Grandma would growl at him through hooded eyes, and then break into tears. Mum shouted, "No cheek here, Sena. My mother is very fragile."

"Like porcelain, no *missie?* If shake too much, will crack, no?"

Sometimes I wondered if he was being nice or was just a cheeky bastard.

Sena slept outside in a hammock tied to the jak tree in the back garden, and to him it was like a first class hotel. He drew a sarong over his bare body at night to hide from the mosquitoes. But when the monsoon rains came Mum would not have him sleeping outside and ordered him indoors.

When it came to finding a place for him to sleep, I had to forego some space. My room was the only one available now that Grandma occupied the guest room and her belongings encroached on every bit of available space in the rest of the house. Still, Mum preferred to have Grandma with us rather than sending her to a nursing home. So I slept on my single bed in one corner of the room and Sena slept on a mat in the other corner by the window; my desk was moved into the centre as the only remaining class barrier between us. He was a good companion for he fell into an exhausted asleep the moment his head met the pillow. His painfully drawn out snores resembled those of someone who was tired down to his soul.

In the months he spent with us, his frame filled out and I saw him eating monster portions of food from the kitchen after everyone else had finished dinner. He ate leftovers—mixing bread with rice, and curry with jam. He seemed always ravenously hungry and did not leave a scrap on his plate.

I asked my father, who worked in the Fort as an executive in a mercantile trading firm, who Somapala and his son were. Dad had taken a couple of shots of scotch that day and was in a magnanimously erudite mood—he normally never said much around the house.

"Somapala—he was a stray like Sena here, sent to us from the orphanage. My father took him in. He was about fifteen years older than me and he looked after us: your Uncle Sam, Aunty Cynthia and me, after our mother died when we were children. He was a good man, very caring. Never spoke much. Just did his duty."

"Sena has some of his father's good habits. He just talks too much at times," Mum said looking up from her knitting. Grandma felt cold on most days, despite our tropical humidity, and Mum was constantly making blankets that Grandma ended up peeing on.

"Yes," Dad mused. "Like his mother. She lived in the paddy field and came from a local family. Somapala fell in love with her or she snagged him, or whatever, by getting pregnant. No arranged marriage as their type is famous for. Somapala gave his notice, married her and went to live with her family. I moved to boarding school in Colombo and lost touch with them. I know they had several children. Finally Somapala left her and now lives in a temple in Kandy. She had quite a foul mouth, I remember. Wonder what became of her."

"You've kept in touch with Somapala?" I asked.

"After he'd gone to live at the temple, he discovered that we had moved back to Kotte. He sent me a Christmas card last year and I wired him back some money. Following the fire, he wrote to me and asked if I could look after his son. I did not know the family still lived in the paddy fields."

"Well, since you are a proper gentlemen, you don't mix with shanty people, Dear," Mum reminded him.

"I know. But I feel I owe Somapala more than just a gift at Christmas."

"Sena can stay, as long as he keeps his mouth shut, his head down, and he does not upset Mummy," Mum said, returning to her knitting. Just then, she looked like Grandma—stubborn and set in her thinking.

***

At nights, after washing up in the kitchen and before slinking into my room to sleep, Sena hung out in the back garden, perched on the lower branch of our mango tree, smoking a *beedi*. My mother forbade smoking in the house and even Dad had to smoke his pipe out on the porch. One night, returning from cricket practice, I wheeled my bike and padlocked it in the back shed. I saw the red flare of his foul smelling weed up on the tree.

"Make sure you are not out late," I said calling up towards him. "I need to sleep early tonight."

The flame flickered. "Boss—you hitting balls and catching. Then you are tired?"

"Don't give me your bloody cheek." I could see why this guy got into trouble. Maybe he got his cheekiness from his mother.

"Boss, Boss, please. Do not get angry with me. Your room only place for me to sleep now. Mummy not letting sleep outside."

"Who started the fire in the paddy field?"

"Police, sir. Officer not getting his cut."

"Why couldn't you go live with your father?"

"Father teaching me English all the time. Saying, without English cannot make it anywhere in this world. I tried sir—only can speak, little. Writing and reading can't. Somapala living in temple now, wants to be like Buddist monk, you know—when get old and cannot do the jig-jig, then want to become priest."

I did not know whether to laugh or commiserate. He'd certainly learned to speak like a gutter Burgher, the ones we called *lafais*. "I'm sorry to hear about your mother."

"Damn stupid woman, sir. Talking, talking, talking. Spreading gossip all over. Neighbours throwing stones, sir. After my father left, she sleeping with a man half her age. Bugger drinking *kassippu* and fucking my mother in front of all of us. I tried to kill him once."

"They would have put you in jail for that."

"What bloody jail, sir? My mother's man—he making and selling *kassippu* behind the house. Police looking other way. Why? Because they are getting free supply."

"But they burned the place down in the end?"

"Because, my mother's man cheating, sir."

"So, it is true that your mother died in the fire?"

The flame on the tree went out and a gust of *beedi* odour made me gag. Sena eased himself off the tree and landed on the ground in a crouch. "Yes, sir. She running inside to get her money under the bed. Cadjan roof falling top of her. She coming running out like *vesak* lantern, sir— fire all over body. I threw her on ground and rolled her in sand. But too late. I knew she gone. At least, no more talking, sir."

I remained frozen as he passed me, bent in his recollection. Then he paused at the kitchen door and his impishness resumed. "Come on sir—you must sleep. Too much hitting balls, no?"

***

The day that Bada's bull reversed course is etched in my mind, like so many memories of my old home. Bada was the neighbourhood farmer who operated a vegetable plot and had several cows, although no one bought his "fresh milk"— there was always a thick brown residue inside the bottles of milk he peddled from door to door. In conformance to his name, Bada was a short fat man who constantly chewed betel and spat red in all directions. Even when he talked, red spittle crept out of the corners of his mouth and dripped onto his faded white singlet that could never travel beyond his bulging gut. He also fancied himself with the ladies, even though no women in the neighbourhood gave him a second glance. To attract attention, he ran his solitary bull along our narrow lane, a short cut that connected the paddy field and his farm.

The running of Bada's bull was a perilous activity. The half-fed black creature had two chipped horns and caked dung hugging its arse, and we wondered whether it ran only when provoked or to outrun the flies that hummed around its backside in a constant halo. Whenever Bada slapped the bull hard at the entrance to our lane, the creature bucked and kicked and headed straight up the narrow pathway for the farm, and everyone and everything in its path had to get out of the way. Children playing cricket were seen grabbing bats and wickets and jumping over fences, *ayahs* ran screaming hugging babies in their arms, and teenage boys used the opportunities to embrace their girlfriends in public "for their safety." And Bada sauntered after his bull looking from side to side, for adulation, a satisfied look on his face. Most often, people stayed indoors until after Bada and the bull had returned to their abode, but the wily Bada kept altering his entrance times just to liven up the show.

The day the bull turned around, I was cramming for my final 'O' level exam on the front porch, anxiously looking forward to the holidays that were on the horizon. Sena was cutting down coconuts from the tree in our garden at the fence line. Of late, he had been seen up that tree whenever the bull ran.

"Safe place, Boss. Bloody bull can't climb trees."

That day, in addition to the kriss knife that Sena used to cut the coconuts, a catapult hung from his waist belt, along with a cloth bag with, what I later found out was, pebbles.

I pushed my books away as the farmer and his bull entered the laneway. This was always an interesting sight, a temporary distraction from my studies.

As the bull commenced its run—mercifully only old Mrs. Jayawardene's servant was outdoors, and she ran scrambling for safety—Sena loosed a shot from his catapult. It hit the bull right between the eyes, slowing the animal's lumbering charge. Two other stones struck the bull in rapid succession, one hitting it near the eye, causing the animal to emit snorts and hisses of pain. The bull came to a standstill halfway up the lane and slowly turned on its heel when a coconut launched from the tree impaled itself on one of its horns sending the animal into a mad charge in the opposite direction. Too late, Bada saw his cash cow, or bull, running headlong at him. He spun around and wobbled as fast his bow legs could carry him. The bull bumped him hard as it fled back to the safety of the paddy field. That nudge was enough to send Bada skidding into the culvert at the edge of the road where he lay moaning, cursing and shouting for help. Suddenly, all the doors and windows in the houses along our lane were full of people looking , laughing and jeering at the hapless man who was too short to get out of the hole. No one offered help. I saw Sena slide down the coconut tree and run to Bada's aid.

"Don't pull that stunt again," I heard him admonish the muddy, shivering and groaning Bada, after hauling him out. "These are respectable people living here."

Bada hurled invective upon the boy and tried to chase after him, but with a skip and a laugh, Sena was scooting up the lane for the safety of our garden, which Bada had no nerve to enter.

And strangely enough, after that day, Bada found an alternative route to take his bull home every day.

***

After an initial scolding for doing such risky things and upsetting the neighbours, Mum settled down to accepting Sena once again.

"*Missie*, don't worry, I even taking *Loku Nona* for a walk down the lane soon. We are free of these bully buggers."

Grandma's ears pricked up at the mention of a walk down the lane. She had been imprisoned in her wheel chair in the confines of our garden for over a year now—a walk down the lane was like a ticket to Hollywood.

Grandma began making plans: she unearthed her best hat from amidst mothballs and tissue paper, she selected one of the least ruined blankets that Mum had made her, and she kept counting the money in her purse. When I asked her why, she replied, "I am going to ask Sena to take me to the shops at the junction."

Mum was not happy and warned Sena not to dare follow the old lady's orders.

"But good for her, no, *missie?*" he argued. "Freedom, no?"

"If you give her 'freedom', you can also have yours and leave this place. *Loku Nona* is my responsibility." Mum stormed away to her room.

Grandma gave Sena a pleading look.

***

I was at school that day when the fracas took place, but I pieced events together from various sources, mainly the neighbours.

At about 3:30 pm (around the time Mum took her afternoon nap) an elderly woman draped in a navy blue blanket and wearing a plumed hat was seen exiting the gates of the Bernard residence, pushed by a nervous Sena. The old lady was excited and had her hand raised as if ordering the young man to push her faster.

At that propitious moment, Bada's bull rounded the corner, and, as if stepping on an un-extinguished cigarette butt, began a relentless charge towards the couple. The young man was seen to let go of the wheelchair and rush headlong at the bull, shouting "You bloody bull, I'll fuck you." The old lady was supposed to have used even more colourful language. Sena swerved just as the bull was about to gore him, and gripping one of its horns, swung himself onto the back of the creature. By pulling its neck to the right, he steered the bull away from the helpless old lady.

However, the wheelchair had started to gather momentum as it headed unaided down the lane, and when onlookers pulled their gaze away from the charging bull and its fearless rider, it was to the scream of Grandma who was being deposited into the same culvert that Bada had ended up in a few weeks earlier.

Sena jumped off the bull, smacked its rump to send it scampering off into the farm and ran back to help Grandma. A hoarse, earth-shattering, bellyful laugh was heard from the direction of the paddy field and the neighbours were sure it sounded like Bada, although the short fat man was nowhere to be seen.

By the time I got home, the worst was over: an ambulance had taken Grandma to hospital, Dad had rushed home from work, Mum was in hysterics, and Sena had vanished.

"If that rascal ever comes this way again, I'll break his head," was all Mum said, over and over again.

And Bada never brought his bull through our lane again. There was no reason to.

***

Grandma went quickly downhill after that. When she returned home from the hospital, she came back to die, she told us. Mum felt that she had let her mother down, but Grandma kept saying that her whirlwind ride down the lane, facing the bull in the eye had been the most thrilling experience in her life and there was really nothing more for her to look forward to, so it was better that she died. And she did, three weeks later.

Sena showed up outside the gates of the cemetery and fell at Mum's feet wailing like a dying goat, asking her to forgive him. The sobs that wracked him were more sincere than all those we had shed for Grandma. Completely spent by her own grief, Mum laid her hand on his shoulder and asked him to get up and not make an ass of himself in public. She did not "break his bloody head" as she had repeatedly threatened but walked back to our car with head bowed. Dad had a few words with Sena, and I even saw him slip the guy a note from his wallet.

When I neared, Sena looked like he had not slept in weeks. His nylon shirt was torn, and the pair of shorts that I had lent him had huge stains on them. His bottom lip hung in a permanent droop.

"Boss—I very sorry. *Loku Nona* wanted to go for walk. Boss, you believe me, no?" he kept following me as I made my way towards the car.

"Boss, please believe me. You are my only family now." His voice trailed into sobs and I did not look back as the car headed out of the gates of the cemetery. His weak pleas followed me. They rattled from a chest worn dry with grief, like a well giving out its last drops of muddy ooze. I held back my tears too because I had nothing to say to him, nothing to offer. These many years later, I realize that it was an opportunity lost. But we are not all built for greatness, and he was greater than me.

Seven Years Later

"Stop at the Majestic, I want to run in and get that prescription for *Ammi*," Shamini said, as I swung my scooter off the Galle Road. I liked the way she hugged me from behind on the pillion, her soft breasts pressing my back, comforting me the way a mother would, only this time it also made me horny and I couldn't wait till I got to kiss her passionately at the gates of her parent's home.

I pulled over into the parking lot. Crowds were rushing in and out of this giant superstore for victuals and other necessities, as no one knew when the next curfew would be declared. The Marxist revolutionary organization, the JVP, had reared its ugly head again by attempted assassinations of politicians, some successfully executed. The Indian Peacekeeping troops had landed in the north to fight the Tamil rebels but were causing more damage than good and there were heavy rumours that the central government would fall—it was hard to fight two wars on separate fronts. And during all this chaos, I was in love.

I watched Shamini disappear into the crush, her raven hair in a pony tail and hanging down to her waist. She was studying to be a doctor like her father: studious, sheltered, virginal, idealistic. I was a budding executive in an airline office, with access to free stand-by airline tickets, which in this cash strapped country added significant soft income to one's earnings. We airline types were ostensibly "good catches," as most mothers of eligible young women would say. I still worried whether our relationship would last—she was Sinhala Buddhist and I a Burgher Catholic. Race, class and religion played vital roles in this country—damn it, we were fighting wars in the north and the south because of it.

I leaned my bike on its foot-stand and surveyed the shoppers. Everyone hurried now: "Don't stand in one place,"

Mum had urged me. Armed policemen stopped vehicles coming into the Majestic's parking lot and held mirrors under their chasses to search for weapons or bombs. I longed for the old days when we strolled the Galle Road, popping in an out of Tamil *thosai kades* and movie houses. Now the *thosai kades* had been burned to the ground in the '83 riots five years ago and the movie houses were mostly empty for fear of bombs.

That's when I saw him. He was across the road by the Muslim sweet shop, one foot on the sidewalk and the other on the pedal of his slanted bicycle. He wore slippers, faded dark slacks and a batik tee shirt. His companion was more interesting—in her thirties, long dark hair, a sari that revealed a fleshy midriff, and a bodice that pushed her breasts out. Her eyes were kohl-lined; she was smiling and being coy. He pulled some money from his hip pocket and kept looking at her as he fingered the notes. Her eyes glistened. She shook her head once and he thumbed an extra note. She nodded and he handed the money to her. She stuffed it into her bodice and mounted side-saddle with him on the bicycle. They pushed off, wobbling at first. He looked back once to find a gap between the madly tooting cars and buses that did not respect traffic lanes; then he merged in expertly and was immediately swallowed up in billowing petrol fumes and dust.

"Let's go." Shamini was at my side and her complexion was darker than usual. "They are out of stock." She swung on to the pillion and sat rigid in her seat; her breasts were no longer in contact. I wondered if kisses by the gate were still on the cards.

"This country is at war, what do you expect? They have other priorities," I said.

"They should not be banning drugs made in India just because we asked their troops to support us. Cutting off our noses to spite our faces. All I have to look forward to after graduation is treating the sick and dying who are getting blown up every day."

"I thought that is why you wanted to go into the government sector?"

"Yes—but that was to help the rural poor with their health problems. Not to help healthy people caught in useless cross-fires."

I did not wish to say anything more. She was right. She had begun to follow in her father's footsteps, but without private practice and well-heeled patients. Her desire to be different from her father and contribute something worthwhile had made her select going into the government hospital system, which these days was strained and overflowing with war victims.

"Perhaps, your father can pull some strings to get your mother her medication?"

She sighed. "That seems to be the only recourse. I told them not to give into this influence peddling—but it seems to be the only way. I've searched ten pharmacies for her insulin."

As we headed down Buller's Road (I still couldn't remember its Sinhala equivalent—they were renaming these old colonial streets too fast), I saw the bicycle again, the woman's feet hanging dangerously off the side. As I neared to overtake I looked at the man. It was Sena, no doubt about it—a bit craggier and weathered, and that moustache had finally taken full root on him. Our gazes met for a moment before I had to look back at the road. I saw his eyes widen and his mouth open before I turned into Baudhaloka Mawatha, towards Shamini's home.

Our kissing was perfunctory. Shamini was pre-occupied.

"Will I see you tomorrow?" I asked. "Pick you up after lectures at the same time?"

She wrinkled her nose. "Exams are coming up. I have to study. And then there is practical work in the hospital."

"Giving you a ride home will not mess up your studies, no?"

She smiled, sadly. "Oh, Jamie—I don't know what's happening these days. I don't know about our future anymore."

"We've known each other for six months," I reminded her. "I thought we were only getting stronger. Your parents like me—right? And mine love you."

It was true, Mum adored Shamini the first day she had come home—for my birthday. She had been dressed in a Kandyan sari with a gold chain and earrings. And Shamini's parents had been polite, reserved and curious when I had visited for her last university batch mates' party. But they were inscrutable. Mrs. Gunewardene had been fussing about with the refreshments and Dr. Gunewardene, who never made eye contact with any of the guests, had talked about the political situation with a group of us but never got into any personal details with me. He had grouped me as one of Shamini's "friends"—relegated to that mass of nameless faces about whom he did not have to bother, for we would all marry other people, or go abroad, and leave him and his family to continue pursuing their careers and social positions.

Now, outside the large wrought iron gates of the Gunawardene residence, Shamini's frown increased. When she got this way, she did not look attractive any more. She looked like one of those people in the shops trying to struggle through the daily grunge of life. Romance, dream building, fun—all that appeared to be trivialities that were of no consequence. I wondered if she too viewed me now as just another average guy trying to hustle a living, instead of the dashing travel executive who had swept her off her feet at our first meeting.

"Yes, *Ammi* and *Thathi* do." She wrung her hands, looking about her. "But there are so many obstacles ahead of us—you know…" She left the obvious unspoken. When she looked back at me there were tears in her eyes. "Do you think we have a future together?"

"Now, there you go with all that marriage stuff again. We've only known each other six months."

"*Ammi* says that by then a couple should be committed. One of these days my parents are going to ask me about you and your intentions again."

"You don't want to be categorized as a loose woman. Is that it?"

She pulled herself up and gave me her steely gaze, the one she normally reserved for cheeky shop vendors and bus conductors. "James—you have no idea. Marriage is the last thing on my mind. There are so many things to fix in this country. And we all have to do our part."

I watched her walk down the U shaped gravel driveway to the high-porched, Roman colonnaded entrance of the sprawling colonial house. Giant banyan and flamboyant trees surrounded the two-storey structure. I felt that she was entering a palace that I could never be worthy of inhabiting. Many of the houses in this area of the city had been converted to embassies, foreign agencies or NGO offices, but the Gunawardenes retained their family home handed down through several generations. A gardener moved lazily under the hot sun, watering the close-cropped lawn that ran up to flower beds, with red roses, pink hibiscus and multi hued hydrangea ringing its perimeter.

The inside of the house was cavernous: seven bedrooms, three of which were used as consulting rooms for Dr. Gunawardene's private practice, a swimming pool in the back yard, a three-car garage and a large outside cook-house for the domestics to work and live in.

A tinkling bicycle bell behind me disturbed my day-dreaming.

"Hello, Boss. How you?" I did not have to turn around to recognize his voice.

Sena was astride his bicycle, leaning one foot on the ground, a wide smile on his face. His female companion was missing.

"You have girlfriend now, Boss?"

"What happened to yours?"

"I left her at top of road, sir. I wanted to talk privately."

"That's not a very nice thing to do."

"She prostitute. Don't even know if she will wait. Maybe another man come and take her."

I felt a mixture of disgust and pity. "Then you'd better get back quickly."

"No sir—she not important. Plenty of time for jig-jig." He winked and fished out a polythene bag from inside his shirt. He extracted a small black booklet and waved it at me. "Sir, now I got passport."

"Congratulations."

"Sir, I hear you are now big man in airline business."

I remained silent.

"Sir—I have to make important decision. Join JVP or bugger off from here. Can you get me job in Middle East? Dubai, Saudi, Oman—I will go anywhere sir."

"What are you up to these days?"

"Not much sir—working in a club. Night shift. Waiter. Very hard to make living, sir."

"It's very hard for everyone. The cost of living is killing us."

"Yes sir, curfews and all. When I go home after work, police always catching and checking if JVP. One day I will disappear sir, and no one will know. That's why I must join the 'boys' or leave country."

He was right. Young men—mainly the innocent ones, not the Marxist cadres—of his age and disposition, were being rounded up for "questioning," and few were returning to their families.

"Get me a photocopy of your passport. I'll see what I can do." I wheeled my bike back onto the road.

"Oh, wait sir, I have photocopy." From the folds of the polythene bag he pulled some soiled papers.

I took the documents and stuffed them into my windbreaker. I tightened my helmet and glanced once more in the direction of Shamini's house; curtains fluttered—that would be Mrs. Gunewardene the Snoop, who always checked whenever I dropped off her daughter at the gate and got amorous. Now she would have some fuel for her fire—the boyfriend was conversing with an ordinary labourer type, and a would-be JVP cadre to boot.

"Okay—I have to go," I said. I fished out a business card. "Come and see me in a week."

***

At breakfast the following morning, after Dad had left for work, Mum engaged me in small talk that I knew had an agenda.

After some cursory chat about the difficulty she was having getting her groceries because of the sudden clamping down of curfews, she got to the point. "That girl Shamini—are you still keen on her?"

"If there was not so much concern by everyone, I might not be. Yes, we are still seeing each other."

"I wish there were more Burgher girls around for you. Most of them have now gone abroad. You have only these Sinhala girls to go out with."

"What's wrong with Sinhala girls?"

"Well, you know, caste and class and all that comes into play, no child? Love marriages—they don't believe in that sort of thing. Too European for them. And now they are running the show with their Sinhala Buddhist posturing. Even the Tamils have become second class citizens after all the *hartals* and riots we've seen."

"You liked Shamini, especially when she came home for my birthday. In fact, you were falling all over her."

"Don't get me wrong, son. She is an outstanding girl—very pretty and very intelligent. And very determined. But at the same time I don't think she will be the right one for you." There was a look of futility on her face.

I rose and straightened my tie. "So you think that I am not good enough for her, is that it?"

She came around the table and straightened my tie a bit more. Then she cradled my face in her hands and her eyes were red rimmed. "This is new for your father and me—this mixing of the races. We Burghers married among ourselves, with only a few exceptions."

"Our European ancestors didn't seem to care much about mixing. Why do we have black Burghers and white Burghers and every shade in-between? And who the heck is talking marriage here, Mum?"

"Oh, but it will come up, sooner or later. That girl is of marriageable age, she is finishing her studies. Soon her parents will want her to settle down."

"Oh, God—settle down! You guys want us to settle down before we can get up and run a bit. I have to go to work. I am getting late."

At the doorway, just to get in an even punch, I said. "I met Sena yesterday."

She bristled at the mention of his name. "Now that is a *rastiadu* fellow if ever there was a rascal."

"And I am going to help him get a job in the Middle East. I have contacts."

She hung her head and sighed. "Better send the fellow off. Otherwise they are the ones joining this JVP and wanting equality."

"At least, the JVP is trying to level the playing field, Mum. Unlike you, holding onto your rung between the *rastiadus* and the Sinhala ruling classes such as the Gunewardenes, always content to be in your place in a lopsided social order, where 90 percent scratch for an existence." With that, I gave her a cold peck on the cheek and made my exit.

***

I went to see my favourite travel agent, Farook, that afternoon. Farook had made his money in the underground economy of the Socialist regime in the seventies when foreign exchange purchases had been banned. The rumour was that he had run a very profitable black market operation in foreign currencies, helping many students go abroad for their studies; those same students were helping fuel the civil war up north by providing ample and generous funding from places as distant as London, New York and Toronto. Farook had also opened a foreign employment service and shipped droves of housemaids and construction workers to the Middle East. I was his point person to get him seats on our erratic flight schedule that was either running full or not operating due to security concerns. When I went to see him that day, he was sucking a lollypop, his greased hair falling in a cock's comb over his pocked forehead. The man was out of proportion—small head and a broadening torso, with his maximum girth occurring around his arse and belly, before tapering off again—somewhat like the Michelin Man.

"Ah, Jamie my friend. Come, come. I have good news. I have a contract for some new airline jobs. Qatar, Oman, they are all opening airlines. You have any friends in the trade you can send to me?"

"I'll think about it. How are the labourer jobs?"

"Plenty, *Baba*—always needing them, no? These days, everybody is rushing to leave or get the necklace in the junction, no!" He grinned and his gold fillings glinted under the fluorescent lights. The "necklace in the junction" was no joke: its recipients were left charred with molten rubber blackening their corpses—testaments as traitors to either the government or the JVP. I wondered if the necklace operators contracted their work to both sides.

"I've got a young man. I need you to get him out. He is a good worker." I gave him the photocopy of Sena's passport.

Farook wrinkled his nose. "How's his health?"

"He seemed okay to me."

"No cough or wheeze."

"Not that I can tell."

After scrutinizing me for any tell-tale signs (as if it was I who had the consumption) he shrugged. "Okay—when do you want to send him? I have two shipments going; one next week and the other in three weeks."

"In three weeks. I am seeing him next week. He'll be happy to receive the news."

Farook fished in his drawer and pulled out some cyclostyled papers—the usual drill handed out to labourers. I knew it by heart: the employment contract would run for one year, passport to be surrendered to the employer on the other side, one month vacation after a year, option to extend employment for another two years on an annual basis, salary approx ten times what one could earn in Sri Lanka plus board and medical, no tax, no booze and don't fuck-up, or you will be on the next flight home. Guys like Sena would feel that they were dying and going to heaven with their new-found income, until they arrived at their destination. "Heaven" was working outdoors in temperatures that hit fifty degrees Celcius in high humidity; board was a camp tent with twenty other workers; food was mainly *chappatis* and chicken curry; illicit booze—if smuggled in—was an eau de cologne derivative called *Siddiqie* (friend!); and the only glimpse of female flesh was a bare ankle extended when a fully robed woman disembarked from a tinted limousine. Masturbation had become an art form in "heaven."

"Where are you sending him?" I asked.

Farook looked at his various lists. "I keep a few reserved spaces to Saudi. Riyadh—that's okay?"

"I guess beggars can't be choosers. Thanks!"
Sena kissed my feet when I gave him the news, right there in my office. The secretaries and counter clerks grinned and taunted me afterwards.

"*Ayyo*, sir, God will bless, sir. Your mother and father and children—all will be blessed, sir."

I picked him up off the floor. There was no use telling him that I got a ten percent commission on all "referrals" I sent Farook. That I also received a cut on the air fare costs the employer paid our airline. I was not doing this out of complete altruism. I had not met a selfless person in this country in my life.

Then he lowered his voice to a whisper. "Sir, can I talk to you outside, please. Something new to tell you."

A sense of unease developing in me, I followed him out of the office.

Out on the dusty street, he bowed to kiss my feet again and I pulled him up, embarrassed and annoyed this time.

"What the hell is going on, man? Enough is enough. I got you a job. You haven't died and gone to Nirvana yet. And it's going to be tough bloody work in Saudi Arabia. You may not thank me when you get there."

"Sir, sir, please understand. I do *not* want to go."

"What!"

"Boss, I am so happy you did this for me. I thought your family had abandoned me. Now I know you did not."

"Then what's up? You've got chicken feet?"

"No, Boss. I am joining the 'boys.'"

"Now, that's the sickest thing I have heard."

"Sir, people like me always poor. If go to Saudi Arabia and come back, after two years, money all gone. Then just like this again, sir. Most of the boys have gone and come, still the same. We need change. Too many rich people sucking off us. Your family is the only good family among rich people."

I could see where he had led me. This whole caper had been to assuage his soul.

"All right then, get the fuck out of here. Go to your 'boys.' You've wasted my time and other people's money processing these papers." That was not quite true: Farook would simply cut his name out and add another of the teeming thousands waiting for a plane out, and probably collect a "consulting fee" as well. Farook waived his fees for my clients. But I was still annoyed with Sena for shrugging off this gift.

Again, that hurt feeling descended on his countenance, the one I had seen at the cemetery the day Grandma was buried. He had let me down and I could see that he was aching inside. I let him ache. I turned on my heel and went back into the office, leaving him floundering outside on the street.

***

The next year was rough for the country and for my beleaguered relationship with Shamini. The universities shut down (again) as the Marxist insurrection ramped up. Shamini decided to use the down time and do her practicals at the government hospital. "No sense in being idle at home and worrying. Better to just get on with it," was her response.

Dad got very upset when his company, which was in the import-export business with India, had one of its delivery trucks hijacked on the Kandy road. The driver was found a day later, tied and dead in a ditch, a smouldering "necklace" around his neck, still smelling of burnt flesh and rubber. The truck and its contents had disappeared and were never found. My father hired Martin Gadoldeniya, a retired police officer, who was now running a growing private security company with branches in many parts of the country, to safeguard the company assets.

Two days following the truck incident, I went to pick up Shamini after her hospital shift. She normally stood outside the gates waiting for me, in her white gown with stethoscope hanging out of a pocket; her attire seemed to give her immunity from other mortals in her vicinity. That day she was missing.

I parked my bike and walked inside the hospital. I counted six ambulances in the driveway outside the Emergency, their lights still whizzing, and two military vehicles with fully armed soldiers. I spoke to the clerk on duty, who was familiar with me by now, as I was often seen picking up Shamini. He waved me inside with a caution. "Some injured soldiers were brought in—everyone is tense. Proceed slowly."

The Emergency ward was full of patients, soldiers, orderlies, doctors and nurses and I couldn't figure out what was going on; normal routines seemed to have been thrown out of kilter. Patients sat on stretchers or on mats out in the hallway, on both sides, leaving a narrow lane for others to walk through. I caught glimpses of open wounds, blood-soaked bandages, dazed looks. A child was sobbing and no parent was in sight, and the shouting of orders from those in charge was high pitched.

I headed for the Operating Room to see how far I could get. Just as I neared, its wide doors swung open and Shamini and two young doctors charged out, discussing something; they dispersed in separate directions down the hallways that radiated from the OR area. I followed Shamini; she was consulting a beeper and her usually starched white coat was stained with blood.

"Sham—slow down, it's me."

She turned around, saw me, and kept walking. "I can't go home just now. I have to operate on a patient."

"You? You're barely out of medical school!"

She swung around to face me. The strain on her face was evident. I wanted to hold her. Cradle her and take her away from this place. Something in her determined look made me hold back. "There are no available doctors. This soldier needs his leg amputated. I have to do it."

"Shall I wait for you?"

"Go home, Jamie. I don't know when I will get off duty. I will call *Thathi* later and he can pick me up. Sorry, there was no time to phone." Then she had turned on her heel and was taking the stairs two at a time.

For the next two weeks, I barely saw her, and decided not to pick her up after her shift any more as her off-duty times were so erratic. She would call me at night sometimes and cry on the phone. Crying was a relief. It was not the strain of work as much as the pain of her patients that she seemed to be unloading. There was very little strength I could offer her. I inhabited a different world.

***

The second revolution in the south of the country, the part in which we lived, hit home one evening when a band of boys in their late teens arrived at our front door. I recognized some of them from the shanty town in the paddy field. Dad opened the door to enquire.

"Put the lights off," the guy in the lead ordered in Sinhala, a cocky smile on his face. The others peered into the house, observing objects and memorabilia that they would never earn or acquire in their impoverished lives.

"Why do we have to do that?" Dad asked, puffing his chest, like he was talking to a bunch of clerks at the office.

"Because it is time to protest."

"We have nothing to protest," Dad said, ready to slam the door when two guys stepped onto the veranda and pushed him indoors.

I grabbed my cricket bat that I had been keeping near the front door in anticipation of incidents like this that we had been hearing about with increased frequency. I stepped in front of Dad, and advanced, trembling, angry and scared all at once.

"Don't you bastards lay a hand on my father. Get out of here. We are not part of your revolution."

The cheeky fellow leaped forward and I jabbed him in the chest with my bat. He was such a lightweight that he went sprawling into the arms of his compatriots.

I saw the two guys who had stepped onto the veranda make their move, and I swung—a square cut for the chap on my right and my best hook for his partner on my left. I got them both on the chest and they staggered off the veranda into the crush of their buddies. Blood pounded in my ears and the smell of victory was overpowering, and like Samson with his trusty ass's jawbone, I hurled myself into the disarrayed gang of youth, swinging wildly with my bat, while Mum screamed from behind. I made a few contacts, bones snapped, and shouts of "*Ayyo*," and "*Budhu Ammo*" emanated before the revolutionaries retreated outside our gate. I chased after them, roaring at the top of my voice, slightly hysterical by now.

That was when I heard a rip and a numbness shot up my arm. I swung around, and one fellow—he must have been hiding by the gate post—was behind me with a rusty knife, and it had blood on it. I raised my bat to crush his head but my right hand was rapidly losing sensation. It was too late to switch hands with the bat so I kicked, and given my size relative to him, connected him in the balls as his knife sailed past my chest by inches. Then I had the bat in my left hand and swung at him, whacking him on the arse repeatedly until he collapsed on the ground, one hand raised, pleading for clemency.

"Jamie—you are hurt." Mum rushed outside the gate.

"Stay away," I ordered her. I faced the gang that had regrouped down the lane and was advancing slowly.

I raised the bat over their fallen colleague's head. He had not fully recovered his wits, still sucking for breath and groaning from my crushing kick. "I will bash this bastard's head in if you take one more step forward." A sinking sensation began to overtake me, I was feeling light headed and suddenly the forces in front of me were overwhelming. I was going to be run over. But not before I took this bastard in front of me, I said to myself. *I will have my kill and they can then have theirs.*

I drew in my breath to stay focussed and I couldn't recall how long we stayed frozen in that frame. Lights—the neighbours down the lane must have complied with these guys' demands and switched theirs off—were coming on in the houses on all sides. Scared faces stared out of windows.

Then Dad stepped between me and the thugs. "If you fellows are here for another two minutes, you can spend the night in jail. I have telephoned Inspector Jayawardene, and one of his patrols is at the top of the main road right now, heading this way."

The gang faded quickly, grabbing the helpless guy at my feet, who was still hunched over, and dragging him away into the shadows.

Mum was by me staunching my blood with the tail of her housecoat. I had to sit down at that point, overcome by the crash of adrenaline. The blood had dripped over my pants. A dull pain was starting to take over my right side and it intensified as I moved.

Dad was shaking his head at the road. "I hope those coppers don't take hours to get here."

The neighbours helped me inside the house, and Dr. Perera, who lived at the bottom of the road, cleaned and bandaged my wound: a gash running from my arm down to my wrist, missing my arteries by millimetres. "We have to get you to the hospital. You will need stitches and an anti-tetanus injection."

After the police arrived (an hour later, for my father had been bluffing), Dad drove me to the hospital with Mum in the back seat.

"You think the house is safe?" Mum asked. She was sobbing intermittently.

"It's safe for tonight," Dad replied as he tooted his horn and overtook a belching bus. "They will be licking their wounds for the next couple of days. But not for long. I am going to call in Gadoldeniya's bodyguards to help out for awhile. I want you and Jamie out of the house for the next month or so, until things settle down."

"Where will we go?"

"Gadol will arrange a safe house. We pay him big bucks for this kind of thing."

I scarcely heard all this as I was gritting my teeth in agony. The extra-strength Tylenols hadn't been adequate and my right arm was a throbbing mass of pain.

I was moaning softly when they got me to the Emergency. I took my turn among the throngs of "common" people waiting for assistance.

When Dad mentioned "insurgency victim," I got a push up the line. I was walked into an outer dressing room where a nurse gave me an injection and told me to wait outside again. The pain began to subside into a dull throb and I dozed in exhaustion.

The cut seemed to have opened something else in me. For all the years I had lived in this country, I had always considered it my home. Yes, I was fair skinned and a minority Christian Burgher, but I had many advantages over my peers. I was fluent in both Sinhala and English, I had come through the school system, I had many contacts in the airline business, many friends, and I had never lived abroad—this *had* to be my home. But the act of being invaded had somehow made this a foreign place. The revolution had to this point been someone else's problem—the poor people's problem. The social set that I belonged to had always been immune to these conflicts, because the economic engine of the mercantile class in Colombo drove the country and no one messed with it. With a stroke of a rusty knife, all that had changed.

There was a rush of feet and I opened my eyes to see the anxious face of Shamini staring at me.

"Jamie, what happened?"

Dad explained as I closed my eyes again. Suddenly even Shamini looked like the enemy. After all, it was her race that had attacked me, the more downtrodden and radical ones of her race. I'd never been called a racist, but I could understand how lines get drawn in these conflicts.

I felt her hands take my wounded arm gently. She lifted the bandage slowly and I winced.

"Let's get this dressing changed, it's soaked." Her voice was clinical, grown up during the recent weeks that had separated us. "We don't have any more blood to give out tonight, so you have to preserve every bit. I am going to stitch your gash. Stay here, I'll make the preparations." Then with a swish of her work-worn coat and a slap of the stethoscope on her side, she was gone.

Within minutes, I was ushered into another room down a long corridor. I closed my eyes to the less fortunate ones waiting on the floor, some even with hands outstretched, begging for attention.

While Dad and Mum waited outside, Shamini quickly ripped my bandage and washed my wound. All I could do was howl in pain.

"Hold this." She stuck a metal surgical tray in my good hand. It contained bandages, gauze, a pair of scissors, a scalpel and a bottle of antiseptic, A roll of rough looking thread spooled into a needle in her hand. Before I knew it, she shot another injection into me and got to work.

"Sorry, I cannot wait for the freezing to take hold. I have to be somewhere else in twenty minutes." She was all precision and concentration. I could have been just any other patient.

"You work with that needle better than if you were sewing a button on a shirt."

"I've had lots of practice." She jabbed me harder and I yelped.

"Sorry. Don't distract me." She worked quickly after that, and I tried to keep my mouth shut. I could hear her heart beat as she leaned against me and feel her stale hurried breath. She must have been in this place all day. Perhaps she might have even slept the night here. I remembered the last time I received stitches—I was ten—when a stray barb from the fence had ripped my foot. On that occasion, there had been a doctor, a nurse and an attendant to look after me. Now there was just this very overworked medical student.

"It pays to have influence around here," I said, reminding her of our conversation on my bike, so many moons ago it seemed. "I could have been waiting here all night for some attention."

"I'm doing this for *you*, Jamie. There are patients worse off that I could be with right now."

"Why, I am deeply honoured." I couldn't bite back my sarcasm.

"I am sorry that you had to be drawn into this conflict, as a victim."

"This is not my conflict."

"If you call yourself a Sri Lankan, then it is. There is no escaping it. That's what I keep telling *Ammi* and *Thathi* who hide in their big house and think that the world stops outside our gates."

"It did stop outside the gates for us middle-class Colombo types. The wars were only happening in the south between the Marxists and the politicians, and in the North with the Tamils."

"Fires spread, Jamie." She pulled back and surveyed her work. "There, that should hold you for awhile. Get your father to take you to a private clinic to have your dressing changed twice a week. There is no point in coming back here. You'll spend a whole day before you see someone."

She rummaged in her pocket and fished out a prescription pad. She scribbled some medicines on it and tore the slip off for me. I saw that it had the rubber stamp of Dr. Lakshman Gunawardene on it.

"Your father's prescription pad?"

"I borrowed it. That's the only way we can get any results around here. I have not graduated yet, remember?"

I handed her back the tray and gently flexed my re-bandaged hand.

"Thanks. Glad you were on duty tonight."

I would have normally reached for her and grabbed a kiss with her in this private room, but looking at her now, she was the professional doctor and I was the patient, and there was a chasm between us. She was no longer the coy student whom I had fallen in love with—the naive, comfortable, idealistic girl who had entranced me. Here was a highly strung woman, fighting some inner demon that was larger than herself. She had assumed the weight of this whole fucked-up country on her shoulders and was trying to save it. She must have sensed my feeling. She pushed a stray wisp of her long black hair back over her shoulder and sniffled as if holding back a flood of tears.

"Glad I was here to help. But then I am here every night. Goodnight, Jamie. Try and get some rest. I'll call you." She picked up the tray and left the room.
She never called me. I guess she was too busy.

My family moved into an apartment on the Galle Road, in one of those monster buildings that were springing up daily, funded by money made from arms imports, petro-dollars or government "deals." It was a concrete slab, ten stories high, with two bedrooms—everything new and sterile; it lacked the emotions and memories stored in our old home. We took as many belongings as we could to tide us over, but several personal items had to stay behind as the apartment lacked adequate storage space.

From the balcony window—the only luxury in our new abode—Mum spent her time looking out across the fabric of tiled roofs, grimy buildings and coconut trees. The railway lines snaked across, parallel to the Indian Ocean, where green waters threw up rough surf. Dad spent more time than usual at the office; twice a week he dropped in to check on the two security guards protecting our house. One evening, I joined Mum on the balcony. The lights of a distant ocean liner streamed past on the cloudy horizon, heading for calmer waters it seemed. I asked her if she was planning to join the next exodus and emigrate.

"We should have done that, years ago when you were a baby. When Uncle John went to Canada. He still asks me why I never bothered to leave."

"And why?"

"Your father has done so well here. A director in his company. What will he do in Canada at his age? Become a security guard?"

***

My wound healed well, but I was left with a jagged scar that was half visible; the other half snaked up my upper arm behind me. The skin around the disfigurement was tight, pulled inward and constrained by Shamini's stitches. My friends told me that this war wound made me look dangerous and that girls would find me attractive, but it did not make me feel any better. I felt like damaged goods. I could not work my hand anymore, and I worried that I would never be a fast bowler again. I also missed my bat, left behind in the old house. We had left only with essentials. At least, if I could practice my batting, I might still be able to play cricket.

Many of the fittings in the apartment did not function—the building had been erected in a hurry and the builder had cut corners, using cheap fixtures. Mirrors threw back warped reflections and the electric burners in the stove constantly blanked out in the middle of cooking. Mum complained about light bulbs fusing out or windows that did not close properly.

On the positive side, I was now closer to my office in the Fort and the beach was a nice place to walk down in the evenings. But I caught myself looking over my shoulder as I let my heels sink in the surf and watched crowded commuter trains hurtle past with passengers hanging off doors. Looking at young lovers seeking refuge on the beach for brief moments of anonymity and privacy made me think of Shamini, swallowed up somewhere in that hospital.

In the confines of my small room in the apartment, with its bare walls and narrow window that looked out on garish lights of the Galle Road, I longed for my old spacious bedroom in Kotte. I missed the posters on the walls of Pink Floyd, Phil Collins and Michael Jackson; I longed to see the picture album of our big cricket match against the Josephians, in which I had scored fifties in each inning and taken a bag of eight wickets. I missed my stereo that sat in the corner of the old room, the one I could play at all hours of the night without disturbing my parents. I had to leave the stereo behind as this new place was too pokey; even on minimum volume, the music would have carried through the paper thin wall and awoken my parents in the adjoining bedroom. I longed for my own apartment one day, like my cousin Alex in

Canada who constantly sent me pictures of his car, his pad, his girlfriend and his golf clubs. But who could afford to live independently in Sri Lanka at the age of twenty-three with the cost of living shooting up the way it did, despite holding an ostensibly "glamorous" airline job? As I was an only child, Dad had promised to partition the old house in Kotte and build an annex when I eventually married so that my family would have a place to live. Yet that would be too small for someone like Shamini who lived in her monster home in Colombo 7.

One day, in a mixed fit of homesickness and recklessness, wanting to reclaim my diminishing self, I decided on a radical action. When I got off work, after verifying from the radio that no curfews were about to be implemented for the evening, I phoned Dad to tell him that I was going to our old home to pick up some of my books and my cricket bat.

Dad sounded alarmed. "Make sure you phone the security guards at the house and let them know you are coming. Identify yourself first. And don't spend too much time there."

"I'll park my bike at the top of the road," I assured him. "I have a large canvas bag in my room back at the house to haul my stuff, so I only have to make one trip."

I phoned the house. The phone rang several times before a hesitant voice answered. "Hello?"

"I'm Mr. Bernard's son, James. Who is that?"

"Security oppicer Gunadasa, sir."

I advised Gunadasa that I would be visiting after dusk to collect my belongings. I described what I looked like.

"Ah, okay sir. We will expect."

I then rode over to Shamini's place. Outside the tall gates, I hesitated. The feel of her lips on mine in this familiar nook returned and I wanted to linger in the memory of it for a while. Why couldn't I just pretend that everything was okay? Ignore what had happened between us. Perhaps this bad time too would pass. No, there was no use negotiating with my cowardly side. I was losing track of myself. I had to find the things that defined who I was. I had to claim back my identity from where I was now, exiled even from my own home. I was not going to be flexible and work around her unpredictable schedules anymore. After all, I had a life too.

I walked up the driveway with a rapidly beating heart. I could feel the sweat spreading under my arms, leaving patches on my shirt. I made it to the long veranda that ringed the building. This large house convinced me all the more of our incompatibility.

Dr. Gunawardene and his wife were seated in wingback rattan chairs on the veranda. He was in business attire, his tie still on, despite the steamy humidity. Mrs. Gunawardene looked tired and was dressed in a housecoat; her arm hung over the side of the chair and I could see the needle pricks where her husband administered her daily doses of insulin, as Shamini had told me.

Dr. Gunawardene feigned a lack of recognition and raised an eyebrow while his wife immediately made me out despite the gathering gloom. She began to rise weakly.

"Please, sit down," I said. "I came to see Shamini."

"Shamini is not at home right now," her father replied, peering down at me over the rims of his half lenses. He straightened his tie. "I'm going to pick her up shortly from the hospital. And then, I am sure she will be too tired for socializing."

"Lakshman, this is James Bernard, Shamini's…friend." Mrs Gunwardene was grabbing for words, trying to melt the ice in her husband's voice.

"We've met before," I reminded him, holding out my hand.

He rose but kept his hands by his sides. I got the feeling they might have been discussing me, even though Dr. Gunawardene pretended that he didn't know me.

"I see…" He said, inspecting me from head to foot.

The strain of the last few months gave way and I let fly, hardly recognizing my words. "Listen, Mr. And Mrs.

Gunawardene. I did not mean to trouble you. But I came to break up with Shamini today. Since she is not home—as usual—you can pass on the news to her. I'm sure this will make you very happy. And if she cares to call me, I shall her give the same message. I also wanted to assure you that your daughter is safe from me. We have all lost her to this bloody war. Good night!"

With that I turned on my heel and walked slowly down that long driveway, leaving them with mouths open.

I rode fast, even recklessly. It had felt good telling them off, and in so doing, telling their martyr daughter off too. The wind rushing at me kept pushing back my mounting sense of loss for breaking off this relationship. I figured that as long as I kept going my feelings would be in check.

When I reached Kotte, darkness had descended and the mosquitoes buzzed in front of my riding goggles. I locked my bike in the parking lot of the local bakery at the top of the main road and fished out the flashlight I had brought with me. Crossing the road, I walked swiftly down a lane that intersected with ours about half a mile down, staying out of the arcs of the occasional street lights; I say "occasional" because not all of them were lit: about one in every three were functioning, just sufficient to provide direction. The fireflies were more reliable. As I turned down our lane, the lights were out in all the houses, either due to a power cut or due to another "protest" from the Marxists. But it suited my purpose, for I was reduced to a shadow.

An ember from a lit cigarette moved in the dark as I neared our gate. I felt myself starting to sweat again. "Officer Gunadasa?"

The ember moved, and I made out the silhouette of a man with a baton resting on his shoulder. "Mister Bernard?"

"Yes, it's me."

"You have house key, sir?"

"Yes."

"Okay—then go."

I smelled arrack fumes, cigarette smoke and sweat as I neared Gunadasa in the dark. "Where is your partner?" I asked.

"Gone dinner, sir. After he come back, I go."

"Okay," I said, moving towards the front door. "I won't be long."

Despite my promise, I took my time, moving from room to room inside the house where I had spent the greater part of my life. It was a three-bedroom bungalow with a kitchen, living room, store room, and a toilet. I decided to take a familiar pee for old time's sake—I could even aim in the dark without hitting the rim of the toilet bowl. This house was hard to give up and I savoured walking through its rooms, now covered in dust. I wiped flecks off Dad's liquor cabinet—locked, as he did not trust the guards. But they seemed to have their own supply of alcohol. I went into my bedroom and flashed the torch over my pop idols—yes, they were still there, pinned up on the walls—arms raised in acknowledgement to adoring fans such as me. I had placed a canvas cover over my stereo; there was a thick film of dust covering the fabric. I worried that if we did not clean this place soon, there would be a lot of damage. Perhaps I could pay the guards extra to dust off some of the more important items.

I took down the Jack Higgins, Wilbur Smith and Frederick Forsyth novels from my bookshelf, dusted them and stuffed them inside the bag I found in my closet. I reached behind the door and picked up my cricket bat—it felt good in my hands. I ran through a few strokes in the dark. I had difficulty and pain with the hook, the sweep and the pull shots. My strokes in front of the wicket were still okay—so I guessed I could still get by as an opening batsman, playing defence, while my partner notched up the runs.

Before returning to the front door, I stopped at the altar in the living room, its oil lamp long extinguished. I reached inside the open lamp and felt the slimy residue on my fingers. It had been a family tradition—when Dad kept more regular hours—to say our prayers together each night. I made the sign of the cross, knelt before the altar and said the Lord's Prayer, and asked God to return us quickly to this house that I loved so much, and which held important memories for me.

As I stepped out of the front door, I failed to see Gunadasa's glowing cigarette on the front lawn. I realized that he was missing. In his place were the bobbing heads of many people assembled just inside the gate. A beam of light struck me between the eyes, temporarily blinding me. Too late, I realized that the "boys" had come calling again.

I let go of the canvas bag and tightened my grip on the bat, but this time I knew, with a sinking heart, that my efforts would be futile. I pointed my flashlight back at them. Right in the middle of the group was Sena, a black bandana tied round his head, wearing a black teeshirt, slacks and rubber slippers.

"You'd better get the hell out of here, before the security guys call the cops," I said, unable to hide the quiver in my voice.

The cheeky guy, whom I had beaten up the last time, stood next to Sena. He shouted back in Sinhala. "What security guards?" Then turning to the rest of his cronies, he started laughing.

Sena spoke for the first time. His voice was calm. "Your guards are both having a long dinner."

"What do you guys want?" I said, biting back the treachery of Gunadasa and his associate.

Sena held his head to a side, avoiding my gaze. "We are going to burn your house down tonight."

As if that was a signal, two of the intruders broke away from the rest. They swung jerry cans off their shoulders and started splashing the exterior walls of the house. The smell of kerosene made me want to puke.

I grabbed at straws, trying to prevent a catastrophe. "Why are you going to burn the house that was your home for months, Sena? Where you were fed and clothed better than in your own home—if you ever had one." I kept pointing my flashlight into his face, daring him to look at me, but he was staring at his feet.

"Do you want to see all the homes you live in burned? Like your shack in the paddy field? Must we pay for your criminal legacy?"

He turned around to his band of thugs. "Hold off for awhile. I have some unfinished business that I have to take care of with this gentleman."

Turning back to me, he ordered in a gruff voice. "Drop your bat and go inside the house."

When I did not move, he advanced and pushed me with a sudden violence that took me by surprise. I staggered back through the open door; the bat fell out of my hand and tumbled onto the veranda. Within a second he was inside the house with me, slamming the door behind him. He had a knife in his hand, a slim flashlight in the other.

He laid the knife down on a coffee table and placed the torch in such a way that it illuminated our surroundings without blinding us. I kept my own flashlight trained on him, my only weapon now.

Then his bravado vanished as he fell to his knees in front of me. "Sir, please understand. This is not my doing. You insulted the boys last time. They cannot lose face in this neighborhood."

"And so you will condone the burning of valuable property?"

"Sir, we are not thieves."

"Oh, give me a break."

"On my mother's grave sir, no one will steal anything from this house. This house is sacred to me too."

"But you will burn it?"

I was trying to figure out how to rush him and break his skull with the flashlight. But could I get away? His cronies had me surrounded.

As if reading my mind, he said. "Sir, I want you to hit me. Make it look like you surprised me. Then go from back door. Nobody there, I know. They are all in front. I will give five minutes and then call for help. Please, sir. Otherwise they will kill you."

I threw the flashlight down and hit him in the stomach even before he stopped speaking, with my bare hands, a blow that sent shards of pain up my stiff arm.

"You bastard! I curse the day I met you," I yelled as I hit him again.

He did not strike back but remained hunched over and out of breath He managed to say, "Keep hitting, sir. If it makes you feel better."

I began pummelling him with everything I had in me. We were both in agony. He grunted, as if in satisfaction, as every blow connected: on his body, on his legs where I kicked him, and finally on his face where my glorious uppercut clacked his teeth and made *me* scream with the recoil.

He was on the floor, gasping, blood streaming from his mouth. I aimed a final kick at him, cursing the circumstances in this country that had pitted us as enemies. I collapsed next to him, panting, spent.

His hand reached out and touched my face. It was cold but gentle. "Now, go sir. Please."

I picked up his knife and made for the back door. As he had said, there was no one around the back. In five steps, I reached the fence, which I scaled, cutting myself on the rusty barbed wire. With all the pain I had recently endured, that cut was like a pin prick. I ran across the neighbour's back yard; I saw figures behind the blinds but no one came out, people knew better. I made it to the road and ran like crazy for the bakery. The scooter was still parked in its spot. As I kick-started it, a crimson glow rose over the trees and I choked back a sob. My books and cricket bat were lying behind in the home that was now being burned to the ground.

Figures came running up the lane, making for the road—the boys were chasing me. I revved into high gear and took off, in the opposite direction, quickly outdistancing them.

Soon, I was out of their reach but the vivid image of my burning home was etched even deeper into my psyche. So many years to build those memories, and the flash of a match to destroy them. I steeled myself to break the news to Dad and Mum.

***

The next day, I phoned Farook.

"Those airline jobs in Qatar. I have a candidate."

Farook sounded hesitant. "And will the candidate travel this time?"

"Yes—this time the candidate *will* travel."

A Year Later

Dear Jamie,

Thank you for sending the money. Now your father and I can afford to buy our tickets to travel to Canada. Your father is busy selling the property; it's been reduced to a piece of land, now that the rubble has been cleared away, like when we first came to it seventeen years ago. Land prices have gone up despite all this fighting. Hopefully, we will get a decent price.

I have some good news, if it is of any relief to you. You may have read it in the newspapers over there—Rohana Wijeweera and his JVP gang were finally rounded up and shot in Colombo two days ago. At least the Marxist revolution will end now, even though the war in the north with the Tigers continues unabated. There was an unconfirmed report that one of Wijeweera's henchmen was seen running out of their hideout screaming and aiming a pistol at the soldiers surrounding the place. The poor fellow was shot to pieces before he took ten paces. I immediately thought of that rascal Sena—he'd do such a thing. Would you believe it that the next day, one of the dead Marxists identified was one Senaratne Somapala Perera? That Sena—poor fellow—he never knew what was good for him!

One other piece of news—your former girlfriend, Shamini, graduated and is getting married to a Sinhala Buddhist MP. It's an arranged marriage. I am so glad you did not get too deep with her. They seem suited for each other: die-hards committed to saving this country, if it ever can be saved. MP's have a very short shelf-life these days with all those Tiger suicide bombers blowing up people at political rallies. Her parents are gifting the couple a luxury condo in Colpetty.

Yesterday, your father and I sat on the balcony of this half-way house, that is now our temporary home, and looked out at the ocean. Your Dad had a sudden pang of regret and wondered if we could just continue to live here, now that the Marxist threat is over. It took him only a little of my silence to agree that even though the war was over, the scars and the loss are permanent. I hope that he is able to get a decent job when we get to Canada.

Take care of yourself and do not work too hard. I cannot wait for the day when we are able to sponsor you and bring you across to Canada as well, and when we could be re-united as a family again.

Look after yourself and write soon.
All our love!
Mum

I fold the letter and put it in my pocket. It will stay close to my heart, as these fragments are the only reminders of a home I lost and the promise of a future home I have still to see.

Yes, that would be Sena all right. I can see him charging into the blazing guns, like he had charged Bada's bovine beast, yelling "You bloody bulls, I'll fuck you." He has finally found his home under the tortured earth of his motherland. And Shamini has found hers, with her high-risk husband, in her high-rise condo above the city of Colombo.

As for me, I gaze out over the mosaic of minarets, white stucco buildings, oil derricks, and skull-capped pedestrians from my apartment window—my half-way house—hearing the muezzin call five times a day, looking out at the waters of the Arabian Gulf and dreaming of a cold country far away that will one day become my new home.

A Lie Oft Repeated...

*D*ear Daddy,
I'm so excited that you finally decided to meet. You don't know what this means to me. I've spent my whole life dreaming about this occasion. I will be at the restaurant at 6pm on Saturday. I've reserved us a table by the window overlooking King St. I've sat at this window a number of times since coming to Toronto, wondering how it would be with you sitting opposite me. Can't wait!
Susan

I haven't paid attention to many events in my life, but the circumstances around Susan are engraved in my mind, while the rest have gone by in a daze. Like growing up in a third world country, emigrating, getting married and divorced (twice), earning degrees and promotions, partying, making money and losing it, having lovers and losing them too—all faded memories now, except for Susan.

Yes, this time I *am* paying attention. You see, I have never fathered a daughter. In fact, I've never sired *any* children that I know of. I wish I had; my marriages may have survived if there had been offspring gluing their parents together after emotion, novelty and sex had waned.

I try going back over the e-mail string. The first one arrived from England three months ago. England! I'd never sowed my seed in that country, although I'd spilt it in plenty of other places. The e-mails began with introductions and questions. At first, I had balked—another one of those immigrant scams, I thought. When memories finally came flooding back, I responded. After we established credentials, the e-mails started to talk of her coming to Toronto in the summer, perhaps immigrating later if job prospects were good. She wanted to know if I'd be prepared to meet her, or would she be too much of a shock to my system?

Then the photographs arrived. She was a dark haired, petite, attractive woman in her mid twenties with intelligent eyes and an optimistic poise. She confirmed my memory of the *other woman,* her mother, dressed in a Kandyan sari with a *pottu,* about Susan's age, a lifetime ago. If there was only a way to go back and reverse events from how they had panned out…

***

Those days of youth were halcyon ones: when kingfishers laid eggs, they said; we were the kingfishers.

Jimmy Ambrose became my buddy immediately, the day I started at the airline office back in the mid '70s in Ceylon, or Sri Lanka as it had been recently re-named. I was studying to be an accountant but my father had insisted that I get office experience in-between and pay my way, and so there I was. I sat nervously, sweating in the humidity that the air conditioner could not dispel, filing reservation forms behind passage clerks, realizing that it would be months before I would perform as confidently as they did. This was in the days before computers arrived and levelled the playing field. I saw a thin, short guy with James Dean features wearing a tie that covered half his chest, sitting on a counter stool, eyeing every customer or prospect walking in the door. He glanced in my direction occasionally with an amused smile on his face.

He suddenly jumped off the stool and extended his hand at me. "Jimmy, Jimmy Ambrose. What's your name?"

"Mark Jansz," I replied, taking his dry hand in mine and wetting it with my nervous perspiration.

"First day here? Don't worry. It gets better. How old are you?"

"Twenty. And you?"

"Thirty-nine, and holding."

His slim figure made him look younger, but at closer quarters I saw the faded look in his eyes: too much drinking and partying, endemic of the airline industry in those days.

"My eldest son's about your age. Nineteen," he said.

"Wow! How many kids do you have?" I was already in awe of this guy, who'd been having children at my age, and who was the only person bothering to talk to me on my first day. The counter clerks had simply nodded and shoved piles of paper for me to file.

"Sore point, buddy. I should be proud but I am not. Seven."

"Seven!"

"I'm a Catholic. What do you expect? Wife doesn't believe in birth control."

His frankness was disarming. I relaxed.

He hoisted his pants and dropped a business card on my pile of papers. "Want to join me for a drink after work? I'll give you the scoop on this place."

***

We had many drinks over the next few months. Jimmy introduced me to the adult world that I had just entered. My focus up to that point had been to get sufficient credits at my A levels and enter university. Due to the standardization system in effect at the time, we city students were having our marks downgraded to compensate for our rural counterparts who were having theirs upgraded— "to level the playing field for university entrance," as the politicians said. I had sat for my A's three times and failed. I was now registered to become a Cost & Management Accountant, the next best thing to appease my soul, and my father who was a retired corporate executive (one of the few who had not immigrated to Australia and ended up working in a factory), and who expected his only son to do better than he had in the land of his birth. Dad pretended to ignore the worsening economic conditions in the country: import controls, export controls, foreign exchange controls, travel controls, any control that added another gate in the distribution process and siphoned handsome bribes to the gatekeepers.

Jimmy and I would go down to the Rider Cricket Club, where male business executives hung out after work, drank copiously, ate fried sprats and devilled tripe, talked politics and spun dreams that they would never realize in a country that was going to the dogs by the day.

"Bloody bull-shitters," Jimmy would denounce. "All they do is talk. They can't do. Let's go to Aunty Bertha's for a massage."

He'd drive me on his scooter to the high-walled house with the red light on its porch on Dickman's Road where the girls were always on call in their transparent clothes, with fresh towels over their shoulders. I tore my foreskin the first time the fat sweaty girl with huge dark nipples yanked my swollen cock too hard. Jimmy laughed later and said that I had just earned my stripes. But he was silent and introspective when we rode home.

"Why do you hang around with me," I asked him one weekend while we were watching a cricket match at the Rider.

His eyes welled as he twirled the arrack in his glass. "You remind me of what I could have become."

"Why didn't you?"

There was a roar in the clubhouse: another batsman had fallen to the dreaded spin bowler who was ripping through the home side.

"See that, boy? *LBW*—leg-before-wicket. That's how I got out. Didn't use a rubber with the missus."

***

The airline business was crazy in those days of socialist government. All foreign exchange transactions required Central Bank permission. Therefore, the purchase of airline tickets had to be accompanied by the dreaded "P form" approved by the Bank. Clerks at the Central Bank were like mini dictators, refusing to approve an application if there was the slightest inaccuracy. After awhile, travellers cottoned onto the fact that there really was no error in the form, but in its presentment. When an envelope bearing a "personal fee" accompanied the completed document, it was mysteriously approved in a flash.

Travel agents waited like hungry dogs, looking for the first tourist to stare into the airline offices located in the inner Fort area. And there were many tourists in those days, as the hippie generation was in full bloom: European hippies trekking overland through India and spilling into Sri Lanka at the end of their rite of passage, and now looking for a cheap one-way ticket home. "Just dip and pick," was how Jimmy explained it. He was busy with clients of two kinds: the hippies whom he picked up by trolling the youth hostel and the YMCA, and rich locals who were ostensibly going abroad for "studies" or on some other excuse and would never return.

I saw how good he was after I had completed my six-month apprenticeship and was promoted to serve on the counter to make reservations and issue tickets. Jimmy brought in an average of four clients a day, while the other rep, an old guy with a snobby attitude, got as many in a whole week. Sometimes Jimmy introduced me to customers he didn't even know, by their first names—they must have been the window shoppers he picked up off the street. But he was always courteous and had perfected his art of the sale.

I had difficulty keeping a straight face in front of the many half-naked women he brought into the office; hippies, unwashed, unshaved and looking like they were ready to screw anything that dangled a male appendage.

"They are good fucks," Jimmy said one day as we were closing up.

Seeing my eyes widen with suppressed curiosity, he elaborated, "The wife and I have not had sex since the last kid was born. She doesn't want to get pregnant any more. We can't afford any more kids."

"Where do you do it?" My curiosity was at an all-time high. Still living with my parents, as most guys of my age did back then, I had often wondered how one could afford the "sex, drugs and rock-and-roll" culture that we saw in an occasional Hollywood B-movie that slipped through our film board censors.

"I have a place. It belongs to a friend. We take turns. Come with me sometime, I'll show you."

In the socially repressed '70s in the old country, we young men were full of sperm with no place to deposit it. The girls we dated only wanted to hold hands, kiss, and plan their weddings, to be followed immediately by babies. The girls who went a bit further than holding hands got reputations as "loose women." Therefore, I had no girlfriend, although I fantasized and masturbated a lot, conjuring up images of those wanton hippie women who came into the office.

After my first accountancy exam, Jimmy took me out to the Rider to unwind. He didn't warn me about the two Swedish women who were in the taxi when he came to pick me up from home. The women looked familiar and I struggled to recall where I had seen them before. Gerta was about thirty, red haired and big breasted, while Anna was in her early twenties and had light blond hair, large innocent eyes and long legs. They giggled and laughed during our ride and I smelled alcohol on their breath. Just before we turned into the driveway of the Rider, I remembered that I had seen them in the office earlier in the week with Jimmy, who had been acting as their travel agent, of course!

After my second beer, Anna dragged me down to the dart board and beat me 290 to 100. She had a gleam in her eyes as she kept hitting the high points; all I did was throw faster and miss. Before each turn she stroked the dart like a penis, winked at me, opened her mouth wide and threw—and scored. I looked around for Jimmy but he was in the dark with Gerta, their chairs pulled far out into the lawn, away from the lights of the clubhouse.

"Do you have a boyfriend?" I asked Anna, after her victory at darts was assured.

"No. But I have *many* boyfriends. Isn't that good? At my age?"

"I guess so," I agreed, unconvinced.

Then she came up to me, embraced and kissed me, her tongue lashing inside my mouth like a loose tow rope in a storm. Her eyes bored through me; gone was the innocence, replaced by an animal hunger. "It is good, no? You want to be another boyfriend?"

This was so simple compared to the local girls I had dated, I almost shouted "Sure!"

As if on cue, Jimmy was at my shoulder, "Time to go buddy, the love nest beckons."

A taxi took us to an address along the coast in Mt. Lavinia. I was in no mood to admire the gently waving palms on the moonlit beach—Anna had her hand on my balls, kneading them all the way, and my cock was about to explode. The house was a two-storey structure with a large wall and a security gate that swung open when Jimmy punched in some numbers. We disembarked in the driveway, and as the taxi drove away, I felt like jumping on board again and heading for the safety of my home. A lick on my ear by Anna dispelled that thought immediately. Jimmy banged his fist on the ornate front door, and after several minutes, a gaunt man with betel-stained teeth, wearing a sarong and singlet, opened it. Seeing Jimmy, the man bowed respectfully averting his eyes from the rest of us, and said in Sinhala, "Ah, Jimmy *mahattaya*, everything is ready." Then he withdrew and was swallowed up in the house and we never saw him again.

Inside, the living room was almost bare: four chairs and a table littered with playing cards and Playboy magazines.

Jimmy was quick and business-like with his instructions, "Marky—there are six bedrooms with toilets attached—three downstairs and three upstairs. Take any of the upstairs ones. I'm taking the master bedroom downstairs." And with that, he grabbed a grinning Gerta and they disappeared through a door in the hallway.

There were many Anna's after that first anxious sweat-drenched encounter, but only after I got through my initiation that night. She jumped me the moment we entered our selected bedroom, making my manhood shrivel in the force of her hungry attack. She was disappointed and pouted. I scrounged around for a distraction and found a half-empty bottle of arrack in the room. So I plied her with drinks and got her to talk about life in Sweden and her boyfriends, while my mind tried to dispel doubts concerning my limp member. She talked and soon the bottle was empty. Mercifully, she fell asleep as soon as the drinks hit her. As she snored, I stared at the ceiling fearing that I could never fuck any woman in my life ever. I listened to the squeals of delight from Gerta downstairs, punctuated by roars from Jimmy. I felt so alone. I dozed. Around dawn, I woke with the biggest hard-on I had ever had. In desperation, I rolled over the sleeping naked Anna and dug myself into her, in case my buddy decided to disappoint me again. She stirred with pleasure and started bucking in her sleep. Before I knew what, we were raising a storm in an otherwise quiet house. As we both exploded in giant orgasms, she opened her eyes wide and exclaimed, "Ah, you were teasing me—this was a surprise you had planned, no?" I was in heaven afterwards and have suffered no penis anxiety since that day.

After I bought my reconditioned 10-year old motorcycle (I began moving up in the world too), it was easy to pick up women who had come into the office earlier to purchase tickets. White women liked us Burgher men—not quite Dravidian and not quite European—we were exotic. Fifty rupees to the caretaker at the house in Mt. Lavinia and "everything was ready."

***

One day Jimmy and I went to the Intercontinental. I bought the drinks that evening as I had just passed the second part of my accountancy exam; two more parts to go and I would be qualified and certified. Some of the guys in the office had come along too; they respected and regarded me now as "the guy who was going places." We drank like crazy that day. Jimmy and I were the last to leave and we were quite hammered by then. He had slumped into his depressed state after being upbeat all evening. "You know, Marky boy, I am going to throw the biggest party for you when you graduate."

"Why don't you save that for your son? He'll be making it through his 'A' levels soon, no?"

"He's not doing any higher studies. He flunked grade 10. He's a *rastiadu* bugger."

"He is not a layabout. You are too hard on him. Besides you've got so many kids—at least one of them is going to make it through."

"I wanted to go to university," he said. "Instead, I'm here."

"But you are still making a lot of money. I counted your commissions last week. Man, you've got it made!"

"You think it's an intelligent way to make money? Scrounging off tourists?"

"You are fulfilling a need."

"With my cock, more likely. Even that is becoming difficult these days—when you get to my age, the girls don't fall too easily."

"You could spend less. You're at the club every day."

"It's better than going home. Screaming children. Wife who only nags now."

"I'm taking you home today. We are both too drunk to ride."

"No fucking way. I ride home myself."

It took two more drinks before I was able to convince him that it was easier to take a taxi. We both staggered outdoors. The humid air and the foul smell coming off the ocean—seaweed season—made him gag. He retched under the hotel's marquee. I slipped the bell captain a fifty rupee note to clean up the mess and take care of our bikes.

Jimmy straightened, wiped the vomit off his mouth and belched. "Ahhh. That feels really good. Let's go home.

But you drop me off at the Piliandala junction, I'll walk the rest of the way."

I had no option because I had no address for him. I only knew that he lived somewhere in the town of Piliandala. And I was quite drunk too.

During the ride, we opened the windows and let in the breeze: clean in stretches, stifling when we got behind a bus belching black smoke, foul when we passed the fish market. It helped dispel the alcohol's grip on us. I felt despondent, despite my recent examination success.

"Why do we use people?" I asked loudly.

Jimmy raised himself from his stupor. "Huh?"

"We are not bad guys, Jimmy, but we use people. We screw women like they are toys, we rip off tourists. I don't like what we do for a living."

He stuck his head out the window and sucked in a lungful of air. "If you don't use people, they use you."

"Life lessons from a great teacher," I mocked. "Since when did you become a philosopher?"

"You asked."

"And where did you learn that?"

"I learned it the hard way. My father beat me as a kid, whenever he was home. Every morning he chased me to get his newspaper, bread and cigarettes. We were ten in the family, I was the oldest. There was no money. My father worked in the port, brokering cargo. Most of the time, he never came home. There was overtime on the ship, he'd say. But there was no money at home, although he wore fancy clothes and owned a car which we were never allowed to ride in. It was as if he was ashamed of us.

"When he wasn't at the port, he was at the Globe Hotel playing billiards—he made money at that too. The times I'd cut school and go into the city, I'd pass by the Globe's window and see him taking cash off the poor suckers who dared to challenge him to a game. He used all of us to get ahead. And then one day, he vanished. They say he went to Australia. We never saw him again. The family split apart after that. My younger siblings left, one by one, when they reached fourteen or fifteen. Many joined ships to get out. I stayed until my mother died when I was twenty five—by then I was married with three children, I wasn't going anywhere. I was used, Marky."

He kept rambling in a daze, as if the vomiting had brought out more than just bile. I was tuning out but caught scraps of his monologue, "...I joined the navy too...wife kept getting pregnant every time I was on shore leave... two babies died. She is super fertile, man, I only have to breathe near her and she gets pregnant...chucked the navy...sold cars for awhile... then they put in this import control shit. Now only the politicians drive new cars and we drive pieces of scrap metal. Don't know how long this airline ticket shit will last..."

We were arriving on the outskirts of Piliandala. When I asked again for his address, he raised his voice belligerently, "Don't you understand English? I asked to be dropped off at the junction."

"You're in no condition to walk the rest of the way. Let me drop you off."

I thought he was going to have a heart attack. I saw him grabbing for words. Then he blurted out. "You don't understand—the road is washed away near my house and the short cut is over two fences and a field full of cow dung. No taxi is going to get through."

"Piliandala junction, sir," the taxi driver announced.

Reluctantly, I dropped him off at the cross road near an all-night tea stall, glimmering like a ship in the dark from the glow of hissing Petromax lamps. The street lights were out—power cuts again. I offered to walk with him the rest of the way but he refused again. "A good tea will straighten me out."

Getting out of the cab, he cupped my face in his hands through the open window. "Marky boy, you are a great chap, buddy. Remember, I'm throwing the biggest bloody party when you graduate." Then he staggered over to the tea stall. A couple of regulars who were hanging around chewing betel and shooting the shit, waved to him as if to a familiar sight in that ungodly hour of the night.

****

Why am I dredging up memories triggered by the e-mails and photographs sent to me by Susan, the young woman claiming to be my daughter? It's all connected in some way, isn't it? The lies that we perpetuate and hold on to so strongly later become as believable as the truth.

There was no washed out road, short cuts over fences, and cow dung to Jimmy's house. The guys from the office and I discovered it the day we went to his funeral two years later. His house, a squat two-bedroom structure, was located in a large garden full of screaming half-naked children, barking emaciated dogs, a communal tap, strings of laundry fluttering in the wind and a row of shared smelly latrines. Our taxi bounced along the stony common garden devoid of any grass and drove right up to Jimmy's house, outside of which were rows of chairs and people milling around in black and white clothes.

His closed coffin barely filled the poky dim living room, ringed with more chairs. Candles and flower wreaths added their stifling fragrance to the suffocating air.

I saw Jimmy's wife for the first time: a pale thin woman, flat breasted, wearing a flimsy flowered cotton dress and slippers, her hair straggly and uncombed, pouches under her swollen eyes. She was throwing herself against the coffin moaning, "My Jimmy, oh my Jimmy," as a toddler tugged at her leg and yelled along with her. Every time a fresh load of visitors arrived, her crying reached a new crescendo. The other Ambrose kids were noticeable, not only for their strong resemblance to their dead father but their clothes were all made of the same material—as if Jimmy had bought a single roll of cloth from a street vendor in Pettah and had them all suited in one fell swoop by a tailor who hadn't seen a fashion book in twenty years. I stepped outside for fresh air.

A group of young adults were under a mango tree passing round a bottle of arrack. One of the boys looked like Jimmy and he appeared quite drunk; dressed in bell bottoms and sporting an Afro hairdo (at least, he was contemporary), he kept swearing that he would get that punk who had caused his father to have the accident. I sat on a chair and closed my eyes, a tear squeezing out of me for my lost friend. There was loss and guilt in that tear: I had let him down. Around me, voices tried to recreate his last moments. "...*aney*, he skidded, child....must have been drunk also...but what the hell was that person doing, trying to open his van door on the wrong side of traffic?" I guess we conjure up myths in our mind, and alter them, until we get comfortable with the ones that fit.

"Do you want a cup of tea, uncle?" I opened my eyes and there was an Ambrose girl, about 12 years old, dressed in that familiar family uniform, holding a tray of mismatched cups and saucers that were steaming with tea. Her eyes were kind, sad and old for her years. A smaller child held onto her dress, sucking a thumb.

I accepted a cup gratefully. There was no sugar but small pieces of *jaggery* to suck on. "What is your name?" I asked.

"Stella."

"Thank you, Stella." I watched her move along the line of chairs, offering her meagre hospitality. I closed my eyes again and pictured her serving Jimmy a cup of tea at the end of the working day when he returned to a house full of bedlam.

One side of me was angry with him for leaving so abruptly. *In the end, you didn't do any better than your father, Jimmy. And you didn't stick around to throw that big party for me either!*
I look at the pictures again. The older woman in the sari; regal posture, lush hair down to her waist. When had she come into this story? After all these years the memory fades somewhat, but I think it was about a year before Jimmy died.

The scenes play back like old movies, the ones you never forget.

She first visited the office with her husband. She was in her early twenties, dressed in a white Kandyan sari with a red border—how striking she was and how elegant, compared to those hippie women we had been processing incessantly these last few months. Her ring finger sported a huge diamond. Her husband looked double her age. He had bushy eyebrows and craggy skin, and was dressed in a tie despite the sweltering monsoon weather. He did the talking, standing up at the counter in our office, while she stood demurely behind him and looked apologetically at me.

"I am Dr. Jayasinghe," he announced. "I have received a scholarship to London, you see." He pulled out a pile of papers from his briefcase, ignoring me as he spoke. "I need to get there by next week. My wife will follow later."

"We are fully booked next week, sir." I said cautiously. "There are only two flights a week and we are in the middle of the school rush. We are currently taking bookings three weeks out."

He threw his half rimmed glasses down on the counter. "Young man, do you know who I am?"

His wife touched his hand, but he shrugged her off. "My father is the Secretary of the People's Socialist Party. Let me speak to your boss."

I don't like political lackeys and opportunists who throw their weight around. I was about to come up with a smart answer when Jimmy appeared out of nowhere. "Let's see what we can do for you, sir," he said, all butter and sugar. I had to give him credit for his suavity under pressure. "Come with me sir, and madam, while my colleague works things out."

After he had escorted and seated them in the visitors lounge, Jimmy returned and hissed, "Find that fucker a seat. He's bad news, man!"

We always had "contingency seats" for problem cases like this, and while the man angrily paced the lounge, staring at us, I processed his reservation from the emergency allotment.

"I will handle all your P forms, exchange control, visa and any other thing you need, sir." Jimmy oozed charm as he escorted the couple back from the lounge after having delivered the news that due to a last minute cancellation we had found the good doctor a seat. "And whenever your wife is ready to travel, I can arrange all her paperwork also. Here is my card."

"Oh, thank you!" The man was pleasantly flushed, overwhelmed by this sudden onslaught of luck and great customer service. Dr. Jayasinghe aimed all his remaining questions at Jimmy. I only qualified for a parting scowl when he finally strode out of the office with his wife in tow.

"She's beautiful, isn't she?" Jimmy said, staring after them.

"Why do good girls marry assholes like that?" I asked.

"Power. And powerlessness. The perfect arranged marriage by the doctor's parents. Their proud son is off to England; time to make him respectable and safe from being led astray by one of those foreign women. So marry him off to a local girl and let him continue to commit his sins under the guise of a happy marriage. I've seen it so many times before. I bet you she's unhappy as hell."

***

I was on airport duty the night Dr. Jayasinghe left for the UK. A lorry load of supporters followed by five Mercedes Benzes pulled up at the airport entrance, fouling up traffic. I wondered about those spanking new Benzes at this time when imports were banned. Dr. Jayasinghe disembarked from the lead car and puffed his chest, waving to his cheering supporters in the open lorry, who were now piling out. He was dressed in a dark suit and tie. His wife stepped out of the second car. She was dressed in an olive green sari with heavy earrings, a gold necklace and a pearl headpiece that shone under the lights. She stood silently as her husband embraced well wishers with many ebullient 'thank you's and 'I'll write soon's. One young man in a national suit, hung onto Dr. Jayasinghe, weeping openly, as garlands were piled upon the departing hero.

When it came time to enter the Customs and Immigration area, Dr. Jayasinghe put his hands together and bowed to his wife, and she did the same, as camera flashlights went off. Then he entered the restricted zone without once looking back at her.

***

I did not see the doctor's wife, Manel Jayasinghe, until two months later. She came into the office while Jimmy was out on a sales call. It was quieter now with the students having departed for universities in Europe; they were leaving in increasing numbers now that their own country, for political reasons difficult to fathom, had rejected them. And the hippies, having shaved and showered, had boarded planes to resume their lives in the non-vegan, materialistic west, probably wondering what the heck had all that trekking and tripping done to their souls.

She was dressed in a sleeveless blouse and pants and had her hair in a pony tail; no earrings, headbands or gold necklace—very western, very beautiful. My palms grew clammy and the sweat began to spout under my arms as she approached. She looked at me with limpid eyes yet smiled confidently, safe from the shadow of the doctor. A hint of jasmine wafted across the counter.

"I wanted to enquire about flights. Mr. Ambrose, said he would help me."

"Jimmy is out at the moment. But can I take down your details?" I cursed myself for being counter staff, chained to this chair processing customers. I wanted to be like Jimmy who was constantly in motion, finding clients and escorting them through the various control procedures that needed unshackling before they were free to leave the country. I wanted to be with Manel Jayasinghe, navigating that bureaucratic maze, gazing at her shapely body, smelling her sweet sweat as we walked the sun-baked dusty city streets, stopping off at a restaurant for a cool drink, watching her wipe her damp brow as we recalled our day's accomplishments. Instead, I sat across this counter, gazing hungrily at her, knowing she would be gone the moment her business was done.

"When are you travelling?"

"My husband is still getting our apartment in London furnished. It's taking longer than I hoped. Perhaps by next month?"

"You'll be getting into the Christmas rush by then. We'd better hold you a seat before that happens. How about the flight on December 7th?"

"That should be okay. When should we start doing the paperwork? I still don't have a passport."

"We can start right now," said Jimmy, who had appeared from somewhere. His tie was askew and his Vaselined hair was spiky.

"Oh, thank you, Mr, Ambrose," Manel Jayasinghe deigned to honour Jimmy with her disarmingly regal smile. "What documents do I need? I only have my birth certificate."

"That's a good start. Why don't we ride down to the passport office straight away and get this show on the road?"

"Right away?" She looked flustered at his directness.

"You are dressed to ride on my pillion, Mrs. Jayasinghe. There is no time like now." His arms were spread wide.

"Okay." She shrugged, a mixture of amusement and excitement on her face.

That scene still flashes before me. They were an oddly matched couple: she tall young and protected, he short old and jaded. I was jealous of him then, one of the few times I felt that way. He held open the front door for her and winked at me as he followed her out.

Jimmy did not come back to the office for the rest of the afternoon.

***

Jimmy drove Manel Jayasinghe on his pillion a lot during the next month. I couldn't keep track of their movements as I also needed to pull away to study. There were times when I had to force myself to visualize a better future for myself and obliterate the sensuous pleasures of eating, drinking, womanizing and clubbing that my colleagues in the travel industry enjoyed. Those were the days I also felt like a monk on a mission in a land of the heathen.

In our incestuous little city, where everyone made it a point to know what everybody else was doing, Jimmy and Manel were often seen going in or out of government offices, or the Cargill's department store, or the rooftop restaurant at the Ceylinco building. He was evasive with explanations, sticking to the usual recounting of what he did for departing clients: passports, visas, export licences, exchange control, tax clearances, including last minute shopping for indigenous gifts for overseas hosts. Whenever I saw them racing by on his motorcycle, she looked happy and carefree, her long hair billowing in the wake of the vehicle; and he drove extra fast, as if he did not want any of us to notice. When I saw them on the lawn of the Rider club, having drinks at sunset, I realized that his assistance had gone beyond merely severing her links with the country we were so procedurally tied to.

Jimmy waved me over without hesitation the moment he saw me descend the steps of the clubhouse. I saw Manel draw her legs in and look away, as if trying to find somewhere to hide.

"Marky, come on over. Pull up a chair. Have a drink."

"I can't stay long," I said, disappointed. I had been looking forward to improving my darts record that day and now felt like I had to make myself scarce as soon as it was polite to do so.

"I am a happy man today," Jimmy leaned back in his chair after the waiter had taken my order and refreshed theirs. "I am with my favourite client and my best friend."

Manel Jayasinghe, who had been quiet and tense up to now, began to relax, and opened up in a rush of words,

"Jimmy has been so helpful with all this paperwork. My, such a bureaucracy, no? I've only got packing to do now."

"Remember, you are only allowed 44 pounds of luggage on board," I said, making my contribution.

She looked quickly at Jimmy and said, "Jimmy has arranged something…isn't that right?"

Jimmy smiled put his arm over her shoulder, drawing her into him, and stared directly at me. She began to pull back immediately but his grip tightened, urging her to stay: *Mark can be trusted*, his embrace seemed to imply. She yielded and let his hand straddle her. I remained impassive, took a large swig of my beer and tried to concentrate on the work crew erecting a giant Christmas tree across the cricket ground.

"My man at the airport will be on duty when Manel checks in," Jimmy explained.

"Oh," I said and tried to gulp down my beer so I could leave. Instead, I choked and began to splutter.

"Hey, slow down buddy," Jimmy tapped me on the back while I caught my breath and looked stupid. "You know Manel, Marky here is going to be a big guy one day. He's going to be a Cost and Management Accountant, and then he is going abroad, like you."

"Come on, Jimmy—I'm still a long way off," I protested, winded from my coughing fit.

"Really?" Manel was looking interestedly at me. "Where will you go when you finish your studies?"

I blushed. Was she actually interested in me?

"I'm not sure," I stammered. "There are jobs in the Middle East, I guess. Or there is—England, Australia, Canada, if one is qualified and lucky."

"If you come to England, you must contact us."

"Give her your card, Marky," Jimmy said.

I pulled out a business card and wrote my home address on it as well. Some romantic notion implied that this beautiful but conflicted woman would deign to write to me.

"Jimmy has my contact information," she said placing my card in her purse. "Please call us whenever you are in London."

***

The day before her flight, Manel Jayasinghe rushed into the office; her hair was loose and dishevelled by the wind, and she was wearing a faded tee shirt that accentuated her breasts and made me gulp.

"Where is Jimmy?"

"Out on sales. Can I help?" I was getting used to being the "other guy."

"I have to postpone my flight. My husband sent a telegram. He is going to Germany on an exchange for six weeks. He wants me to come in February now."

"That's no problem," I said, happy to be of service, reaching for her reservation card.

She gripped my hand. Hers was icy cold. "No. You do not understand. I *should* go tomorrow." There was panic written all over her face.

"But if your husband doesn't want you to come…"

"I'll sleep in the empty apartment if I have to. But I must see him before he leaves for Germany. I'm sorry I am not making any sense. I wish Jimmy were here…"

I led her into the visitor lounge and got her a glass of water, resentful that she still preferred Jimmy to be here. She calmed down as she sipped the water. I wanted to put my arms around her, protect her, but I couldn't in public. Perhaps my nerve would have failed me even in private. She was too good for me, up on a pedestal, out of reach. Damn Jimmy!

I had to return to work as there was a line of passengers forming. When I next looked up, Jimmy had arrived and was escorting her out of the office, his hand behind her back. This time he did not turn to wink at me.

Given the uncertainty, I decided to leave her reservation for departure the following day unchanged.

***

"He is bi, but he prefers boys," Jimmy spat out, knocking back his first scotch for the evening. We were at the Rider after work, that same day of Manel's surprise visit. The Christmas tree glittered across the cricket grounds and lights were on in city streets, heralding the Season To Be Jolly. Jimmy was not.

I remembered the young man crying and clinging to Dr. Jayasinghe, and it made sense. "Then why is she in such a hurry to get to England?"

"She missed her period."

"What? I thought you said you never touched her!"

He merely looked at me and drained his glass. "I never said I didn't."

"You and her? In Mt. Lavinia? Oh, it's horrible to imagine." I groaned.

"It's not horrible when you are in love with someone."

"Oh, no—you can't be, Jimmy. She is just a plaything to you. Like all the other women."

"No, Marky boy—she is not. She is special. But I can never have her. That's what makes her special."

"So, if she goes to England tomorrow, she could still pretend her husband is the father? I thought you said he prefers boys?"

"He does it with her on ceremonial occasions—like when they were married and had to show bloodstained bed sheets to both sets of parents. He also honoured her with a parting fuck the night he left for England. She's hoping he'll oblige her with a welcome repeat performance when she arrives in London, after such an absence and all."

"Wouldn't an abortion be simpler?"

"I'm a Catholic, remember? And she lives with the in-laws, it will be too noticeable, she says."

"So what are you going to do?"

"Drink up and kiss goodbye to the only woman I loved in my life. I've advised her to ignore Darling Hubby's telegram and get on that flight tomorrow."

***

The following day, Manel Jayasinghe showed up at the office once more, just as we opened for business. This time her eyes were red and puffy and she was still in the same faded tee-shirt.

"I'm sorry, but I have to cancel after all."

I did not want to betray the conversation I'd had with Jimmy the previous evening, and reluctantly took out her reservation card again. "You are quite sure?"

"My husband telephoned last night, and my mother-in-law picked up the phone. She told him I was still planning to travel tonight and handed the receiver to me—he scolded me for disobeying his orders. I have no choice now but to cancel, otherwise there will be worse questions later." She had a resigned look on her face.

"Fuck!" came the exclamation from behind us. Jimmy had just arrived for work.

"I'm sorry for giving you all this trouble." She wrung a wet handkerchief, then placed a hand on Jimmy's breast as if grasping for something. Just as he reached out to hold her hand she withdrew it.

"When shall I re-book you?" I asked.

"I don't know," she said, and darted out of the office.

***

Manel Jayasinghe vanished from our lives after that day and into her walled house in Kollupitiya where she ostensibly awaited her husband's summons to proceed to the UK. The house was like a fortress: security guards at the gate, two huge Alsatian dogs patrolling the inner garden, and the ten foot high wall with broken glass embedded along its summit.

Jimmy took me there one day. We parked our bikes across the road and watched the gate open and close to let a car go in or out occasionally, giving us glimpses of the prowling dogs and the marble fountain in the middle of the lawn. The upstairs window curtains were drawn and nothing moved.

"She's killing me, Marky," Jimmy said, lighting his last cigarette and throwing the empty pack on the sidewalk. He'd been chain smoking since Manel ran out of the office that day. "In this country, true love has to hide under cover of darkness."

"You didn't love your wife?"

"I thought I would grow to love her after I knocked her up. We married because I thought that would happen. It didn't. Kids, too many of them, money or not enough of it—they all got in the way. I thought Manel was my second chance. It was a bloody romantic pipedream, Marky. Guys like me don't get second chances."

I shook my head. "You should have seen this coming. She's too high class for us…for you."

"Yes, but you con yourself that it *can* be true, and you say it to yourself so many times it feels real. And when I was with her, it was real. It's the crash landing that's painful. If you ask me would I do it again? Yes, Marky boy—yes!"

***

A month later, Manel telephoned the office asking for me. My pulse quickened as I listened to her silken voice, which was calm and matter of fact. She had heard from her husband. She wanted to book her departure for February 8th. No, she wasn't coming into the office, and she didn't want to speak to Jimmy, and she would courier the ticket to me to have it revalidated.

Click.

I shrugged at Jimmy, who had been pacing and waiting to grab the receiver the moment I could safely hand it to him.

"She didn't want to speak to you. Sorry."

"Fuck!" Some customers in the office, overhearing, looked quizzically at him. I was glad the manager was out, or Jimmy would have been in deep shit. He slumped in the empty customer chair opposite me. "Just this once, I'll compromise my principles and get her an abortion if she wants it. Anything she wants, if only she will speak to me."

***

On February 8th, we were both at the airport: me on my regular shift, and Jimmy who had ostensibly come to "help" one of his "important clients" through Customs. You understood why our sales guys intervened or bribed Customs officials not to inspect their clients' baggage too closely when you saw the stuff that people took abroad those days: chutneys, pickles, curry stuffs, even cooked food—forms of gratitude and payment at their destination because foreign money was prohibited and expensive on the black market.

Manel arrived at the airport, escorted by her in-laws, one on either side. She wore a glittering blue sari loosely draped around her, sufficient to hide any embarrassing bulges. A horde of visitors, who had arrived separately during the preceding half hour, rose and rushed to greet her. Much hugging, kissing and smiling went on; Manel emerged looking slightly dishevelled and there were damp patches under the arms of her bodice.

I was checking-in passengers, so our interaction was formal. She was within her luggage limit—perhaps she had sent her excess baggage by sea. I imagined her swelling belly, hidden behind those loose folds of the sari. She looked pale, like a resigned victim on her way to the gallows.

As she stooped to pick up her bag, the sari parted briefly and I got a glimpse of her full cleavage—inviting and mysterious. I flushed. She straightened, caught my fluster and smiled. "Mark, thank you for all your assistance. I have your business card in my purse. Can I call on you if I need help?"

"Of course." The words jumped out of me. I felt like a powerless serf, served a morsel at the last minute by the queen passing by in her carriage. "Sure, just send me a message."

"Thank you." she said. "You are so reliable. And disciplined. All the best with your exams." Her eyes lingered on as me as she left the check-in counter.

After she had cleared Customs and Immigration and entered the departure lounge, I saw Jimmy emerge from the crowd of well-wishers and follow her, using his employee badge to get through security; those were the days before planes became bombs and crashed into tall buildings—conditions were a bit lax back then.

I began wrapping up at the counter; all passengers were checked in. Then I saw mother-in law and father-in-law Jayasinghe being escorted by a fawning Customs officer; the man mumbled a word to the security guard at the door to the restricted area and ushered the elderly couple through. The Jayasinghes were heading towards the departure lounge, puffed with self-importance, while other visitors could only stare at their departing loved ones through the public barrier.

I dropped my work, muttered an excuse about taking a quick toilet break to my counter colleague and ran for the lounge. I overtook the Jayasinghes, who paid me only a passing glance. Airport employees ran around a lot in those days, especially when walkie-talkies ran out of power or failed completely through overuse—thanks to import controls that prevented the ordering of spares.

I rounded the corner into the lounge and looked for Jimmy and Manel. My eye immediately caught them in the duty free shop, between the perfumes, *locked in a kiss.*

I wanted to shout, break them apart, warn them of who was coming behind me, but I was frozen amidst this mass of travelling humanity. All I desired was to be standing in Jimmy's shoes right then. As much as I envied him and coveted his position, the other side of me questioned who I was to deny Manel and Jimmy the right to this last moment of happiness, deny them the lie that was real for just that one instant.

When I averted my eyes, the in-laws came into view. Mrs. Jayasinghe, recognizing me as the running employee, promptly inquired, "Is there any problem with this flight?"

"No," I stammered. "Everything is okay."

She was glancing over my shoulder, in the direction of the duty-free shop. She grabbed her husband's hand.

"Jaye…is that our Manel? I can't see without my glasses. Can't be, no?"

I heard the inward uptake of breath from Mr. Jayasinghe, then his swearing, "My God! Bloody shit!"

That's when I started jumping and waving my arms like a man gone crazy, creating a mini-spectacle in the lounge. "Attention, attention everyone! We will be boarding in a few minutes."

A traffic supervisor passing by pulled me aside and started to give me a lecture on using the PA system for such announcements. Had I forgotten my training, he pompously demanded. I nodded dumbly and said that I had indeed forgotten in my hurry. Out of the corner of my eye, I looked back at the duty-free area: Manel was perusing the perfume racks and Jimmy had disappeared.

The traffic supervisor finally left, threatening to report me to my manager. I caught sight of the elder Jayasinghes leaving the departure lounge in a hurry with their sycophantic Customs officer in tow. Mrs Jayasinghe was insisting that it must have been someone else they'd seen, while her husband growled and said that he wanted to get out of this place, he felt so embarrassed.

After the flight had departed and my shift had ended, I met Jimmy outside, by the office bus.

"That was damned stupid," was all I could say.

He had a dreamy look on his face. "She hasn't forgotten me, Marky. The feeling's still strong."

He was silent for the rest of the drive home. We dropped him off at the Piliandala junction and I last saw him walking towards the brightly lit tea-stall, whistling. He looked like a man in a desert, blissfully happy and pursuing his mirage.

***

Jimmy drank a lot in the months that followed, months when there was no news from England. He went off the female tourists completely, and so did I—one night stands were beginning to lose their appeal. He said that he was accompanying his family on their weekly excursion to Sunday mass, something he hadn't done in a long time. When he finally opened up on the subject of Manel at the club one day, he was pretty drunk.

"She asked whether I would marry her if her husband gave her a divorce."

"And…"

"I said I'd like to…" He didn't elaborate, looking dejectedly at his glass, as if wondering whether to order another drink.

"Does she know about your family?"

"Shit, no. We'd never even have gotten off to bat if she knew how many kids I had."

"So you lied to her."

"I didn't lie to her. I just didn't tell her everything…"

"It's a sort of a lie. Would you marry her, if you were able to?"

"Let's not even think about that, Marky boy. You and I know that is never going to happen. I could never leave my family, like my father did."

***

We were both in the office the day the overseas call came. It was during the hot days of June and the city was labouring: the students were getting their admission papers ready before rushing to us, and the tourists were hiding from the heat on some beach or watering hole, out of the humidity of the old Fort area.

"Call for Jimmy, from London," the telephone operator piped out from her cubicle.

Jimmy dropped his newspaper, spilt his afternoon tea and grabbed the phone, all in one swoop. "Put her through."

Her? How did he know?

First he listened, then he tried to protest; there were a whole lot of "but"s, yet she kept overriding him. I saw his face turn pale, then white. Finally, there was a pause on both sides, while the clock ticked and the air conditioner droned, and the other guys in the office tried to guess at what was going on; many had taken bets on various outcomes, as Jimmy's affair was no longer a secret. I heard the polite metallic voice of the operator on the UK end come on and ask if the connection was still required. "Yes, yes," Jimmy growled but remained silent afterwards. Finally, he said, "I'm sorry…I just can't. Maybe if you knew…" Then the line clicked and he was left staring at the dead phone, and me.

***

We didn't talk about that phone call until the aerogramme letter arrived addressed to me at the office. It was brief:

> *5ᵗʰ July 1976*
> *Dear Mr. Jansz,*
> *Your baby will be born at the end of next month. My husband does not want to have anything more to do with me or the child, and has left me, or rather, turned me out. I am living in a woman's shelter right now. I have no money as I have not been able to get a job since arriving in the UK.*
>
> *Given your connections in the airline business, can you please arrange to have the baby brought back to Sri Lanka? I cannot bear to face the anger of my husband's family, so I will continue to live here, if that is at all possible.*
>
> *You promised to help. Please do not let me down. Too many people in my life have done that.*
> *Manel Jayasinghe*

My baby? What the heck was she smoking? I showed Jimmy the letter.

His eyes were red brimmed after he finished reading it. "She's washed her hands of me, Marky. She asked me to marry her again on the phone that day. I said no. What else could I say? Now she's wiped me out of her life. And she knows that being my good protégé, you will show me this letter."

Suddenly this was all becoming very clear to me. "She must have been very unhappy to go to these lengths to leave her husband."

84

Jimmy looked up, his jaw dropping. "What do you mean? Stop being such a smart little bugger, Marky."

"Lies—she fed you lies, Jimmy. I bet you her husband never went on an exchange trip to Germany."

He was silent, digesting my words, looking for solutions.

"I've still got to help her. I can't bear the thought of her living in that derelict shit-hole, having a baby. My baby."

"Or mine—as she is now forcing herself and the world to believe."

"Can you help, Marky? She needs help."

"How?"

"When the baby is born, I can arrange for a pre-paid ticket in the black market for the child. You can apply for a staff ticket, take a trip to England and bring the baby back. I'll cover all your expenses."

"And then?"

"And then…" he was groping, "and then I'll arrange for an orphanage, adoption whatever is required. Just do this for me, buddy."

I felt burdened with this cross of instant parenthood, something he had accepted many times over, at an even younger age than I.

"But I don't want to be the father."

"You won't. You'll just be the…the Good Samaritan!"

I blurted about needing time to think this over. We still had about six weeks before the baby would be born.

I didn't go out for drinks with Jimmy for about a month after that. I locked myself in my room at home after work and focussed on my studies instead. Accountants always measure other people's risk and never take any of their own; that is why the discipline has appealed to me all these years. But during this time I would wake up at night with weird dreams: of screaming babies, and Manel Jayasinghe spewing milk from her swollen breasts, and Mr. and Mrs Jayasinghe locking me in handcuffs pronouncing that I was their prisoner for life. Normally, studies were a way for me to lock out the real word when it became overbearing, but my intake of knowledge and output of work exercises during this period were the worst I'd ever done since embarking on my accountancy course. At the end of two weeks I even considered quitting. Then the thought of ending up like Jimmy with his loveless marriage, umpteen kids, brainless job and no way out, spurred me to greater effort. At the end of that month, I was a wreck, having slept very little, with an overburdened brain full of accounting ratios, balance sheets, investment scorecards and other abstract concepts. Better the abstract; the real was too frightening.

***

I sip my scotch sitting at the corner table of the Ambassador restaurant on King Street in Toronto. In the gilt framed mirrors running around the room, I catch my reflection: a full head of grey hair blackened with a good coating of hair-dye, progressive lenses concealing my terrible eyesight, a thin beard hiding my weak chin—advancing age well camouflaged. The mirror does not reveal the limp from a skiing accident of a few years ago, a recreational sport I was never any good at but which I took up to appease my second wife, to look Canadian and *belong* in this country. I should have known that adopting Canadian culture was not what my wives had wanted—they had wanted me, and *me* was what I had been reluctant to give them. It would have meant risk beyond what I was willing to commit.

The mirror also disguises my height: five feet eight inches. In Sri Lanka that would have passed for average, but over here I am short, and getting shorter as my frame thickens and my belly presses out. Will Susan be pleased with whom she meets?

I see her the instant she steps into the restaurant, looking expectantly around her, ignoring the hostess who is asking her if she has a reservation, striding towards me with glowing eyes, running the last few steps and falling into my arms with an "Oh Daddy...!"

I hold her—this pulsing bundle of energy—smelling the strawberry in her hair, the lilac in her perfume, her breasts pushed up against me in trusting abandon; I marvel at how easy it is to hold her in my arms compared to attempting that with her mother a generation ago. I smell life again. I must be out of breath for she quickly invites me to sit down. She takes the chair opposite me, a dreamy look on her face. "I just want to look at you for a minute. I have imagined you in so many different ways." Her British accent takes getting used to.

After a pause, she concludes, "You are handsome." I blush and exhale.

"Can I get you a drink?" I stammer, noticing Jimmy's piercing eyes, and Manel's shapely tilted nose; a beautiful amalgam of the two people I had betrayed present in this woman before me.

We order wine followed by dinner. I have to filter the information she gives me in between the many asides she makes about missing the life she wished she'd had. She is determined to pursue her dreams now that she has found at least one of her *real* parents.

From the age of six months, she had been adopted by a generous middle-aged childless couple. She had never known her birth mother. Life with her foster parents, both teachers, was comfortable, though not extravagant, nor was she indulged. She aced university. I smile distractedly when she says that—at least, one of Jimmy's kids had finally made it! She was working as a marketing executive in Brighton by the sea. Her adoptive parents had both entered a nursing home recently and their care was provided for by good pensions. Being free and unattached, she was interested in immigrating to Canada and had studied the points criteria required to qualify: with a parent in Toronto, it would be a slam dunk for her.

"I guess, I am anxious to discover how you found me," I ask when our plates are cleared away and coffee served.

"Six months ago, a package arrived at my foster parents' home. It was from Wales. My mother, Manel, was working as a housekeeper for a retired executive and his family. She had saved all her money for me, which was enclosed in a certified cheque. She apologized to me, and you, for betraying us and running away to England to live with her lover, who left her just before I was born. I am sure that this must be hurtful for you, raking up this past."

I keep my eyes on my coffee. Lover? More lies? "Go on. Tell me more."

"She urged me to leave England and go to North America or Australia if I could. She said she regrets not having done so herself, but the fear of change, after all the things that had happened to her, had kept her rooted to Wales and a safe job."

"Did you try to contact your mother?"

"The parcel came from her employer." Susan pauses to take a deep breath. "My mother had died the month before—ovarian cancer that took her very quickly."

There are tears in Susan's eyes, and there are tears in mine too, a vision of that elusive damsel that I had wanted to embrace, now gone forever. I reach out involuntarily and take Susan's hand in mine; her touch signals her gratitude.

She wipes her eyes with a tissue. "I know this must be hard for you," she says. "You knew her. I didn't."

"You still haven't explained how you found me."

"In the package were some photographs, and my birth certificate. You were listed on it as my father, with the address as 'Colombo, Sri Lanka'. There was also your airline business card. I contacted your former office in Sri Lanka and one of the senior staff remembered that you had gone to Canada. A web search did the rest."

The years fall off me. I am racing back to those fateful last days when I made all the wrong decisions.

Susan interrupts my thoughts. "Well, look at what I have ended up doing—reduced myself into a pile of tears and put you into a sulk. I'm really sorry. This is not how I planned this evening."

"Crying is okay. I wish I had cried more, instead of burying myself in work and letting life pass me by."

"But you moved to Canada and are a successful accountant."

"And I drifted through two marriages in this country because I did not know how to love."

Susan looks crestfallen. "But you loved my mother, no?" Her pleading look suggests that everything will crash and burn and this whole reunion will be written off in a flash if I don't say "yes." What harm would one more lie create in this already entangled web?

"Yes, I did," I say looking down. "From afar, at least."

"That's a relief." She relaxes and becomes conscious of the pile of wet tissues in front of her. She looks at her appearance in the gilt edged mirror. "Well, I think I need the loo, right now. Will you excuse me, while I freshen up?"
I watch Susan head for the washroom and recall the final letter I received from Manel.

30th August 1976
Dear Mark,

Your daughter was born two weeks ago. She came early. She is a beautiful girl—six pounds and 10 ounces, and I have called her Susan.

I still have not heard from you regarding the arrangements you are making to bring her back to Sri Lanka.

My husband has filed divorce papers and has threatened to kill the son-of-a-bitch that did this to him. I cannot stay here much longer in this shelter and need to find employment. If I don't hear from you, I have to pursue other alternatives.

Please reply as soon as possible.
Manel

I was shaken to receive that final letter and needed to consult Jimmy, but he was hardly in the office those days. He was usually found at the club even though his bar credit was in the danger zone. His sales at the office were petering out, and I knew it was only going to be a matter of time before the sales manager hauled him in for a "chat."

I rode to the club that day, the letter burning in my hip pocket. I found him drinking alone on the lawn, his chair pulled away from the circles of other members. People were giving him a wide berth that day. It was too early for the Season and there was no Christmas tree across the grounds to remind me that it was only last year that Manel had been sitting with us in this very spot.

Jimmy looked happy to see me. "Marky, have a drink with me, please."

"Only if you can hold your liquor."

"Sure I can." For a moment, he was the Jimmy of old: false bravado, living life in the moment. "See those assholes over there," he gestured towards the club's regulars. "They ignore me now. I told you, didn't I—people take advantage of you, all the time. Then they dump you."

The old waiter, indentured to the club until he would drop dead one day, brought our drinks, but balked when Jimmy asked him to run a tab. Jimmy growled and was about to throw his drink in the poor man's face when I intervened and asked the waiter to put the drinks on me.

"Bastards!" Jimmy yelled at the back of the fast disappearing retainer. "I've spent so much money in this fucking place. Now they quibble over a few drinks."

"Your credit here sucks, Jimmy. And your sales are dropping at the office."

"Don't be such a fucking smart aleck. I'll come back. I've come back a hundred times, *putha*. Even those bastards following me in that Hi-Ace van don't scare me."

A chill ran through me. I left my drink untouched, although that was what I needed just then. "What Hi-Ace van?"

"Old Jayasinghe's goons. He's been after me ever since he saw Manel and me together in the departure lounge."

"You'd better tell the police."

"Are you crazy? They are all in cahoots. You know what scares me, *putha*? It's not my life—it's the life of that little child who will be born any day now. I witnessed all my children's births, even though I haven't been able to do much for them. But this time…I'm so fucked."

Despite my inclination to show him the letter, the news about the Hi-Ace van and Dr. Jayasinghe's threat to "kill that son-of-a-bitch," held me back. I didn't want Manel using me again to hurt him.

"Marky boy, promise me one thing, Will you go to England and bring this kid back? I've arranged the pre-paid ticket and rustled up some Pounds Sterling on the black market for you."

I remained silent and concentrated on finishing my drink.

He kept talking, "And I've arranged a spot with an adoption agency—a reliable one. The kid will be adopted by a couple in Sweden. Everything will be okay, buddy." He forced a grin as if life was normal again.

He sensed my reticence and suddenly reached out and grabbed me. The stench of alcohol and cigarettes on his breath was revolting. "You promise, don't you? Marky? You are not going to be like one of those assholes, are you?"

"I promise," I said hollowly. He released me and slumped back in his seat, drained, drunk and dejected. That picture of him is frozen in my mind forever. So this is what happens when a man falls in love? I didn't want this to ever happen to me. The distaste and fear of loving has dogged me to this day and contributed to my many failed relationships. I knocked back the rest of my drink, left him to his misery and went home. Midway, I realized that I had not even told him that his daughter was already born.

I guess I never got to tell him after all, because that was the night of his accident. An eye witness said that someone carelessly opened the passenger door of a Hi-Ace van while in motion, sending Jimmy skidding towards his death. The van, or its occupants, was never found.

And after Jimmy's funeral, looking at his hysterical wife and lost children, and contrasting it to the prospect promised by my impending accountancy diploma as a passport out of this madness and lies, I chose to mitigate my risk. I tossed Manel's second letter into a garbage container on my way home. Jimmy was dead—there were no more promises to keep.

***

I watch Susan picking her way back from the washroom, composed, fresh, and optimistic again. I wonder if she is lying to herself that I am her father. I don't look like her at all. But there have been lies throughout this story, both overt and hidden, so why not a few more?

"You are still sulking," Susan says, a frown of concern creasing her face.

"I was remembering the years in Sri Lanka."

"And I was thinking of what you said, about not knowing how to love. I can't believe that of you."

"I must have had the wrong teacher, or taken the wrong lessons. Or like a good accountant, I never took risks. Women were a convenience, nothing deeper—that does not make for long relationships."

"Did you use my mother too?"

"No. Surprisingly, she was the only one I could not use."

She picks up her purse as we get ready to leave. "I admire your honesty. Being an accountant, are you going to insist on DNA tests and everything, now that I have surfaced out of the woodwork?"

I smile. Staring across the table is Jimmy's parting gift to me—his final lesson—of loving, and taking all the joys and hurts that come with it. Manel had clinched it by sending Susan her letter: I have no option now but to play this new role and not expose Manel's final lie. I wonder if I can grow to love Susan as a daughter; if I can live the lie long enough so that it becomes real, for both of us. Then something good would have come out of all of this in the end.

"No. That will not be necessary. You are my daughter. I would like to get to know you better over the next little while. Today has been a good start." I sign the bill and slide my credit card back into my wallet.

She holds her hand out to me. "I would like very much to call you—Daddy."

I put my hand over her shoulder and guide her out of the restaurant.

Survivor

The First Coming

He came like Poseidon, over the water surrounding our house in the old country. That is my first memory of him. The tropical rains had been pouring down on us for weeks and the river had overflowed its banks three days earlier, covering the paddy fields and the road, stopping just short of our house situated up on the hill. Mum had kept me home from school since the flood, as the only way to the bus stop, half a mile away, was to go downhill and wade waist high in muddy water full of leeches until you got to higher ground by the town.

He came on a raft strung together with banana tree trunks skewered by wooden stakes. He was bringing old Mrs. Perera from next door and her bags of food; she had gone into town a few days ago and was presumed drowned on her way back home.

As I watched through the window, he jumped off the raft and pulled it to dry land up the hill. He helped a wildly excited, happy-to-be-home Mrs. Perera, and then eased polythene- wrapped packages of groceries onto the stony ground above the waterline.

The man looked hesitantly about him and narrowed his gaze on our house, and at me peeking out. He was in his late twenties, dressed in a faded shirt with its top buttons open or missing, and khaki shorts that had seen better days. He wore no footwear—with this water, shoes, even slippers, were useless. He was short and muscular and his hair was a rusty brown. He was fair and burned red by the sun. His European genes stood out against the darker Mrs. Perera.

Holding her hand, he gently helped the old lady carry her bags to her house as her starving dogs started barking inside. She stopped at the gate to thank the man and stuff something into his hand.

When he neared, I realized that his face was terribly disfigured. A hair lip split his mouth apart and ran up into his nose.

I felt Mum's presence at the window behind me and heard her sharp intake of breath. "Burke? Burke—what are you doing here?"

The man smiled shyly, and when he spoke I could not understand him—his words were mashing into each other. It was only over the time he subsequently spent with us, that I finally understood his speech. "I um noo nay wi' u. (I've come to stay with you)." He put his hand inside his shirt and pulled out an oily polythene bag. " 'Ere mought you some 'ake (Here, bought you some cake)."

Mum had her hands on her hips. "After all these years? After all your boozing and carrying on, you come to stay with us during a flood?"

"I ot ticked out fom de boding (I got kicked out from the boarding)."

"Serves you right. It's your ganja smoking that does it. I have an eight-year old boy to look after now," she threw back at him, placing her hand on my shoulder. "Can't have your sinful ways around this house."

" 'At yo boy?" He looked at me and broke into a smile. The rain had started falling again from skies that had swelled to a dark grey since the last cessation.

"Who is that man," I asked, getting nervous at this altercation.

"Ralphy, go inside and do your school work." Mum pushed me away from the window.

I held firm. "Who is this man?"

Mum shook her head in frustration. "My brother," she replied. "My long lost little brother."

***

Uncle Burke stayed with us for a month that first time. Mum gave him the servant's shed in the back garden to live in (Mum was between servants at the time as they were always getting jobs and going away to the Middle East in those days) and he bathed at the outdoor well we used when the tap water was cut off several times a week. He used the communal latrines in the nearby municipal housing project. "Too messy," was all Mum would say when I asked why Uncle Burke could not use our indoor bathroom. My father, who was in the merchant navy and away on one of his regular voyages overseas, wasn't at home during Burke's stay with us. I was forbidden from going into my uncle's temporary home in the shed.

Burke spent the first few days reinforcing his banana boat with stronger stakes and ferrying people and goods over the flooded neighbourhood—always courteous, always careful to escort his passengers and their goods off the raft without getting them wet. I saw his passengers hand him money which he gratefully accepted. He rowed me to and from the bus stop so I wouldn't miss school: it was comforting, to see him standing there waiting for me as I got off the school bus on my way home. I got the seat in the stern beside him when he had other passengers. Before long, others started water taxi services with similarly constructed boats and rafts and Burke started to lose interest. By then the waters were receding and life was returning to normal. One day, he ripped his boat apart and set the banana logs floating in the thick sludgy flood remnants that still hugged the land.

Mum cooked him a plate of rice and curry for lunch and dinner, daily, and kept it on the back porch wrapped in a napkin. Without an exchange of words he would pick the food up, and leave the empty plate, washed and dried, for her an hour later. One day, I saw Mum pick up the empty plate and shrug, "Hmm, at least, he has learned some good habits now."

Choosing my moment, I asked her, "Why do you treat him like a servant?"

Her fair face went red. She tucked a stray lock of dark brown hair behind her ear and looked towards the shed. "He disgraced the family."

"Why? Because of his face?"

"No—that we couldn't fix because we did not have the money. No one could understand him speak. He was an angry child. Getting into scrapes all the time. One day he threw a stone at a Catholic priest in his school. They sacked him. Then he went to the dogs. Drugs, drinking. Some other bad things which I can't tell you."

"When did you last see him?"

"When you were a baby. He came to see *you*, but Grandpa chased him away."

"How did he live?"

"I don't know. Burke has always been a survivor. Makes things with his hands. Comes up with all sorts of schemes. See what he did during the flood? That's our Burke." She suppressed a sad smile. "That's why I don't worry too much about him—he'll get by."

One day, when Mum had gone to the post office, I was reading my junior edition of *Kidnapped* but was more interested in finding out about our shed dweller. Book in hand—just in case Mum came back unexpectedly—I slipped across the garden. He had cleared a space amidst the tools and knick-knacks and was lying on the rickety stained camp cot. A cigar dangled from his mouth, and it gave off a foul odour. He raised an eyebrow when I peeped in the doorway. His eyes arched up, as if he were about to pounce on me, then he broke into a smile, the crack in his mouth widening to reveal betel stained teeth. " 'Ow are you?"

"Mum says you are getting better," I said nervously, hoping he would not devour me with that blood-red mouth.

He laughed into the rafters, so loud that dust from the thatch fell down on his bare chest. "She 'ont tell me dat. What's the book?"

I told him.

"Will you read to me?"

I was starting to get accustomed to his funny speech now and did not have to force my ears to catch his meaning.

I read to him. It was much more interesting than reading alone. I couldn't remember when Mum had last read to me, now that I was considered "a big boy." And Dad was never around. Burke was a patient and rapt listener, and even when his cigar went out he did not notice it. I forgot the time, immersed as I was in dramatizing the events in the story for my audience of one, until I heard Mum calling for me.

"I've got to go," I said in a panic.

He rose, lithe and fast, like a cat, stubbed out his cigar and peeped through the dusty window towards the house. "Okay. But come back sometime. I like that story. I never could read."

The following day, he showed up on the back porch, just as Mum was placing his plate of food down on the steps. I peered at them through my bedroom window which overlooked the backyard.

"I like to make something for you," he said. "I can't stay here for free."

"I know you are good with your hands, Burke, but there is nothing that I need. Bernard brings back everything from his overseas trips."

"I bet you he cannot bring you a marble garden seat."

"A marble garden seat? How on earth would he bring one of those? They must weigh a ton. And why would I need a marble garden seat?"

"See! So there is something I can make for you. Your neighbour Mrs. Perera has one."

"And since when have you been making marble garden seats?"

He placed his hands on his chest and bowed. "Burke's Marble—that was my company, until I ran out of cash."

"Is this a way for you to get money from me?"

"No, no. You can buy me the materials. I will make it. I don't need any money. Please Mary—please, let me do something for you." He had gone down on his knee. Mum dabbed her nose on her apron.

"Okay. I'll think about it," she said and quickly retreated indoors. Later, I heard her grumbling under her breath in the kitchen, "Useless things…garden seats. If only he made me some storage for the bathroom…"

I knew why she was frustrated: if she wouldn't let him use our bathroom, how could she ask him?

***

The marble garden seat was Burke's grand project. Mum relented and gave him the money to buy the materials after he provided her with an elaborate list of what he needed: cement, rubble, black marble stones, river sand, bricks, six-foot long planks, twine, a saw and a trowel. And Mum could not forbid me from looking, as Burke had decided to erect his worksite in a section of flat ground in the backyard.

He laid old newspapers on the ground. On them he placed bricks in the shape of a meshed rectangle to form a sand-free work platform. He sawed the planks into four-foot and two-foot sections and created a rectangular frame that he placed on top of the platform. Then he mixed the cement, marble, rubble and sand with water into a goopy mortar and poured it inside the frame.

He chomped on his cigar and said, "Now, we let it sit."

The following morning when I awoke, he was spraying water on the slab that had hardened overnight. When I enquired, he said, "Like plants—you have to water it. It gets harder and stronger every time you water it."

From then on, I sat in the garden and read to Uncle Burke as he gazed lovingly on his creation, solidifying daily before our eyes. We read a lot of books during that first week of construction. I ran through my pictorial editions of *Moby Dick, Call of the Wild, Swiss Family Robinson* and *The Adventures of Gulliver in Lilliput.*

One day, I asked him, "Mum says you are messy, but I don't see it. Are you?"

He laughed silently. "I was an angry child. I broke things. Smashed them."

"That's why she wouldn't let you in the house?"

"I'm better now. A Buddhist monk cured me. He taught me how to turn destruction into construction. That's why I only *make* things now. But your mummy only remembers the past. It's sometimes hard to let go of the past. I know. That is why I went to the monk."

"Will you make her a marble cupboard for the bathroom, next?"

He didn't look very convincing when he replied, "Maybe…"

***

Mum got distracted when a telegram arrived from Dad saying that his voyage had been cut short in Singapore and that he would be flying home shortly.

She rushed outdoors, telegram in hand. "Burke, we have to clean up your mess in the backyard. When will the seat be ready? We should have it installed before Bernard gets here."

"Another week," he replied.

"A week? We don't have a week. Bernard will be here in four days."

Burke scratched his head but did not reply.

***

I'll never forget that day, four days later, because we had just finished *Robinson Crusoe* the evening before and Burke had remarked that he had been like Mr. Crusoe all these years, lost in his world that no one could understand. And that I was like his Man Friday. I felt proud to be included on his island.

I woke that day in anticipation and dread. It was a school day. From my window, I could see Burke tapping off the planks that supported the marble slab. I dressed quickly, took my satchel and went into the back yard.

"It is time," he said. "Your mother says so."

"But what do you think?"

He puffed on his smelly cigar. "I wish I had a say in this."

"It's your marble block."

"Your mother has spoken. All my life, *they* have told me what to do. That's why I cannot stay long with anybody."

He broke off, for Mum was on the back steps, hands on hips. "Well, is it ready?"

"Yes," he said. He lifted the block and set it down on two upended rows of bricks placed at both its shorter ends.

"It doesn't look solid enough to me," she observed.

"Ralphy will stand on it. He will show you how strong it is. Go on, Ralphy." His eyes were imploring me not to let him down. "Show her." I didn't realize then that he was reluctant to stand on it himself, and was hoping that my lighter weight would not damage the slab.

I took my shoes off and gingerly stepped onto the block. It was cold even to my socked feet. Its surface was rough and its colour was granite.

"Walk all over it." His eyes had a maniacal glow, as if he were trying to defy the world. "My Man Friday, go on."

Buoyed by his encouragement, I stepped out into the centre of the slab just as it emitted a sharp crack, formed an erratic line under my feet, and collapsed right through the middle.

Mum shrieked and Burke lowered his head like a kicked dog. "It needed a full week," he said.

I felt like I had betrayed him and tears flowed from my eyes. I shut them only to feel two strong arms and a whiff of cigar smoke lift me from the midst of the wreckage and place me on the firm earth again.

"I'm sorry," I said, holding onto his hand.

"It's okay." He kept rustling my hair with his calloused fingers.

Mum's eyes were alight with anger. "Bernard will give you beans when he comes in the evening. And he'll be mad at me for wasting all this money on you."

"But he said he needed more time," I interjected.

"Ralphy—don't argue. You will be late for the school bus." She stormed indoors.

Wearily, Burke knelt over his broken marble slab and picked through the pieces. He retrieved an undamaged square, about a foot on each side. "Might be good for the bathroom, no? Your mummy can put her toilet things on it."

***

When I returned from school that day, Burke's garden workspace had been cleaned up—there were only traces of mortar to disturb its original appearance. The shed door was locked. Mum was sewing in her bedroom and did not look to be in a mood for talking.

"Where is Uncle Burke?" I asked, stubbornly breaking her peace.

"He left."

"He never said goodbye."

"He never does. He's a gypsy."

"Why did you not listen to him? He said he needed time."

She put her things away. "I am so used to his screwing things up that I sometimes cause him to screw up. He needs to live away from us, from me."

I was annoyed with Uncle Burke too, for coming into our lives like Poseidon parting the waves, and then exiting like a thief.

A horn tooted outside. Mum jumped up, anticipation, excitement, even a trace of fear mixed in her face. "Bernard! Your Daddy is home." She rushed out to the porch.

I followed her, but paused when I saw the small slab of marble on the dining table; it looked like the piece Burke had salvaged from the wreck. Its sides were neatly sanded and the top was polished. There was a note wedged under the block. It had an illegible scrawl that I think read, "From Burke."

But Mum wasn't paying attention. I heard her excited chatter outside, the slamming of the taxi door and my father's gruff voice in greeting. Normality was returning to our home.

The right players were back in place. All that remained of the stranger who had come into our lives and elevated me to his Man Friday was that piece of black marble, and the fast fading smell of cigar smoke in the air.

The Second Coming

The year after Dad left the merchant navy was rough. Civil war broke out in the country and the economy went into tailspin. Dad bragged that he would land a job in a flash, but everywhere he applied they said that he had no experience—after all, a guy who had spent ten years as a purser on a ship did not have much scope on land. One thing my dad could do well was talk; he said it was a gift of being a Burgher. And he could drink—another gift of the Burghers. So, as he talked at every job interview and was declined, he drank more, and at the end of that first year of his return home, most our savings were gone. Mum kept things afloat somewhat by taking on dressmaking jobs for people in the area.

Mum and Dad did not know each other much anymore; his long absences had contributed to their distance. There was even a time, after he had returned from a voyage, when he slept in the spare room during his entire month onshore and Mum had remained silent about his behaviour. He went to the doctor a lot during that time and now I realize what had probably been the problem. After that, they tried to avoid each other as much as they could and only talked when I was around, and then too, it was always small talk.

I was pumping air into my bicycle that day, about to head out to give tuition to a ten-year old kid who lived in the neighbourhood, when I heard this voice from the past come from behind me.

"Ah, you are a mig moy now!"

I swung around. The rusty brown hair was scantier, the face craggier, the frame fuller, the horrible crack in his face covered partially by a full moustache.

"Uncle Burke!" I exclaimed. I was pleased to see him. My resentment over his last abrupt departure quickly fell away.

He held out his arms and when I grabbed him in an embrace, he was a good head shorter. I don't think he could have lifted me as he did the last time. He smelt of the sweat of several days, and of that infamous cigar which brought back memories.

He was pulling a cart behind him. On it, sat a rickety metal-and-wood contraption with two circular openings at both ends and a coiled cylinder in the middle. A pile of coarse brushes with new wire and garish handles lay to the side, tied in a bundle with rope.

"I os massing by (I was passing by)."

His speech began returning to me.

"Dad's home now. For good," I informed him.

"Good for your mummy. She will not be so angry all the time." He gave me a mischievous leer.

"I wish." I sighed.

He looked concerned. "It's not good?"

"You'd better talk to them," I said, mounting my bike. "I have to give a tuition class—that's how I make my pocket money these days. There isn't a lot of cash at home."

"Did your mummy use the marble slab I left her?"

"It lay around in the shed for a few years but she would not part with it. Then I installed it in the bathroom for her. She puts all her things on it now."

"Oh, good."

"Are you planning to stay with us again? The shed is vacant. We can't afford servants anymore."

"If your mummy and daddy will have me. The people I was staying with sold up and went to Canada."

"Canada! That's where we should go. But Mary is full of doubts." It was Dad coming out from behind me, dressed in just a singlet and shorts, barefooted. "Hello Burke. What's all this shit you are carrying around with you?"

Seeing Dad, Burke immediately looked cowed. Dad towered above us and weighed over 200 pounds; that's why he threw his weight around in this country where everyone was scrawny, small and dark-skinned. Dad even had blue eyes, a throw-back to his Dutch ancestry and one that gave him a superiority complex over the "natives," as he called his fellow-countrymen.

"I am making brushes, now."

"What's that? Speak up man. You still have that bloody hair-lip thing. Why didn't you get it fixed?"

"He makes brushes," I translated.

"Brushes?" Dad squatted to inspect the goods. "Huh, pretty dammed good."

"And brooms and rugs," Burke continued, starting to pump up with hope.

"With that machine, huh?" Dad looked sceptically at the appliance on the pull cart. "Where did you buy it from?"

"I made it," Burke said.

My heart swelled with pride for this bedraggled uncle who seemed to re-invent himself every time I saw him.

"I'll be damned," Dad said, scratching his balding head, inspecting the device.

Dad straightened up after a few moments of jerking the machine's parts. "Well, come on in. Let's have a drink. We've got to talk about this." He raised his voice and shouted indoors. "Mary, guess who blew in—your long-lost brother!"

"I have to go," I said, pushing off on my bike. "I hope, at least, you will be around for dinner when I return."

***

He stayed for dinner all right, and for a whole year afterwards. Dad had sensed opportunity. My father was all plans during dinner on that first evening, fuelled in part by a bottle of arrack. I noticed that Burke did not join him in the alcohol, but sported a cautious look right through the meal. Mum was in high spirits too—somehow she seemed to have transferred all her affection that she normally had reserved for Dad (before he came home from that suspicious voyage) to her prodigal brother. She cooked up a superb meal of rice, chicken curry, fried brinjals, dhall and okra: a feast we would normally expect at Easter or Christmas, given how low our fortunes had sunk.

"You make them, I'll sell them," Dad said, belching after the dinner had gone down, reaching to drain the dregs of the arrack bottle into his glass.

"Burke, take some more food, child. You are looking haggard since I last saw you." Mum gestured to the leftovers. Burke did not seem to need much encouragement. He was already licking his fingers and tipping the remaining chicken leg onto his plate. I passed the bowl of rice to him.

Dad carried on, addressing no one in particular. "The problem with this bloody country—everything is based on influence. Now that the Tamil Tigers have given these Sinhala buggers a scare, they will hunker down even more by favouring their own kind. We Burghers should have left long ago."

"But if we hadn't been Burghers, everything we owned would have been burned last year," Mum lashed back. I was surprised at her sudden outburst, even though it was over the events of June 1983, a year ago, when the bodies of those 13 Sinhala soldiers were brought into Colombo, an event that had started the *hartal* against the Tamils. Perhaps she felt emboldened to chastise her useless husband now that she had the protection of her deformed younger sibling at hand.

Dad ignored her outburst. "How can you live in a country where they come in mobs and kill minorities. We are minorities too—don't forget that. Our turn could be next."

Burke swallowed his last morsel of food, drank some water, burped and looked up. I think his deformity made him a silent witness in company. He also looked uncomfortable in his chair, and kept glancing at the furniture in the dining room and the veranda beyond. I suddenly realized that during his previous stay he had not eaten even once at our dining table—in fact, he had never been inside our house.

"I sold the brushes," Burke said. "I make them *and* sell them."

"How can you sell, man?" Dad looked impatiently at his brother-in-law. "With your hair-lip, people cannot even understand you. You need my help."

"Is is because you need a job?" Burke asked politely.

Dad's face reddened. "Listen—how many brushes do you sell a day?"

"Depends. Sometimes a dozen, sometimes two or three."

"And you walk door-to-door?"

"Yes."

"You are not going to get rich that way."

"And how are *you* going to get rich?" Mum butted in, looking at Dad.

"By selling to the wholesalers. That's how. Batches of a hundred at a time."

"But I can make only ten a day," Burke said.

"If you are not gallivanting all over the place trying to sell your products, you could make ten times that," Dad countered without missing a beat.

Burke looked down at his plate. "I suppose I can."

"You could make another machine," Dad said, "a bigger one."

Burke smiled. "Or I could make a machine that does many brushes in one load."

"You made that rust box by yourself?" Mum asked. She was having difficulty with comprehending her brother, I could see. After all, he was the guy known for screwing up, and here he was turning out industrial strength brushes, rugs, mops and carpets with the turn of the screw in his bizarre contraption.

"My friend and I made it," Burke explained with downcast eyes. "But he decided to do something else. So I went on my own."

"Listen Burke," Dad leaned over. "The shed is vacant. You can turn it into your workshop. Let's go into partnership."

Burke looked at Mum then at Dad then at me and then back at Dad. Mum was looking expectantly at her brother. Finally, Burke said, "Okay, I guess it is settled then."

"It will be wonderful for you to stay with us, Burkey boy," Mum said.

"And you will let him use the bathroom and the dining room and enter the house without asking for permission?" I added my two cents to the negotiation.

Mum blushed and glinted at me. "Of course, of course."

***

And so B&B Brushes & Brooms was born. Bernard, my father, was the sales manager and Burke was in charge of production. And I helped during my free time, preparing the wooden handles (we did not paint them anymore as that took too much time) and arranging the various batches of coir or wire needed for the bristles of the brushes. There were various kinds of raw material to deal with, for the products varied from floor mops to rugs to toilet brushes to baby feeding bottle cleaning brushes to toothbrushes to shoe brushes. Burke made a larger machine that, once set to the size and shape of brush, could spew out a dozen units at the other end by a turn of the handle at his end.

Dad was highly motivated. After months of inactivity, he now had a purpose and a goal. He loaded his old Vespa scooter with product every morning and disappeared, to return in the evening with his pillion empty. And Burke worked from dawn till late at night trying to fulfil the orders that Dad brought in. This activity also kept the interaction between my parents to a minimum and focussed them on the business.

Therefore, it surprised me one evening, after dinner had been cleared away, when Dad banged his hands on the table spilling a pile of invoices on the floor. "We are still not making any real money!"

"What do you mean, Bernie?" Burke asked tentatively.

"We have too many product lines—we are selling two-three pieces of each everywhere. There are no economies of scale."

Burke could not understand Dad's bombastic word pulled straight from the Economics text book. "What do you mean? But we are making and selling more brushes than when I was on my own."

"That's the point—we are making too many damn things. Let's cut out the rugs, feeding bottle brushes, and toilet brushes—too little of that stuff moves. I met a new dealer who exports to the Middle East, and he could sell big quantities for us, but only brooms and mops. He can buy them from us in hundreds, even thousands. Make a bigger machine, but only for these items. And turn out a hundred per batch."

Burke scratched his head and looked forlorn. "But I liked the variety."

"This is not about likes, man—we have to make a living from this."

"Okay, I'll see what I can do." When Burke left the dining room his shoulders were stooped.

After Burke had departed to his shed for his late-shift production run, Dad dropped his voice to a whisper, "I also got the papers from the Canadian embassy today. We are going to apply to immigrate. Now that I have 'Sales Manager' on my list of experiences, I stand to get points under the Jobs category."

Mum sucked in her breath and said nothing. I could feel the steam coming out of her ears. But she refrained from saying anything in my presence.

"What will happen to Uncle Burke if we leave?" I ventured.

"He won't get passed with his speech defect and all," Dad said.

"But we can't leave him behind. He's put all his effort into B&B." Mum had found her voice.

"You said it yourself—he is a survivor. He'll manage."

***

"How do you to get to Canada?" Uncle Burke asked. It was three months later and he had just finished upgrading his machine to a larger one, which had meant working seven days a week: five days on regular production, and the weekends on building the new machine. Money was still tight, Dad said, so Burke had improvised with old parts from cars and motorcycles that he had rummaged from the nearby scrap yard.

"Lots of luck, that's what you need to get to Canada," Dad laughed, downing his fourth drink. They had been celebrating the new machine and Burke had indulged in a Churchill cigar that Mum had bought for him from Miller's department store in Colombo. It was like they were trying to cushion him for the news.

I tried to explain the process as we had experienced it. "Well, there is the application, and the interview and the medicals. We have to go for our medicals next week."

"And don't forget the police check," Dad said.

"Police check?" Uncle Burke looked puzzled.

"They want to see if you have a criminal record."

"Oh," Burke looked crestfallen. "But how are all those criminals who burnt down the houses in Colombo in the *hartal* going across? I knew some of them."

Dad looked taken aback, as if relegated to the class of criminals that Burke was referring to. "Perhaps, they never got caught. Or perhaps you are mistaken."

"Do you want to apply to go with us, Uncle Burke?" I was hoping he would say yes. I could already imagine him running a huge factory in Canada, exporting his brooms and brushes all over the world.

"No thanks, son." Then he almost whispered to himself, "Criminal record checks, huh."

It had all started a bit earlier that evening when Dad had taken his third drink and told Burke that he could have the whole of B&B when we left for Canada.

Burke had sputtered on his cigar and coughed. "Canada?"

Mum looked down at the table, and I did not know where to stick my face. After all, the three of us had been part of this conspiracy not to tell Burke, in case he was distracted from building his larger production facility. "It's for his own good, the bigger machine," Dad had cautioned us, so we followed suit, even though I had felt like Judas ever since.

Dad shrugged, downed his drink, and poured his fourth shot of arrack. "We did not want to tell you Burke, and distract you from your work. It was a long shot to begin with. But we had our interview this week and things look promising."

"And I thought you were going to a wedding—all dolled up like that," he said, shaking his head from side to side, sucking on his cigar.

"Just think of it—you will have a bigger operation—selling a hundred brushes a day."

"But *you* sold them. I could only sell two or three, maybe a dozen a day if I was lucky."

"Hire someone, Burke—you can do it." Dad seemed to be suddenly tiring of his motivational speech.

Uncle Burke scratched his head. "I am not sure about that." That's when he asked me the question of how one got to Canada.

***

Six months later, we received positive results to our medicals and police checks and needed only the visa documents to follow in the mail. I went across to the shed that day. There was a different set-up inside now. His three generations of production machines sat in the centre of the floor: Father Bear, Mother Bear and Baby Bear, I called them. The whole place was swept and utilitarian. Bundles of wire and racks of wooden handles covered one corner. A huge work bench with machine tools stood in another. There was also more light as Burke had installed track lighting along the perimeter of the shed and cut out an extra pair of windows on the east and west walls. Bales of wrapped brooms and brushes were stacked by the door awaiting shipment; I was surprised that there was so much production for distribution. And most surprising of all, Burke was lying in his old camp cot by the window, smoking, when he normally would be working.

"Lots of orders I can see," I said.

He glanced over at the piles by the door. "That's last month's production. Your daddy has lost interest. I have no more space until that batch goes out, so I am taking a break."

"Are you going to hire someone?" I asked.

"Your daddy says that we are still not making any *real* money."

"That's not what I heard him tell Mum. How do you think he got the money to pay for our tickets to Canada?"

He sat up this time and stared at me. Then he laid his cigar in an ashtray on a nearby stool. The cigar rolled off and spilled its ashes on the stool but he ignored it. "Are you telling me that you have been passed already?"

I looked down. I could not meet his steely gaze.

He rose slowly and walked over to the work bench and fiddled with a wrench.

"Why didn't you want to come along with us?" I persisted.

"They wouldn't pass me. I have a criminal record. I stoned a priest, remember."

"But that was long ago."

He pointed to Baby Bear. "After I broke up our business, my partner made an entry in the police station that I had stolen his invention. The police didn't get around to investigating."

"You stole it?"

He laughed bitterly and pointed to Mother Bear and Father Bear. "Do you think I could have made these others if it was *his* invention?"

"What will you do? After we leave?"

He looked at me. There were tears in his eyes and I was trying to hold back my own. "You will do well in Canada. Everyone does well in Canada."

He went back to the camp cot, stuck his cigar in his mouth and closed his eyes.

***

That night, the shed burnt down. We awoke to bright lights glinting off the windows. What had been the B&B factory was a ball of flame. Dad rushed downstairs and tried to use the garden hose. Mum phoned for the fire brigade, who came two hours later, all whistles blaring, only in time to sift through the embers.

Mum was devastated and hysterical and had to take a sleeping pill. Dad cursed and swore and drank a whole bottle of arrack to calm his nerves. The fire chief reported that the shed and all its contents were burned down. There were no human injuries.

"All…all the mach…machines were destroyed?" Dad stammered in drunken self-pity.

"Two machines were destroyed, sir," the fire chief confirmed.

"Only two?" I asked. "There were three."

Dad and I toured the site with the fireman to verify his statement. Mother Bear and Father Bear had melted into each other. Baby Bear was gone. So was Burke.

"There was a melted ashtray full of cigar stubs on a burnt camp cot inside. We also found a lighted cigar on the ground outside the structure. It may have caused the fire. Was anyone living in the shed, sir?"

Before Dad could reply, I interjected, "No. No one lived in the shed."

***

Three months later we left for Canada to begin a new life. As the aircraft circled our little pearl-shaped island of Sri Lanka before setting off on its long journey, I looked down on the dark green foliage below, wondering how and where Uncle Burke would re-emerge.

The Final Meeting

We only think of dear ones when times get tough. Uncle Burke slipped my mind for several years. But there had been plenty to occupy ourselves in the interim. I qualified for scholarships to get into university after two years of high school in Toronto.

Dad, for all his grandiose plans to become "Mr. Super Salesman," ended up selling appliances in an electronics store on straight commission. He wanted to do a real-estate course but we were always short of money in those early days. When he made sales bonuses during the Christmas season, he drank a lot and cursed this cold unfriendly land that was intent on thwarting his moves to make it to the top.

Mum, on the other hand, forced to take a job to make ends meet, flourished. She joined a craft store and in a few years was designing her own creations. She made cloth dolls for children and doll houses and other custom articles that began to fetch good prices. Within months of her joining the store, her proprietor began pushing Mum to stage her own exhibition, the route to the top of that industry, but in her typical cautious manner she kept putting him off, "Later, later. I have a husband and son to look after first." I never realized that my mother had such a talent until I remembered that she was Burke's sister.

I came out of university loaded with student loans; the scholarships had only taken me so far. I was greeted into the real world with my father collapsing on the floor of his showroom, felled by a massive heart attack that killed him in the ambulance on the way to Emergency. He was just a few days short of his fiftieth birthday. His Canadian dream had never materialized. I wondered if he would have done better to have remained a partner of the burnt down B&B Brushes and Brooms. Perhaps it never would have burned down if he had stayed.

Mum's cautious side got hold of me immediately and I took the safest possible job: I joined a bank as a management trainee.

My Canadian dream was made up of lurching from one debt to another. It seemed like the common Canadian's dream, and I had fallen in with the masses, destined never to stand out. After the student loans, came the car loan, and then the mortgage, when my wife Jean, whom I met in university, and I, decided to buy the new house in Oshawa. Thus began the record commuting into downtown Toronto—one hour in each direction if I was lucky. When the kids arrived in fast succession—Richard and Sally—our whole world quickly revolved around them. It was baseball for Rich and skating for Sally and swimming for both, and any other artistic or recreational sport we could squeeze in for them in our already extended schedules. Jean was a primary school teacher and had her own share of workload and stress to deal with. The years went by fast and when I hit the ripe old age of 40, Jean and I took our first vacation to the Caribbean, leaving the kids, 10 and eight, with Mum. My mother was also taking her first real break in Canada at the time, by retiring at 65. Eighteen years earlier, she had relented to her boss and staged her first craft exhibition, soon after Dad died, an event that had put her on a trajectory to fame (not necessarily wealth) in her field. Her only way out had been retirement.

Two years after that first vacation, the axe fell on my world. I lost my job in the wake of the crash of 2008. It was clinical and fast. I had risen to the rank of director at that time—a mindless job in a hierarchy where decisions were pushed up until someone ultimately called the shots. I didn't call any shots, I was expendable, and so were a large number of my colleagues. I was thrown into a job market glutted with guys like me, or better than me. What the heck was I to do with my young family and my pile of debt?

My boss gave me some advice as she handed me my pink slip and an eight-month severance package in consideration of my tenure at the bank. "Get out of this business altogether. Start your own, you are still young. They can't take your own business away from you, unless you mortgage it."

I spent a week, cocooned by my loving and sympathetic family who tried to cheer me up. But cheering-up was one thing; I realized that my Canadian dream was founded on money—and when that eventually dried up, my dream would be in tatters: the thought of repossessed cars, houses and property, divorce, suicide even, was common in this land of milk and honey, especially when the milk went sour and the honey dried up. And how could I start my own business without getting into more debt?

My thoughts eventually turned to Uncle Burke, the master of re-invention. I guess I needed to see him again. Perhaps he had some answers for me, some inspiration—if he was still alive, that is. Very soon, the desire to see him became an obsession in my depressed state. I went to see my mother. She lived in a modest apartment that her pension and savings could now afford her.

"I have no idea where my brother is after all these years. He sent me a surprise Christmas card, with only his signature on it, five years ago. I was worried at the time because it was from a hospital of all places. I wrote to the hospital, but they advised me that he had checked himself out. So I knew he was okay. He contacts me only when he is in trouble."

She had kept that card. She went over to her family album and carefully flipped through the pages. I looked at Mum during her hunt for the card. She was the only one who had, in the most unlikely way, achieved her dream in this new land. She was now a well known (retired) designer of children's crafts. Having eased out of the exhibition circuit, she now worked when she felt like it and did many charity projects for underprivileged and immigrant children. Her one-bedroom apartment was littered with dolls and cloth animals and playhouses. I wished she had demonstrated this gift when I was a child, but back in those days she had been pre-occupied with maintaining a house and raising a son, with an absentee husband, in a country of shortages.

"Here it is," she pulled the card out triumphantly, and the envelope it had arrived in. "See—he mailed it from the Kalubowila Hospital. What does that tell you? That he had no fixed address—nothing unusual—but that he was in some kind of health crisis."

I fingered the card; a cheap, mass produced piece from Hong Kong, with snow and pine trees and sleighs by an artist who had probably never seen the real thing.

"I am going back to Sri Lanka," I announced. "I'm going to track him down."

A worried frown crossed her brow. "Be careful, child. I hear they are planting bombs all over the place now. Even in Colombo."

"I'll be careful. Besides I have time on my hands."

She pulled a photograph from the album. "Here, take this with you. It will help in your search. But bring it back safely, it's the only one I have of him."

It was a black and white picture taken of Burke standing next to his "Three Bears" inside our old shed. Burke had a downcast expression on his face even though he seemed as if he was trying to smile.

"You took this before we left?" I asked.

"Yes. I am so glad I did. That was the day after your father broke the news to him about of our plan to immigrate to Canada."

"I can't help but feel that we let him down, leaving like we did."

"What to do, child? Let bygones be bygones. Your father ran everybody's lives back then. I had to obey him."

"You were a bundle of talent waiting to blossom, the moment he died," I said.

I tucked the photograph in my pocket and got up to leave. As I embraced and gave her a kiss on the forehead, she trembled. "Please tell Burke…that I…" She was groping for the words.

"Yes?" I wanted her to say it. Get it off her chest after all these years.

"Tell him…" she bit her lip and turned her back on me.

"I'll tell him," I said finally. There was no sense in dragging it out any more. I guess, my mother, for all her accomplishments, still had her issues.

"Please look after that photograph," she said before rushing into her bedroom.

***

I started my search in Colombo, at the Kalubowila Hospital. The city of Colombo was dirtier and more congested than I had ever seen it. Every bit of street front had been overbuilt several stories high, shrinking the old colonial-era roads even further. Armed policemen at regular intervals and the frequent military check-points were new and disquieting. I had to remind myself that this was a country at war with itself.

The hospital scared me with its hordes of patients standing, sitting, lying on the floor, waiting for a minute of attention from the few overworked doctors who barked orders and looked like they were due for a nervous breakdown at any moment. My fair complexion, clothes and accent classified me as a foreigner and I drew more attention than the patients, but heads shook negatively when they looked at the picture of Burke. Five years was too long in their memories, too many atrocities and disasters had happened in the interim.

A nurse suggested that I talk to Raju, a male intern who had been in the hospital for 30 years and who knew more stories about the place than anyone else. I found Raju, chewing betel in the cafeteria, wearing a faded green uniform and rubber slippers. I spoke to him in halting Sinhala, which had been returning to me in dribs since my return, and showed him the photograph. Raju had once been a body builder, you could tell from his frame, but now his shoulders were stooped, and he carried a hairy belly that poked through his uniform which was missing two buttons down the front. He surveyed the photograph and spat a red stream into the spittoon by the side wall.

"His crutches did not fit. So he stuck broom handles in them to make them longer," Raju said with a smile on his face.

I sat forward in my seat. "So you remember him then?"

"Yes, Burke *mahattaya*. We used to chew betel together."

"Why was he in the hospital?"

"He was almost dead when they brought him here. Bomb blast. One of the innocent pedestrians. Both his legs were shattered and had to be amputated."

A chill crept through me. "How long was he here?"

"A month or two maybe. I can't remember now. But he was determined to get back to selling his brushes."

"How the heck could he do that in his condition?"

"He even offered me a job—as his assistant. He said there were great sales to be made at the Pettah market. He knew a stall owner who was retiring. Burke *mahattaya* had offered to buy the spot from him in exchange for twenty percent of every sale. Burke *mahattaya* wanted me to help because now that he was going to be in a wheelchair for the rest of his life, he could not chase after urchins and thieves who stole his wares."

Raju rose, folded another betel leaf into the corner of his mouth, popped a strip of dried tobacco along with it, chewed firmly, and started to walk away.

"Wait," I followed him. "What happened to Burke? Where did he go?"

Raju turned and there was shame written all over his face. "I said no to him. And I regret it now. I chose the safety of this place which has been my home for all these years. I chose to see the human misery of sickness and the damage done to people by bombs and fighting. They come in here every day—young and old—maimed and put on waiting lists for years to get artificial limbs so that they can try to function again. He offered me a way out, and I said 'no.'"

Raju bowed his head and shuffled down the hallway with its chipped cement floor and grimy walls.

***

By now I was on fire in my hunt for Burke. I felt destined to find him. I scoured the vendor stalls in the crowded and smelly Pettah market. The stalls hugged narrow streets which were a melange of belching busses, trishaws and motorcycles. Bullock carts jumped sidewalks to escape throngs of pedestrians who commandeered the throughway with impunity. There was fear in the air—downcast eyes, nervous scurrying—for bombs had exploded in these close confines in the past, killing disproportionate numbers of packed humanity. The heat, humidity and stench of human effluence in the enclosed stalls made me nauseous. I had to drink copious amounts of water to keep going. I showed his picture to every stall keeper only to receive vacant expressions in return; they lost interest as soon as they realized I wasn't buying anything. The picture was looking frayed and had curled its edges when one man recognized Burke.

"He gave up his broom stall on the next cross street, around the corner. The new owner is still selling brooms and rugs there. You can go and ask."

"When did Burke leave?"

"Oh, about a year ago." The man looked hesitantly about him and lowered his voice. "He was being harassed by our local security people...you know... the mafia that we have to pay to keep the cops off our backs. He said he couldn't afford their fees. None of us can, but we pay and survive, no?"

"Does the mafia protect you from terrorist bombs?"

The man scoffed. "No sir, only from the police. The terrorists—no one can protect us from them."

I thanked the man, slipped him a thousand rupee note, about ten dollars, and went over to the next cross-street.

The broom stall keeper was in his thirties: thin, dressed in a sarong and open shirt, revealing a tawny body and ribcage. He had a fanged moustache and a scar that ran across his cheek. He did not look very welcoming. I recognized some of the brooms; they had come out of the bowels of Baby Bear, and were on display with other, newer models. The man was washing his fingers from a bottle of water into the flowing drain behind the stall. The smell of curry and sewage was oppressive.

"This man," I said getting down to business and holding up the photograph. "Where is he?"

The scar-faced man's eyebrows arched slightly when he saw the picture. He belched. "Are you the police?"

"No, I am a business associate from abroad. I'll pay you well for the information. More than you will make in an afternoon selling brooms."

"How much are you paying?"

I peeled off two thousand-rupee notes from my cash belt and held them tight in my hand. "There's more if you give me accurate information," I said.

The man studied me closely. I wondered whether I was being stupid. How could I trust him or his information?

"Burke *mahattaya* moved to the upcountry, towards Haputale area."

"You will have to be more specific. That's a lot of area you are talking about." I looked at the brushes again. "I see you have some of his old goods. Did you buy them off him? Or did you just scare a cripple on a wheelchair away from his only livelihood?"

The man started at my direct approach and began to fidget.

I played my last card and hoped I hadn't overshot the mark. "I buy exports from this country," I lied. "I have connections. Burke is a key supplier and my relative. I wouldn't like to see any harm come to him."

"Sir—no harm was done. He was finding it too hard to run things. Business was down. I was his assistant at the time. One day, he just said that he'd had enough of brushes and wanted to go and see his bhikkhu in the mountains in Haputale and plan the next stage of his life. So he just gave me the shop as a gift and left. It was easier than having to go through the hassle of finding a buyer."

"How could a cripple get up to the mountains?"

"We arranged a sleeper train ticket to Haputale and then a bullock cart was going to take him to the temple. I don't know exactly where. He did not want to say, in case someone followed him."

As fantastic as this sounded, the information was not implausible. I tried another angle. "Was he harassed by the local mafia?"

The man stepped around the stall, right up to me, and dropped his voice to a whisper. "Not so loud, sir." He pointed to his scar. "See this? This is what they did to me one night, when Burke *mahattaya* refused to pay his *santhosam.*"

The scar was jagged, made by a Kris knife. I realized that it was this deformity that gave him the shady appearance. His eyes, at close view, were entreating.

"I am sorry to hear that," I said.

"Burke *mahattaya* was also sorry, sir. It was after this incident that he decided to leave. He said that when he had finally started doing what he wanted, and not what others told him to do, it was causing harm to those nearest him."

I thanked him, peeled two more notes and gave him 40,000 rupees. Hopefully, he could now meet his next *santhosam* payment.

***

I took the overnight train to Haputale, a small town perched on top of the most spectacular scenery: distinctly shaped mountains bearing their own names, tea plantations falling down rolling hills and the majestic green mara, red flowered flamboyant and purple flowering jacaranda trees spreading their branches and fragrances on the edges of a dozen waterfalls. Had Burke finally found his heaven on earth?

Arriving in the morning, I enquired at the station regarding temples in the area, and there were several. I narrowed my quest down to those that could be reached in a few hours by bullock cart, hired a trishaw, and drove out to each one in turn. The temples were noticeable from a distance as one approached—located strategically on hilltops like forts guarding the country from invaders. Buddhism had taken on an all-encompassing role in this country: enmeshing itself within lay life, politics, business and even fermenting recalcitrance among its adherents towards sharing the island with the Hindu Tamils. That's why there was a civil war that seemed as if it would never end.

After a day of visiting half a dozen temples, inhaling leaded petrol fumes from the open air trishaw, and making no progress, I decided to call it quits and find accommodation for the night. The main guesthouse was closed for construction and the smaller one had gone out of business now that the tourists came only in trickles.

My driver suggested that we travel downhill to the next town, Belihuloya, and try the rest facilities there. I was relieved to find out that the place was open and had most of its rooms available. My driver, wanting to hang onto this crazy foreigner who was driving up a storm, enough to keep him in the money for an entire week, promised to come back for me in the morning, in case I wanted to see more temples or head back to Haputale for the train to Colombo.

After a cool night, lolled by the slow rolling river beside my bedroom window, and only bothered by an occasional mosquito, I awoke refreshed, and went down to breakfast. There were only four local patrons in the restaurant although there were covers for over a hundred—I guessed the tourist groups had stopped coming even to this beautiful place.

Having arrived after dark the previous evening, I was unprepared for the broad vista that awaited me from the open veranda restaurant of the guesthouse. A courteous waiter, dressed in the traditional sarong, ushered me to a table that looked out into a gorge between two steep mountains; one side was dotted with cascading tea plantations and the other was thick with wild, unchecked vegetation. The view was immediate, and I felt that if I took two steps away from my table I would fall off the precipice.

Dallying over a breakfast of milk rice, *lunumiris* and fried eggs over-easy, and not wanting to leave this exquisite perch, I took out my field glasses and surveyed the two mountains forming the gorge. On the ordered side, the tea plantations were close-cropped lush green bushes on steep inclines with turbaned dark-skinned Tamil women, carrying large baskets, plucking the leaves that would go into tea sachets that eventually made their way into urban households around the world. The other face of the gorge was a profusion of bamboo, banana and mara trees at the base and pine trees at the higher altitudes—a curious mix of south and north. No wonder the Brits had considered this country their home away from the foul British weather during colonial times. And those two mountains faced each other like colonial master and vanquished colony, the latter never being able to replicate the order, method and productivity of the former.

A whiff of smoke coming through the trees midway up the forested mountain drew my attention. I focused my binoculars and saw the stupa peeping through the undergrowth, the white parapet and the giant Bo-tree camouflaged by tangled vegetation. The discovery set my heart racing.

My driver was walking across the lawn towards the veranda. I pointed at the sight I had just seen. "There is another temple in there. Here, take a look." I shoved the glasses at him.

He waved them away. "Yes, I know. But that temple is a very old one. A rock temple from King Walagambahu's time in the first century. Only Bhikkhu Wimalasiri lives there. He was once world-famous, but has chosen to live like the Buddha, in solitude."

"Take me to him."

My driver looked nonplussed. "But sir, even my trishaw can't get up there. How could your relative have made it in a bullock cart?"

"My uncle has done stranger things." I tossed some notes on the table and grabbed my travel bag. "Come on. I have to check-out. Take me as far as you can up that mountain. I need to visit the temple. Something tells me that I am nearly at the end of my search."

***

The trishaw stopped where the road ended about a half-mile uphill. My driver said that he would wait for me. I followed the plume of smoke and made it up a damp cow path the rest of the way. In minutes, my shoes were covered in red mud, and mosquitoes snipped at my exposed skin. The sun beat down relentlessly as I climbed higher. After about 30 minutes of swatting insects, parting bushes and plodding through mud, I found the temple, standing behind a barbed wire fence: a brick whitewashed structure built into the mountain. The Bo tree offered shelter and protection by swooping down its hanging vines over the building. A thin boy, about 10 years old, dressed in a tee shirt and sarong, stood like a sentinel behind the closed gate. He looked nervously at me.

"I want to see Reverend Wimalasiri," I said.

"He is doing his morning meditation," the boy replied hastily. "He does not see visitors anymore."

"I have come about Burke."

The boy's features lit up at the mention of the name. "Burke *mahattaya*? You know him?"

"Yes. He is my *maama*. I have come all the way from Canada to see him."

"Wait here. I will go and check." The boy turned and ran inside the temple while the gate swung open on its hinges behind him.

I stepped inside the compound and saw the guest house across the valley. The vista from over here was even more stunning. Through a crack in the mountains I could see clear to the distant game park of Yala, once teeming with wildlife, now riddled with guerrillas and closed for tourists. I sat under the Bo tree. This was definitely a place of reflection, with the world, in all its beauty and flaws, spread out before me. I closed my eyes. A sense of peace descended and my mind floated. When the boy next tugged at my sleeve, I even resented the intrusion.

"Reverend Wimalasiri will see you now," the boy said. "Come."

I took off my shoes at the entrance and followed him through the sparsely furnished temple building smelling of burnt coconut oil and frangipani flowers, into an opening at the back that led directly into a cave in the mountain. I had to stoop inside due to the low rock ceiling. Light came from a dozen oil lamps scattered about the room. Faded frescos adorned the walls and the ceiling, and the shrine before me held an array of garish red, orange and indigo figures from Buddhist and Hindu mythology, reminiscent of a time before the people of this country had polarised along religious and ethnic lines. The cement floor was cool to my bare feet. A shrunken figure, clothed in a saffron robe, with a trace of white fuzz on his head, was sitting in a lotus position. When he saw me enter, he waved an emaciated hand.

"Go and sit next to him," the boy whispered. "Rev. Wimalasiri is almost deaf."

When I sat next to the bhikkhu, he leaned forward. His eyes were clear like the droplets from those waterfalls I had passed. He smiled. "You have come."

"How did you know I would come?"

The bhikkhu leaned even closer and squinted his eyes. I repeated my question, louder this time.

Another smile creased his benign face. "If you had not come, Burke's life would have held no lesson for his family."

"Where is he?"

"He came to see me several months ago. He could not climb up here, and I could not go down." The bhikkhu found that amusing and began to chuckle. "So we sent Sunil here as our translator. The poor boy ran up and down the mountain several times that day."

"Where is Burke now?"

"I sent him on to the next stage of his evolution. His life experiences had prepared him for this phase."

I was getting anxious and irritated by this circular talk. "Where can I see him?"

"Sunil will take you. You have a vehicle? It is some distance from here."

"Yes. I will take the boy and bring him back safely."

We talked some more and Rev. Wimalasiri gave me more details about Burke. "Thanks to my connections, I was able to get him an interview. The people managing this project could see and feel the pain he had endured. How do you say it in your modern language—he was the 'right fit?' "

I thanked the bhikkhu, bowed and rose. I stuffed some money into the bright red collection box that no one could miss. At the entrance, I paused and walked back into the dim interior. "How did you know about me?" I asked loudly.

The small figure looked up and his voice reverberated sharply in the close confines. "Burke talked about you a lot. He said that you were the closest to a son he could ever expect to have in this incarnation."

***

The boy Sunil and I rocked in the back seat as the trishaw cut off the main Colombo road and went down a smaller branch leading through thatched houses and half erected bungalows.

The boy told me that his parents also had a similar house and that they would build sections of it from time to time, whenever his mother, who was working as a maid in Saudi Arabia, had saved enough money to send home,. The road was badly washed away in sections and complete stretches had become shallow waterholes that our driver gingerly tipped us into and rode through slowly. Sunil issued instructions on which forks in the road to take and which ones to avoid.

Finally, we rounded a bend and ended in front of a large white two-storey building, which looked like some kind of a factory. It had no signage, and had been recently erected with bits of masonry and wood shavings still in the muddy and furrowed front yard. A logo of an international aid agency that was partially funding this initiative adorned the front door.

Sunil led me into the building. There was no reception area, just a bare waiting room with two cane chairs and a door that led into the interior. This was beginning to look like another work-in-progress building to me, until I stepped through that next door.

Several lathe machines stood in rows along a large hall with operators stooped over them under dim lights. Fluids and lubricants gushed onto revolving spools churning out various sizes of metal parts; grinding noises, squeals and the slapping of running belts comingled in a hive of activity on this production floor. Finished parts were being placed on a slow-moving dolly that gently rolled towards a loading dock at the far end.

I saw him, in a wheelchair, greyer, thinner but energetic, moving between the machines, talking to the operators who strained to catch his words. He was discussing and inspecting the output as the components were being placed carefully on the dolly.

"He is helping our injured soldiers to walk again," Sunil said, his voice full of awe. "My older brother got the first artificial leg that was manufactured in this factory."

I sucked in my breath. This was beyond the scale I had ever expected of Burke. But there he was, calling the shots for once, telling people what to do instead of being ordered around and manipulated. I got out my camera and took several pictures of him in action. My blinking flash caught his attention, and he stopped his supervisory work to gasp with joy, "Alfee (Ralphy)!"

Then I threw my camera away and ran down the steps towards him. No picture could capture this priceless moment. I felt that if I could embrace him again, his powers of re-invention would seep into me and my life would be back on track. And he just beamed at me with his deformed mouth hanging open and his arms extended: Burke in his wheelchair, like Poseidon ordering the waves, as I had first seen him on that day of the flood…

Paradise Revisited

I am late. The police and army roadblocks, all the way from Colombo and into the mountains, are not obstacles I have accounted for. As I near my destination, I have a sense that I am arriving too late.

I hurry from the bus stop, through the swirling mist that now comes only at dawn and at sunset in the central hills of this tropical island. Hopping across the open ditch and ignoring the two planks laid across it for vehicular traffic, I enter the crumbling gates of *Paradise*. The addition to what memory holds is a skyward facing spike at the top of each gate; these long shafts support opposite halves of a lion to form an identifiable whole of the animal when the gates meet in the centre. The gate posts had once been whitewashed and visible for a long distance down the hill, now they are moss-covered and blackened. The property's name sign is faded and the last four letters have dropped off, leaving only their shadow; from a distance the sign now reads like the Sinhala equivalent for "rotten"—*Para*.

The gravel driveway, sprouting grasses that poke out between pebbles, twists and turns through giant pines and teak trees before arriving at the large house, now shrunken in adult perspective, except for the giant bay window of the living room, through which I had peered into the house the day Emma first invited me in. Today, instead of roses and hydrangeas that once decorated the inner windowsill, a bed is drawn up to the window and an emaciated figure is propped up in it, staring at me as I approach.

I stop in midstride, in shock, then in relief, when it dawns on me that the figure in the window is Emma herself, her once strong nose now bending like a beak; her large eyes are still alive, yet the fire that once raged in them looks like a slumbering ember. She is wearing an oversized dressing gown with a blanket draped over. A night cap covers most of her once auburn hair, now silver and stringy. A finger crooks, summoning me, and a smile cracks her thin wide lips, stoking the fire in her eyes. Just as I had first entered her house in trepidation, I find that I am doing the same again, forty years later.

***

I came to live in Nuwara Eliya in the hill country when I was 10, after my mother died trying to birth the only sibling I wished I'd had. She left a hole in my life, which, psychiatrists in Canada later told me, was never filled. My father was an engine driver in the railway and travelled all over the island, staying away from home for days. I enjoyed the trips, whenever he was able to take me along, riding with him in the engine car. With soot in our eyes and fire on our cheeks, we propelled over hills and through paddy fields, with Dad telling me stories of nights away at remote railway stations with only a deck of cards, a bottle of arrack and a wireless radio for company.

Dad drank more after Mum died, and my grandmother came to stay with me whenever she could. But Grandma suffered from a rheumatic heart and couldn't always show up. Six months after Mum's passing, Dad requested and received a transfer to Nuwara Eliya; it was the axis of his route network and he did not have to spend more than a night away from home, if at all. During those one-nighters, I was passed around to other railway families to be put up for the night. I preferred to stay on my own, but was considered underage. Dad promised to get an *ayah* to look after me, but they were never available in those days and I did not know if he had the time to look for one. And the available ones were untrustworthy—they stole things. I remember staying over nights with the Jansz's. Mr. Jansz, who was an engine driver like Dad, drank a lot too, but he beat his wife, and his children huddled in fright along with me in the big bedroom where we slept together. I also stayed with the Shoecroft family, who smoked and played cards until the early hours of the morning, making sleep a pipe dream. And the one time I stayed at Mr. Neydorf's, he crept up to my bed and started feeling my penis while his wife snored in the adjoining room. I screamed and Mrs. Neydorf charged in with a cricket bat, as if she had been waiting for the signal, and started whacking her husband, shouting, "You bloody homo, you promised me you will never do it again!"

Dad put up with these disasters in the caring of his only son, by drinking an extra shot of arrack whenever I rendered an account of my most recent sleep-over. He even had words with Mr. Neydorf and promised to report him to the railway authorities. However drunk he was, Dad was always kind to me and promised that one day we would leave to a better life in Canada, where his brother had ended up soon after Independence. But I could see the anguish in his face; I was an enigma to him; a child was a woman's problem and he felt that he had been unfairly treated with this twist of fate. I knew that because one day I caught him violently masturbating in his bedroom, cursing Mum for leaving us. I went pale and slunk away before he could see me. I recognized what he was up to because I had seen our former servant boy Gunadasa doing it behind the shed in our house in Colombo when I was six. Mum had thrown a stick at Gunadasa and yelled at him, "Get the hell out of our house, you pervert. Bloody disgrace, corrupting young children." I did not go into Dad's bedroom after that—perhaps he too was a pervert and a bloody disgrace.

When Dad wasn't home, I spent my days after school wandering the tea estates, playing imaginary cowboys and crooks, and hiding behind the giant Mara trees whenever I saw phantom Indians or monsters coming to attack me. It was safer to inhabit this imaginary world than the real one. I did not get much satisfaction playing rough and tumble rugby with the other boys, where you had to get your front teeth knocked out in order to earn your stripes. I was no good at cricket either. I think it was these peregrinations around the tea estates of the "up-country" that got me charting imaginary worlds and led to my becoming a successful young adult fiction author later in life. My speciality was dropping off young heroes in exotic tropical locales and bringing them home to their parents through various misadventures. That formula worked all the time. However, during my days in Nuwara Eliya, I felt as if I was continuously adrift, that I was never going home, for my parents were either dead or never around. I found that I was crying less at night, although I still missed Mum very much.

One day, Dad came home, sober, and announced triumphantly that he was sending me to boarding school at St. Thomas' in Gurutalawa.

"I've saved the money for you to go. You will be better looked after there, than I can."

"But I don't want to go," I protested. "Who will look after you?"

He laughed and poured his first drink of the day from a new pint. "I will manage. You'll be back for the holidays, so I can take you on the train to Colombo to visit your aunts and grandmother."

I knew that protest was useless. Dad considered this move a parental success from his perspective and I could not disappoint him. I resigned myself to going to St. Thomas' after the Christmas holidays, only two months away.

That was the loneliest time in my life as Dad did many day-runs into Kandy and back, out when the first cocks crowed and back late at night when I was already in bed. The mist and rain were severe that year. Mud slides kept me from running through the tea bushes that hung down to the side of the narrow mountain road. Even though this was November, I tried decorating our old Christmas tree at home, but the decorations were all crumpled from our move and the lights had fused. And there were no Christmas lights for sale in the shops because everything imported was banned and Christmas was still far away. Then I had a grand idea: why not check out the other houses in the neighbourhood? Perhaps I could request, cajole or threaten, and extract some decorations for my tree. I was sure Mr. Neydorf would be most obliging, even though it gave me the shivers to enter his house again.

My plan proved successful. After visiting just ten houses in the neighbourhood, I had a pillowcase full of decorations, and Mrs. Neydorf even invited me in for a cup of tea and gave me the lights from her tree, saying with a syrupy steeliness, "Don't worry, child. Mr. Neydorf is in Colombo. I will telephone him tonight and tell him to bring us some new lights from Cargill's department store." I'm sure Mr. Neydorf would have bought his wife anything to get out of his self-created dog house.

As I hauled my bag of loot up the hill to our house, I passed the whitewashed pillars of the property called *Paradise*. I had been intrigued by this house ever since we had moved to Nuwara Eliya but had never stepped inside its imposing wrought iron gates. My school mates had said that a witch lived there. A witch in Paradise? I didn't think so. My friends also lacked the intellectual curiosity that I had at that early age—that's why they played sports while I daydreamed in the hills.

Concrete blocks covered the municipal ditch opposite the gates of *Paradise* in those days. I pushed the left gate—it was ajar—and entered. The long driveway was elegantly paved with white stone markers on the edges—for night driving. After about two hundred yards, the house came into view around a bend. The bay window ran the length of the front of the house and glimmered in the sunlight that had peeped out for a few hours after the rain. A flower bed below it was lush with pink roses, red anthuriams, and dense hydrangea—blues, purples and whites. The inner wall of the bay window was a profusion of red that, on closer inspection, unravelled as vases of roses and pots of geraniums catching the elusive sun.

I stepped off the driveway and onto the moist lawn, neatly mowed, and peered in the window. An elegant grand piano faced me. Behind it, a teak and glass cabinet, filled with ornate blue and white Delft crockery, leaned against the wall. A fuchsia floral-patterned sofa-set stood in front of the piano, with a coffee table in the middle of the room; by the window, and inches away from my nose, a round marble table and two wooden chairs stuck out. Several open magazines strewed this table, with scrawls on them, as if someone had been studying. I was about to turn away when a voice behind me boomed, making me drop my loot bag.

"Well, who do we have here? An intruder?"

Behind the stentorian voice, a tall woman peered down at me. She loomed through the mist that had swooped down on the driveway again. The wind gusted and the mist lifted momentarily. The woman was dressed in a khaki shirt and skirt with a sweater slung loosely over her shoulders. She wore half-stockings and black laced shoes. Auburn hair swept into a bob at the back and her rimless glasses balanced on a long nose as she inspected me. A thick black leather book was lodged under her right arm.

I grabbed my bag and looked for an opening to dodge the woman and run away. A firm hand reached out and grabbed me by the shoulder and I knew that there was no escape.

"What are you doing here, young man?" Her eyes were magnified by the lenses; they were stern, but kindness played at the edges.

"I am collecting Christmas decorations," I explained, expecting the grip on my shoulder to relax. Instead, it tightened.

"What! That pagan ritual?"

I did not know what she meant. Christmas was usually a fun time with fireworks and gifts, the adult males getting drunk on scotch or arrack, the women getting "tipsy" on milk wine, a sumptuous dinner, and a Christmas tree.

"Here—take a look." I thought that opening my bag would help. She glanced into it cursorily and sniffed, the glasses on her nose inching up a bit.

She let go her hold, took the book out from under her arm, thumbed to a page and read:

For the customs of the peoples are worthless;
they cut a tree out of the forest,
and a craftsman shapes it with his chisel.
They adorn it with silver and gold;
they fasten it with hammer and nails
so it will not totter.

Like a scarecrow in a melon patch,
their idols cannot speak;
they must be carried
because they cannot walk.
Do not fear them;
they can do no harm
nor can they do any good.

She peered at me over her glasses. "Jeremiah 10, verses three to five. People have forgotten the spirit of Christmas." She grabbed me by the collar. "Come with me," she ordered, and pulled me toward the house.

A wicked witch, who reads the Bible? That's when I *really* got scared—she was taking me into her lair. I struggled, but her grip was firm.

"What? Do you think I am a witch or something?" She let go of me. "All right—then go. Run out of here and be damned forever. I have a message for you and all those heathen out there. But run along—go to your doom." She flicked her hands, dismissing me and strode towards the house.

In my panic, I misunderstood what she had said. I thought she had already cursed me and if she did not break the spell I was going to melt into liquid before I got home and no one would find me.

"Wait!" I implored her.

She turned around and a smile creased her thin lips, devoid of lipstick. In fact, she wore no makeup at all but her cheek bones and chin were prominent in profile—an intelligent woman, I sensed. Very fair of skin, almost European. Not a witch.

"Do you want to be saved?" She arched an eyebrow.

"Yes," I stammered. "But can we do it outside."

She threw back her head and laughed; the bun came loose and her thick hair unravelled on her shoulders. If not for her glasses, and her height, and that booming voice, I would have said she was beautiful.

She opened her book again. "'You are my hiding place; you will protect me from trouble and surround me with songs of deliverance.' Psalm 32, verse seven. Now will you come inside? I don't bite, you know. Do you take chocolate cake with your tea?"

I could not remember when I had last eaten chocolate cake. "Yes. But I have to be home in half an hour."

"That will depend on how fast you eat." She turned on her heel. "Come along then. Oh, and leave that bag of pagan objects on the porch before you come in."

As she held the door open for me, I got the faint smell of lavender talcum powder, mixed with fresh perspiration. She was human. Despite my sense of dread, there was a promise of reward as I stepped over her threshold on that first occasion.

The living room, the one with the grand piano, smelled of the roses in the windowsill, and of old print. I noticed stacks of files and papers by a writing desk in an alcove. An ornate but worn typewriter sat in the middle of the desk with a sheet of paper still in its platen; a small book case, lined with old hard-bound volumes, lay within arm's reach of the desk. I took a seat in one of the wooden chairs by the window, while the woman disappeared into the kitchen, where in minutes, I heard a kettle whistle. Faded pastel paintings of English country scenes adorned the cream coloured walls. The opened magazines on the table had drawings of Jesus and various quotations were underlined with pencilled notes on the margins.

My mouth watered when she returned with a tray bearing a teapot and assorted dressings, cups and saucers, spoons, and a heaped plate of chocolate crème biscuits. "Help yourself," she said, laying the tray down in front of me. At close quarters she appeared to be in her mid-thirties, although her severe bearing made her look older. She smiled as I reached hungrily for a biscuit. She poured the tea with proper poise and decorum, like I had seen the church ladies do at Mum's funeral.

"How many sugars?" She arched an eyebrow, the heaped spoon poised over my steaming gold-rimmed cup in its gold rimmed saucer.

"Three, I think."

"Diabetes will get you early," she said and complied.

She raised her cup delicately to her lips, studying me. "What is your name?"

"Paul."

"Hmm…the great convert. Do you know the story of your namesake?"

She noticed my hesitation. I had not learned anything about the Bible. Religious Knowledge classes in school were boring with Fr. Stanislaus yawning through most of the lesson and spraying us in the front row with spittle whenever he woke up to read us from the Good Book.

On that visit, I learned the story of Paul, or Saul as he had been called originally. My hostess launched into a vivid tale of marauders and a long trip to Damascus. She rose and rolled on the floor demonstrating how Saul was struck off his horse. When she rose as Paul, her eyes were tightly shut, indicating his temporary blindness. Her tall figure expanded and radiated and her voice boomed, "Saul, Saul, why do you persecute me." Then she was on her knees, playing Paul again, asking for forgiveness with a quiver in her voice. I was enthralled—this was better than watching a movie.

I spent over an hour with her on that first visit. I ate all the biscuits and my tea went cold in its cup. We both forgot the time and were at the point that Paul was sent to prison for his convictions when my hostess looked at her wristwatch and said, "My goodness, you will be late getting home. We must continue another day."

I wanted to tell her that I really did not have to be home as I had indicated (there was nobody home, anyway) but that would have meant I had lied earlier and somehow I did not feel that lying was going to be tolerated in this God-abiding house.

She took down a dark leather bound book from her book case and handed it to me after inscribing something on its inside cover. "Here, read it every day. And come and see me again. We will have tea and talk."

"Thank you." There was a peacefulness radiating inside that living room that I did not want to leave for my lonely abode. She waved as I walked down the driveway. I turned back many times and, every time I did, she was still waving.

On the main road, I opened the Bible she had handed me. On the inside cover, in very ornate script, was written, "To my disciple Paul—may you bring light to many— Emma."

***

The next time I visited, I felt a change in the atmosphere. It was a sunnier day and I picked the same time, thinking that Emma would be at home. A battered open-roofed truck, with its side panels lowered, was parked outside the house. A burly man, in his mid forties, was unloading bags of cement. He grunted as every bag hit the ground, raising clouds of grey. After the last bag had landed, he picked up a shovel and began pushing river sand from another part of the flat bed onto the driveway. He was dressed in a dirty white shirt, unbuttoned to the belly, and khaki pants. As I neared, I could see his thick matted hair pouring with sweat, his jowly cheeks wobbling under the strain, and a half used cigarette sticking out from behind an ear. He had a chocolate coloured complexion—one of those mixed breed types that Dad railed about constantly, especially when he'd had a bit too much to drink.

The man caught sight of me and stopped his exertions.

"What do you want?" He spoke in English and his voice was raspy, like Dad after a hangover. I didn't think the man was a labourer, although he looked like one.

"Is Emma at home?"

"No. She is on her rounds. Converting heathen." He threw back his head and laughed. His laughter became violent and tears streamed down his cheeks. "You…you want to be converted?"

"No."

"Then you'd better bugger-off before she returns."

Just then the front door swung open and a young woman, not more than twenty, stepped out. At first I thought she was a servant; she wore a batik lungi and a white bodice that emphasised her shapely figure. A gold chain disappeared between large breasts that stretched the bodice, which outlined the dark aureoles beneath it. Black oily hair in a pony tail swung down to her hips. She had the same mixed chocolate complexion of the man; a nose stud pierced her right nostril, and she wore rubber slippers. She carried a bottle of Arrack and a glass in her hand.

She gave me a coquettish smile and reached over the open side of the vehicle, handing the bottle and tumbler to the man. He flung the glass back at her with a grimace, opened the bottle, took a long swig, swirled the liquid in his mouth and gulped, grunting, as the stuff went down his innards. I remember Dad saying that he always had to chase his arrack with soda water because the grog was so strong and raw. This guy kept going until half the bottle was empty. Then he wiped his mouth with his sleeve and tossed the bottle down to the young woman who caught it as if on cue. He picked up the cigarette from behind his ear and lit it with a lighter that he fished from his trouser pocket. He blew smoke rings in the air.

"This guy is Emma's new victim," he said, hiccupping and laughing.

The woman looked at me and waved her arms, as if shooing me away. "Come back later. Emma is not home." There was a look of concern in her eyes.

The man jumped off the truck and circled his hands around the waist of the young woman. "Yeah, but I am home, baby." His mouth descended onto the woman's bosom and he began kneading her with his groin. The woman feigned encouragement but her eyes were looking at me, imploring me to go away. The man had his hands on the woman's lungi now and was lifting it up her legs, pushing her against the truck, grunting louder.

"Not here, Brian—let's go inside," she managed to say before the man put his hand on her mouth and wrenched her lungi over her hips. I got a glimpse of a thick shadow of hair between her legs before he blocked my view with his thrusting pelvis.

"Stop it!"

The shrill scream caught us in freeze frame. I swung around to see a charging Emma, heading up the driveway, hurling the Bible in her hands that struck Brian on his ass, thrusting his pelvis even deeper into the younger woman.

"You bloody cad! Taking your lust out in broad daylight. And in front of children. Get out of here. Leela, go to your room. I gave you a room for that purpose. Now get out! Both of you!"

Emma stopped in front of the couple, hands on hips, breathing down on them like a dragon, blocking me from their view. Brian uncoupled and emerged, looking strangely cowed. He hoisted his pants up and jumped back into the truck. "Later," was all he said, as he resumed shovelling sand onto the driveway. The young woman picked up the Bible, bottle of arrack and glass, and ran back into the house.

Emma turned towards me and I could still see her lips quivering. "You will never come to this house until I tell you when. Do you hear me?"

"Y…yes." I wanted to run home and never return but my step was shaky. I turned away dejectedly instead, and as I walked away I could hear her footsteps behind me. She caught up with me at the gates.

"I am sorry. Come tomorrow at three o'clock after school. I will be at home expecting you. We can continue your Bible lesson. And I want you to read from the Book of Daniel, chapter six verses 13 to 24, before you come."

Her trembling had given way to tears that flowed freely down her fair cheeks.

***

Thus began my biblical education—daily at 3.30pm sharp, after tea and cookies had been served in the living room. We sat at the bay window and went through The Book—we covered Daniel and Genesis and Exodus and Elijah and Kings, and I was beginning to get good at finding passages whenever she called them out. I seldom saw Brian or the young woman after that.

Brian, whenever he was seen, puttered about in the garden mostly. The cement and sand he had been unloading that first day was for building a birdbath that, once constructed, attracted mynahs and sparrows and even the odd king fisher. They shat all over the structure and Brian would curse loudly and aim the water hose at his creation, trying to keep it clean. He also worked at tidying the flower beds, at weeding, and was constantly planting or moving flowering plants that grew in abundance in this climate. Despite his unruly and arrogant appearance, he took pride in the garden and scowled every time any human, animal or bird interfered with its symmetry.

Leela spent her time mostly in the kitchen, cooking; or washing clothes by the outdoor well. If she had a free moment, she was out by the mango tree, singing to herself.

Between lessons, Emma dropped snippets of information on the residents of *Paradise*.

"I grew up in our home estate in Bandarawala, about 20 miles away. It was a sprawling place. When my father died five years ago, he left the property to me. It was just too big to manage so I sold it and bought this place. I have a manager, Mr. Hendricks, who looks after this estate for us. Brian and Leela live with me because they have no means of their own."

"Are they your relatives?"

Emma wrinkled her nose at my question. "My father took an estate woman as his mistress after my mother died. Leela is his daughter from that woman, and my half sister, I guess. Adultery is such a sin."

"Where is Leela's mother?"

"She died when Leela was twelve. I have raised her since. She is not very smart and needs looking after."

That was all the information I received as we returned to our lesson, in which I had to answer a question on how Solomon solved the problem of the two women who each claimed a single baby as their own.

***

Another day, when I arrived for my lesson, Leela was seated on the floor of the living room and Emma was combing the younger woman's hair with repeated brush strokes. They were unaware of my entry and I watched them luxuriate in the shared experience: Emma lovingly trailing the brush through Leela's long tresses, and Leela laying her head back, half asleep.

I must have knocked over the newspaper that was delicately balanced on the sofa's hand rest, for Emma immediately glanced at her watch and exclaimed, "Heavens! It's gone past three, and here is our Paul. Leela, I think it's time for tea."

Leela scrambled to her feet, tied her loose hair into a bun, and hurried out to the kitchen without a glance at me.

We studied Ezekiel that day. I was getting drawn to Emma's teaching. She knew how to energize the lesson, so that it was never boring. It beat staying at home alone, reading comics. She made the oracles and the visions of Prophet Ezekiel come alive with diabolic drama, using the entire room as her stage. As she gesticulated and sweated out her part, I wondered if she had been an actress in her past.

I asked her about it.

"An actress? Never. They are harlots. Besides they don't have minds of their own; always playing someone else in order to be whole. No, I wanted to be a nurse."

"And why did you not become a nurse?"

"I got married, instead. Then my father fell ill, and I had to give up nursing altogether."

"You were married? Where is your husband?"

She sipped her tea. "An unfortunate incident…" and did not elaborate.

"Do you have children?

She looked at me and smiled. "No. You have become the closest thing to a child to me. And Leela, of course."

I wanted to tell her that she had become the closest thing to a mother to me over these last few weeks, but I was too shy. Instead, I let her stroke my head.

I hadn't been offered a chance to explore the house at *Paradise* because all my lessons took place in the living room. The opportunity arrived the time I wanted to use the toilet and had to venture beyond my comfortable nook. I remember that day well, because I had just come in, late, due to the school bus breaking down, and Emma had the radio turned up loud. When I asked to be excused, she looked up at me in dismay then nodded in understanding.

"Use mine. It's attached to my bedroom." Emma said, shrugging to herself, and began to mark my answers to the homework I had brought back with me. "It's down the hall at the very end, on your right. And don't go wandering around."

I walked down the carpeted passageway which had rooms leading off on both sides. The first doorway led into a kitchen and I couldn't resist peeping in, despite my bursting bladder. It was a large room full of that same Delft crockery that gave it a bluish tint. A cutting board lay prominently on a counter in the centre and cabinets against the far wall contained tins of assorted condiments—all properly labelled in large letters: CINNAMON, CARDOMON, CLOVES, RAMPE, KARAPINCHA. Unlike our kitchen at home, this place was tidy and there was no smell of open cooking or leftovers. I stepped back and walked further down the passageway.

A door on the left was ajar. I peeped in again. Brian was lying comatose on a king-sized bed, naked. His large penis lay flaccid over his thigh. Leela was rising, adjusting a brassiere around her large breasts. Again I saw that thick mat of pubic hair before she pulled on her panties, and stretched out on the bed, extending her arms wide and sighing contentedly. I felt a stirring below my belly, the early arousal of desire I was to learn later, and my heartbeat began to accelerate. Leela looked back at the sleeping man and then started to pull on her housecoat that had been lying on the floor.

"Paul?" I heard Emma calling from the front of the house—an enquiring, anxious call. At that point, a floorboard creaked under my foot, and Leela swung around. Our eyes locked as she took a sharp intake of breath and pulled the housecoat tight around her. I pulled away and hurried down the hallway towards the last doorway on the right, my footsteps hitting every creaky floorboard remaining in the house.

Shutting Emma's bedroom door behind me, I felt safe and did not want to re-emerge into that passageway again. I leaned against the door and adjusted to the darkened interior.

Warmth enveloped me in this space. A woman's warmth. Drawn white lace curtains decorated the window that looked out into the garden, letting in diffused light. A large queen-sized bed looked soft and inviting, draped in an oversized pink and aquamarine floral duvet. Two large embroidered pillows stood up against the solid teak bedpost and a teddy bear reposed in the centre of the bed. A side table held a copy of the Bible and a large alarm clock. An oval reading table and chair were placed beneath the window, and a floor- to-ceiling bookcase propped up the other wall. As I headed towards a door, which I believed led to the toilet, I glanced at a shelf on the bookcase that had no books in it but displayed photographs propped up in frames. They were sepia prints of older people whom I took to be Emma's parents, and even grandparents: sitting inside horses and carriages, sporting golf clubs, dressed in Victorian era clothing, and more recent Colonial togs; there was even one black-and-white photograph of a teenaged Emma, slim and beautiful, dressed in blazer, skirt, and white hat, carrying a dark skinned baby. One picture at the far end, almost tucked into the recesses of the bookcase, caught my attention. It was a bust-sized portrait photograph of Emma, in her early twenties, with a man in his thirties. The latter looked stern, with a droopy moustache, dressed in a suit. I looked again and gasped. The man was a younger thinner version of Brian! My bladder was starting to give way at this point so I tiptoed into the toilet and eased myself. My head was spinning with this new information. I tried to distract myself by surveying the contents of my surroundings. It had the same Spartan efficiency of the kitchen: a pink plastic shower curtain separating the bath tub from the porcelain sink, Ponds soap in its dish with no residual watery scum, pink matching towels on the rack, neatly folded, a container of moisturizing cream, a safety razor, a bottle of Dettol antiseptic, a bowl of cotton balls, a tin of talcum powder. No heavy perfumes or paraphernalia like those that had littered our bathroom when Mum was alive. I pulled on the flush and started my long road back, thinking that I must have been gone for well over half an hour. The clock in the living room said that I had only been away for ten minutes.

As an added precaution, I kept massaging my stomach when I returned. Emma raised an eyebrow and surveyed me all the way back to my seat.

"Sorry," I said. "I must have eaten something bad at school."

"I see," she replied coolly, that eyebrow still arched. "Then you'd better not have any tea. The milk might upset your stomach. And that goes for the chocolate cookies too."

I spent the rest of the lesson salivating at the cookies that stayed in front of me the entire time, realizing that this was my penance for lying.

***

As the winds of Christmas descended upon us, the days got colder and the mists thicker, and I had to wear double sweaters to keep warm. Blue skies were difficult to find now as the days were cloudy and wet. I had decided that I was not going to put up a Christmas tree after all. I was also sad that my time with Emma was coming to an end and I would soon be going off to boarding school.

"You will receive a fine discipline in the boarding," she told me. "I was in a boarding school in Colombo right through my high school years, returning to Bandarawala only during the holidays. Cheer up—you can still come and visit me during the school break. But before you go away, you need to accompany me on one of my home visits."

I did not like the idea of these home visits. Adventists, Born-Again's, and Witnesses used to tap on our doors regularly. When Mum was alive, she would slam the door in their faces and tell them not to pester us. Dad did not even bother to answer their knocks.

"Are you scared of rejection?" Emma pre-empted my hesitation. "Let me tell you that rejection is the essence of life and the forger of character. Jesus was rejected when he came down to earth, what does it matter if poor us get the occasional door slammed in our faces?"

***

We set out on a wet day, umbrellas in hand, wearing raincoats. The rain was a thin steady drizzle that penetrated the bones and made the thick foliage of the up-country droop and sag, filling the air with foreboding. We took the bus halfway to Talawakele as Emma had already covered most of the houses in Nuwara Eliya. Off the wet windswept road that snaked up, down, and around the mountains, we trudged up steep muddy lanes and pathways to ramshackle houses, climbed improvised stone steps and spoke to the families of estate workers. The younger men and women were out earning their livelihood, and we had the attention of just the grandmothers and young children who were at home, or the disabled men cast aside to fend for themselves. Our audiences invited us into unlit rooms and sooty kitchens, and listened to us with curiosity. They were kind and attentive, despite the poverty and tragedy that embraced their lives.

Emma surprised me with the fluent Tamil and Sinhala that she spoke to address these people. Everyone smiled and put their hands out hesitantly to accept the magazines that this fair lady and her protégée handed out. They were of many faiths, some lasting many generations, others daubed on them by colonial masters during their passages through this country. We were often invited to share a cup of plain tea and jaggery. One woman even ran into her kitchen and came out with stale *kavums*, while another served us piping hot *massala vaddes* that were deep-frying on a makeshift fireplace. Some scratched their heads at Emma's words and looked surreptitiously at an oil lamp in front of a Buddha statue, or at a faded garland around a Lord Shiva picture, or even at a flickering candle in front of the Virgin Mary, symbolic reminders of their diverse and blind faiths tucked away within the private recesses of their homes. No one slammed doors in our faces.

Emma explained to me as we concluded our home visits that day, "People are rude only in cities and towns where affluence interferes with the Message. These poor people are waiting to hear the Good Word—any word of hope. They are only restricted by culture and history."

Despite our umbrellas, we were soaked by the time we reached the unsheltered bus stop to head back to Nuwara Eliya. There was no guard rail and the road fell down immediately behind us into a sheer precipice of wild green foliage. On the other side, the asphalt was rimmed by a jagged face of rock, dynamited by the British when they had brought roads to the up-country. Emma turned into the wind and the rain beat down on her face. She held her arms out wide, one holding the ineffective umbrella and the other her remaining magazines. She breathed deep and exhaled, and her countenance glistened with the water streaming off her face.

"I got my calling on one of these roads during a rainfall, five years ago," she said.

"Where?" I was curious and uneasy, wondering if I was going to get hit by a bolt of lightning next, now that thunder was rolling about in the distance. Perhaps it was something to do with having the name Paul.

"Oh, in Bandarawala. My father had just passed away. I walked the hills in the evenings asking God for a message of what I should do for the rest of my life. And then out of the blue, it came to me. I knelt on the side of a road like this and accepted my new role. I was to be a messenger."

"Is that when you moved to *Paradise*?"

"No, that came later, about two years ago. What the Lord did not tell me was that the path I had chosen for myself was not going to be an easy one. But I should have known. Did Jesus have it easy?"

The bus came around the bend, sloshing water on either side, splashing us as it squealed to a halt.

***

When I arrived at *Paradise* the following week, Emma was lighting a candle on a small cake in the living room.

"Shh," she whispered. "It's Leela's birthday. We used to always give her a surprise."

"Where is she?"

"In the kitchen, making tea."

"I thought you did not celebrate pagan rituals, like birthdays and Christmas and stuff?"

She turned to me and winked. "There is an allowance for history, sometimes. Leela will be so happy. I cannot take that away from her."

Just then Leela came in, bearing a loaded tea tray. Her eyes widened and she broke into a knowing smile, wagging her head from side to side. She put down the tray hurriedly, ran up to Emma and put her arms around her.

"Emma, Emma…thank you!" Leela's English was more locally accented than Emma's. I often wondered whether Emma had been educated in England, she had such perfect diction.

They twirled in a laughing pirouette. I could feel their abandon overcome me as well and the tension that I usually felt, whenever I arrived at this house of secrets, fell away.

We cut the cake and sang Happy Birthday, which Emma played on the grand piano. Then she fished out music sheets from a folder and launched into perfect renditions of her favourite classics: Beethoven's Moonlight Sonata and Tchaikowsky's Swan Lake, and even my favourite: Chopsticks. As Emma played, I saw Leela tapping her foot and looking on in awe at her older sister.

"Do you play?" I asked tentatively.

Leela shook her head. "No. I don't read…the music."

Leela switched her attention to the books that lay open upon my satchel.

"Paul, you read a lot of books." Again, that awestruck look on her face.

"I had English today. I have to read Huckleberry Finn. It's very funny. Do you want to read it while I take my class with Emma?"

Leela, smiled nervously, "No. It's okay."

With a crescendo, Emma brought her piano recital to a close and ran her fingers across the keys. She stood up and took a bow, while Leela and I clapped.

"Well! That was most exhilarating. Thank you, dear Leela, for giving my fingers that exercise."

After we had partaken of the cake and tea, and Leela had cleaned out the leftovers and retired once more to the kitchen, Emma lowered her voice to me. "Don't ask her to read again. It embarrasses her."

"Why?"

Emma sighed. "It's always questions, questions, questions from you, isn't it? Leela is functionally illiterate. She was born severely dyslexic."

***

Our lesson was interrupted that day when Brian barged in.

"There is a fucking dead cat in the pond," he growled.

Emma betrayed a hint of embarrassment, and then regained a straight face. "Well, you will have to clear it out, won't you? How much will it cost me this time?"

Brian grinned, flashing his crooked, tobacco-stained teeth. "About five hundred rupees. I have to rent a pump to drain out the water."

Emma sighed again. She looked beaten. "Very well, then. Get on with it. And leave us alone."

Brian hung around, his thick fingers rubbing the wall, as if checking the plaster. "Where will we bury it? The cat."

"Oh, I don't know. I suppose we could bury it in the back garden. Do we know whose it is?"

"It's one of those bloody strays who are running on the road. That's why we need a gun. I've been telling you, forever. We could get rid of the crows, the strays and the bloody beggars who come crawling around here."

Emma rose. Her cheeks were flushed. "And before you know it, you will be shooting the coolies, the drunken tea pluckers on pay day, the neighbours, anyone you don't care about. And there are a lot of people you don't care about, Brian. *There will be no guns*, do you hear me?" She strode across to the alcove, sat at her writing table, and wrote on a pad. She returned, extending a piece of buff coloured paper.

"Here's five hundred. Now, leave us in peace."

He stuffed the cheque in his pocket, stuck an unlit cigarette between his lips, chewed on it and rolled it across his mouth, then walked out, slamming the front door.

Returning to our lesson, Emma paused. "I bet you, he threw that cat into the pond. I must check how much it costs to rent a water pump the next time I am in town."

***

When I returned for my class the following day, there was a visitor at *Paradise*. He was sitting on the sofa while Emma was at her writing nook, puzzling over a ledger. The stockily built man was in his mid forties and wore planter's togs: white short-sleeve shirt, long baggy khaki shorts, hose and black pumps. He rose as I entered, taking off a Panama hat and dusting it against his thigh. He had a plump florid face. "Well, Emma—I must be off. I hope we are able to secure that loan…"

She swung around on hearing my step. "Oh Winston, this is my protégé Paul. My stray. Paul, this is our estate superintendant, Mr. Hendricks." Then she laughed while looking at me. "While Brian wants to shoot strays, I adopt them, don't I?"

"How do you do, young man?" I took his warm hand and bowed my head in respect.

Emma carried on, "I'll speak to my bank manager, Winston. I think they will give us the loan, despite the temporary blip in tea prices."

Mr. Hendricks shook his head. "I don't know, Emma. The Indians and Africans are flooding the market these days.

And now our Burgher boys are immigrating to Fiji and developing that market too."

"Don't worry, Winston. God will provide. Remember the Israelites in the desert for forty years?"

On that note, Mr. Hendricks bid us a hasty "good afternoon" and made his exit.

Emma threw her head back and laughed. "He is nervous about religion. His wife is more receptive. Come, let's get to work." She was already stowing away her business papers. Then she picked up the Bible and headed towards our table by the bay window. I got the feeling that she looked forward to our meetings as her high point for the day. Just as it was mine.

***

I returned all the Christmas decorations and lights to the neighbours who had donated them to me. They looked surprised, even disappointed, Mrs. Neydorf in particular, who now could boast of two sets of lights; her husband had bought her a very elaborate set, which she showed me over a cup of tea. All my neighbours appeared to be leading superficial lives by the time Christmas rolled around that year. I seemed to have emerged into a deeper dimension and they did not interest me anymore, like Emma did.

And yet, there was a tragic aura around Emma that I could not understand. I spoke to Dad about her one day.

"Ah, ha! So the rumours I've been hearing about where you've been spending your afternoons after school are true," he said, nonchalantly turning the pages of the newspaper at breakfast that morning.

"She's nice," I replied. "But her sister's husband is a bad man."

"Hmm. He has a bit of a reputation at the Bandarawala railway station. Got into a drunken fight with the station master there a few years ago. One of the engine drivers who came by here recognized him in town the other day."

"How do you know about them?"

"When I heard that you were visiting them, I made some enquiries. This is a small place. Everyone knows everyone else's business, although your Emma and her relatives keep to themselves. They don't seem to have any friends."

"What do they say about Emma?"

"That she is a bible-thumping, sex-less zealot, all out to convert the world. People shut their doors to her now in Nuwara Eliya. Please tell her not to come this way."

Dad was making me mad. "She is not a zealot. According to the Bible, zealots were the ones who killed Jesus. She loves Jesus. And she works with the poor people living out of town now."

"Good. Ask her to stay there."

I decided not to tell my father that I had accompanied Emma on one of those excursions. I was surprised that Dad had not forbidden me to go to *Paradise*. But I guessed he had seen how engaged I was with my Bible studies and all, and must have felt that something good was coming out of my visits to the "zealot." Besides, there were only two weeks left before I headed off to boarding school. What could go wrong in-between?

Dad shut his newspaper and stood up. "I have to do one more run to Colombo next week. That bugger Jansz fell off the engine last week and we are all taking turns subbing for his run. I'll be gone for two nights. Can I arrange for you to stay at the Shoecrofts?"

"Oh, no." My groan was loud.

"Then, do you want to stay at your bible-thumper's house? With the big bad drunkard?"

"It's better than the Shoecrofts—they are *all* drunkards!"

Dad laughed again. "They are all Burghers—that's why."

"I'll stay with Emma. If she will have me."

"Do you want me to go over and ask her?"

"I'll ask her."

Dad narrowed his eyes. "Are you sure? It's usual for a parent to ask, you know."

"I'll ask her first. Then you can." I really wanted to stay those two days with her, before I went off to Gurutalawa, and I did not want Dad to screw it up.

***

"Stay here?"Emma looked taken aback.

"I don't want to stay with the Shoecroft's. They drink and gamble all the time."

"What a den of iniquity! Your father is a sinner for exposing you to all that. But I only have the spare room opposite mine. The bed is creaky and very uncomfortable."

"I've slept in worse," I said.

I guess the pleading look on my face must have won her over. "Of course. Tell your father, that I will be happy to look after you. That's next week, already. I will have to clean that room out and make it habitable."

***

Dad accompanied me to *Paradise* the next Friday, to drop me off in person. He always did that. It was his way of salving his conscience for leaving me. Emma met us at the door. She was dressed in an ankle length pale blue cotton dress, sandals, and she had done her hair up in a bun at the back. She even wore a pearl necklace, and I saw lipstick for the first time.

"Hello, Mr. Van Dort. Nice to meet you. We are so glad to have Paul with us for the next couple of days. Do come in and have a cup of tea before you leave."

I could see Dad hesitate and stammer, gazing upon this tall, beautiful, intelligent woman, who was in control of the conversation while shaking his hand firmly.

"No. I...I have to get down to the station. Thank...thank you for looking after my son. I hope he is no bother."

Emma shook her head and placed her hand on my shoulder, drawing me to her side. I could smell the fresh lavender on her. "Oh, no. Paul is no trouble. He brings us such joy, with his questions on… everything." She turned her wide grin on me and winked.

Dad dragged his gaze away from her and tried to look like a disciplinarian. He didn't quite achieve it. "Well, young man, don't go asking too many questions. I'll see you in two days."

Dad left, hesitating and looking back several times before disappearing from view down the driveway, as if he was still not sure whether the apparition holding me close was a real woman, or not. Serve him right for calling her sex-less!

***

Before dinner, we took a walk in the garden that bordered the tea estate. The pond was clean again after the recent draining. Fallen white *Araliya* flowers from the tree by the pond floated on the surface of the water. Brian was still at work, repairing the stone barrier between the pond and the grass verge.

"All the pumping and moving damaged the stonework," Emma explained as we paused by the pond. Brian had stripped down to his trousers. His hairy chest may have once been muscular but now a beer pot threatened to burst his trouser buttons. A half empty bottle of arrack stood on the ground next to his abandoned shirt.

"We need to repair the fence over by the boundary line." He stopped working and pointed in that direction. "Bloody coolies will be crawling in here pretty soon."

Emma nodded and shooed me on. Under her breath she muttered, "And I wonder how much *that* is going to cost?"

Tea pluckers, mainly women in multi coloured saris and makeshift turbans, hauling large cane baskets full of tea leaves, were making their way downhill to the workers' huts through lines of tea bushes that converged upon their living quarters. The sun was going over the west mountain and the mist was starting to bite.

Emma pulled on the sweater she had tied around her waist when we left the house, and inhaled the air deeply. "I've known these hills from the time I was a little girl. It's very difficult to leave despite all the bad things that happen."

"What bad things?" I ventured.

She smiled sadly. "God sends us challenges from time to time. I would still rather face them here, in a place I love, than anywhere else."

We had dinner at 7:30pm. Emma said grace after Brian—the last to take his seat—came in, still in his work clothes. He had put his shirt back on, with three top buttons undone. Leela, our resident cook, had prepared a sumptuous meal of rice, chicken curry, potato curry, fried *brinjals* and fresh *mallum*. This was a treat for me because meals at home were often what we could scrounge at the tuck shop in town, routinely string hoppers and stale coconut sambol and—whenever we could get it—beef curry, in which the pieces of beef were hard to find and the curry too hot to handle.

Brian and Leela ate with their fingers as was the local custom, while Emma and I used cutlery. I would have used my fingers too, but Emma's elegant table manners made me reconsider.

"Why are you such a *mahattaya*?" Brian asked me during the meal. "Trying to show-off?"

"Brian, leave him alone,' Emma said, putting her knife and spoon down.

I flushed and coughed on my food. Then I decided to stand up for my decision. "Well, my father and I always eat with a fork and spoon."

"Railway Burghers—what bloody forks and spoons for you, man?"

I tried to focus on my food but I had suddenly lost my appetite.

"Brian. I will not tolerate any more rudeness at this table." Emma had risen, her face was flushed.

Brian pushed his plate aside. He had wolfed most of his food down. He burped loudly. "This is just my lucky day: to be stuck with two women—one who will not fuck and the other who cannot—and a stuck-up little *sudu mahattaya* aping a *pukka sahib*." He kicked back his chair and walked out of the room.

Leela burst into tears. "And just because I told him I had my period."

Emma looked like a deflated zeppelin. "I'm sorry Paul, you did not have to hear that. Leela, I'll help you clean up. Then we can all sit around the piano and play some music."

We played for a long time that evening. The music helped diffuse the bad vibes stirred up by Brian. Emma ran through every tune in her repertoire; she played waltzes, country and western ballads, and even those old plantation songs that Dad used to sing whenever he'd had a few drinks: *Old Black Joe, Don't Fence Me In,* and *I Dream of Jenny with the Light Brown Hair.* We put a log in the fireplace and I got dreamy with this concentrated dose of nostalgia. I thought I saw a vision of Dad and Mum dancing—a recollection from some party the three of us had attended long ago where I had been more interested in playing with my toy train engine. I did not want the evening to end.

As Emma gathered up her music sheets, and Leela started to extinguish the lights in the house, I caught a glimpse of Brian through the bay window, sitting in the cab of his truck which was parked in the driveway, the dull glow from his cigarette illuminating a face suffused with anger.

That night I tossed and turned in my lumpy bed. Emma had been right, the bed was old and unused, and despite her putting on a fresh sheet and blanket, decorating the room with some pictures and setting up a side table with a night lamp, a Bible and a tumbler of water, I did not have the best rest. It must have been about 2:00 am when I wanted to pee. I remembered Emma's instructions before she retired for the night: there were three toilets in the house, one was attached to the master bedroom used by Brian and Leela, another to Emma's bedroom which I had used before, and the remaining toilet was at the rear of the house by the back door. She had asked me to use the night lamp if I needed to get there in the dark, or to wake her up if it was too much of an ordeal. I decided to take the easy way out. I went over to her room, across from mine, knocked on the door and peeped through the keyhole.

A table light went on inside and I saw her rise, a thin nightdress revealed her long boyish body; I caught a glimpse of small breasts with tiny nipples that were quickly hidden by the housecoat she threw on and firmly tied around her. She slid into slippers and advanced towards me from the other side. I stepped back as she opened the door. She swept back her tousled hair from her face.

In the dim light, I saw her pout in amusement. "So, it was tough going out to the back, hah?"

"I did not want to make a sound by knocking into anything," I said lamely.

"Come along then. Make it quick. We all need our sleep."

I entered her room. Again, that warmth, and the smell of lavender. I took my time peeing. I remembered my Mum and the times I had been in her embrace, especially when the world had become a scary place following a nightmare. It had been so long since I had felt that way. I wanted to linger here.

When I came out of the toilet, she was sitting up in bed, studying me. "You look like a lost child, Paul."

I guess I must have looked like one, so I said nothing, just dragged my feet toward the door and to my uncomfortable bed.

"You can sleep here if you like," she said. She rose and pulled out two pillows from a closet. A spare blanket came out of its resting place. She lay them down on the unused side of her Queen bed. "Go on, make yourself comfortable. I don't snore, I think."

I climbed in beside her. This was the softest bed I had slept in, ever. She placed the blanket over me. I was snug and drifted off to sleep in no time. The last I remembered was her gentle hand stroking my head. I had a momentary difficulty in associating that tender stroking with the stentorian and strident woman walking the land converting the heathen with her Bible. I only knew that her stroking was sincere and that I trusted this woman even more than I trusted Dad.

When I awoke the next morning, the curtains were drawn and sunlight streamed in from the garden. Emma was already up and gone about her daily chores.

I took walks in the garden and into the adjoining tea estate that day. I saw Mr. Hendricks hard at work, panting up the hills of tea, mustering his staff as all good *sinnathurais* are expected to do. The gardens of *Paradise* were well cared for. Despite Brian's erratic outbursts, he seemed to pour his attention on the upkeep of the property. I asked Emma about that when we were returning that evening from another of her missions to convert the heathen.

She explained, "Brian lost his desk job in Colombo due to an argument with his boss. He swore never to work again, unless he could get an 'executive' position as he called it. Men of his bearing did not do junior jobs, according to him. But there was no 'executive' work up here for him. He has put all his energy into the gardening and maintenance of this place, and for that I am grateful."

***

But peace and tranquility were not what we found when we arrived home.

Brian was in the front yard, yelling at one of the estate workers, an older man in a white shirt and sarong, who had his head bowed. An overripe Jak fruit lay on the ground between them.

"Brian—," Emma hurried to intervene.

"Don't interfere!" Brian had his hand up. "This bugger was stealing fruit off the Jak tree. He deserves to have his hands broken."

"No, *missie*," the man explained in Tamil. "Fruit had fallen on our side. Badly damaged. I didn't think lady and master would need. This for my family only, *missie*."

"Let him have it Brian. You would not eat it anyway. Besides, he is Mr. Hendricks's problem to deal with. Not ours."

Brian's lip curled. He swooped down, picked up the oversized fruit, raised it over his head and hurled it to the ground, shattering it into myriad squishy pieces. "Okay, now let him eat the bloody fruit then." He turned on his heel and walked away.

Emma reached into her purse. "Selvam, here's ten rupees. Go and buy your family something to eat. And don't tell Mr. Hendricks that I gave you this, or I will get another lecture. And please clean up this mess."

She put her arm around me, as if to shield me from the inequity. "Come along, Paul. Our lesson beckons. We need to attend to your spiritual upliftment."

***

Dinner was a sombre one, even though I relished the crunchy *rotties* with *lunu miris* and beef curry (and there were real pieces of beef this time). Brian did not show up for dinner which made me eat even better. Leela advised us that he had taken the truck into town, and Emma sighed. Leela was nervous throughout the meal, darting looks at me. I felt as if she wanted to tell Emma something but I was in the way.

Emma looked calmly at her sister and added another roti to her plate. "He gets that way when you are…indisposed. I think he is better off at the club."

"Yes, but then he comes back drunk and demands."

"It won't be long before you are free. Lock your bedroom door tonight." Emma's voice was steely.

Then Emma changed subjects and we talked about my school project: Huckleberry Finn. She suggested that after dinner we read from Mark Twain's *Life on the Mississippi* to get a feel for what it was really like to live the life of young Mr. Finn.

I found Emma's recounting of Samuel Clemens's life on the river boats fascinating. Again, with biblical drama, she enacted the gambling, rambunctiousness, randomness and tragedy behind the superficial humour of those times. Leela joined us and sat with an entranced expression throughout the performance.

Emma explained, "Mr. Clemens was against organized religion. He even tried to write his own version of the Bible. But he failed. It proves the power of God over man—even men of such talent as Samuel Clemens."

***

I had another troubled sleep that night. This time I heard voices, sometimes loud, sometimes hushed. A man was yelling somewhere and a woman crying. They were all part of my jumbled dream, I thought. Then I shot up, bolt upright. They were real voices. The clock showed 2:00am. Damn, I needed to piss again, badly this time. But I was not going to wake up Emma again. I had imposed on her kindness enough. Taking the night light from the bedside table I inched out into the corridor.

There was a dim light under her door and hushed voices coming from inside. Surprising. But attending to my bladder was more important and I made my way over to the toilet at the back of the house which I had scouted out during the day for just such an emergency. I peed in the dim light, and cursed for splashing over the unfamiliar seat in my haste. I pulled the chain flush, and it seemed to explode the silence of the house. Adding to my clumsiness, I stepped on a creaky floorboard as I returned to my room, and froze, thinking that I had woken up everybody. The light was still on under Emma's door and the voices had changed into grunts. Savage, inhuman grunts.

I guess that was when, like Paul the apostle, I had my revelation that blinded and scarred me for life. I drew close to the door, and just as I had done the night before, could not resist the urge to peep through the keyhole.

What I saw made me, at ten years of age, suck in my breath and hold onto the door knob lest I fall. I saw a man's bare buttocks thrusting forward and a woman's pair of legs curled around his sides, drawing him in. The grunts came from the man with every thrust of his pelvis. The bed sheets were a mess. I was riveted. *This is what having sex is all about*, a voice pounded in my head. Suddenly as if electrocuted, the man tensed, gasped and shuddered. He withdrew from the woman and rolled over on his side and—if only by his long cock that was still twinging, shuddering and shrivelling—I recognized Brian. I did not even want to look at the woman with her spread legs revealing a tangle of dark wet hair at their apex, but I heard Emma's voice ring out icily. "Now, you'd better go."

I stumbled back into my room and managed to shut the door before Emma's door opened. I remained frozen in a bath of sweat, praying for my legs not to give way. I heard heavy footsteps recede down the hall. Another door slammed—the front door. The truck started after a few moments and chugged down the driveway. I staggered towards my lumpy bed and fell in, drawing the blanket over me and pulling the pillows over my head, as if that would shut the world out. Emma's words, from not so long ago, kept ringing in my ears—*Adultery is such a sin...*

The hypocrisy of everything I had just witnessed overcame my spirit, and after sobbing my heart out, I fell into an exhausted sleep.

***

The following morning I packed my bag. Dad would be home in the evening, but I did not wish to stay here anymore. When I came into the living room, carrying my things, Emma was in her housecoat, having her tea by the window. She glanced at me woodenly. "Leaving so early?"

"Yes. Thanks for putting me up."

"Have a cup of tea, at least. And a muffin. Leela has just baked them."

"No thanks." I picked up my Huckleberry Finn book which was lying on the coffee table from the previous night's reading, and stuffed it into my sling bag. "Good bye, Emma."

She remained sipping her tea, her gaze now out into the garden, away from me. I knew there were tears in her eyes, just as there were in mine. We did not have to say that we each knew what the other knew. As I stepped out the front door, I heard her breaking voice behind me, "I hope God gives me the chance to explain things to you one day."

That day was a long time in coming, for a week later I left for the boarding in Gurutalawa. And the following year, my industrious father, despite being unable to find us an *ayah*, yet true to his promise, was passed to immigrate to Canada, thanks to the efforts of his brother who had worked hard at the sponsorship end. And as Dad's sole dependant progeny, I got to immigrate along with him.

***

The living room is the same, except that the grand piano is gone and the rest of the furniture has been pushed back into its space to make room for the bed by the window. A wheelchair reposes behind the bed. The air is stuffy and there is no scent of flowers, for there are none on the windowsill. There is the smell of must, a hint of human waste and stale urine. I am glad that I have arrived before it is too late.

"Come over here, Paul." Her voice is still firm, though less strident. "Let me look at you."

I pull a chair over to the window and sit facing her. We look at each other for a long time, the years falling off. "You have aged well," she says with a nod.

"Thank you. I have not had spouses or children to wear me down." I retrieve a book from my knapsack and hand it to her. "My latest."

She closes her hands lovingly around the book, her eyes misting over. "Oh, I hope you have brought Allen Hamilton home for good in this one?"

"Yes. I was getting tired of his ramblings. I want to start another book soon. An adult novel. I think it's time I grew up."

She looks up at me and her jaw drops in disappointment. "But you have given children all over the world such entertainment. They even make movies of your books now. You really are a messenger, Paul."

"I had good practice growing up. I peeped into people's lives, I guess."

"The eternal child…" She waves a weak hand towards the bookshelf behind her. "Your books are all there. Do you mind bringing them to me, please?"

I go over to the bookshelf. In prominence, lies my oeuvre: seventeen young-adult books written over the last twenty-five years. I pile them up and bring them over to the bed. The earlier ones have frayed covers. I stack the books with their spines facing her, and she adds my latest, the eighteenth, to the collection.

Over the years, instead of the letters I had wanted to write, I had sent her an autographed copy of every new book of mine that was published. And she had sent me back a card thanking me for each gift—no other explanation. Then last month, I had received a letter, forwarded to me by my agent. In shaky but ornate handwriting, Emma had finally broken her silence:

My dearest Paul,

I have been diagnosed with one of those illnesses that only give you a few months to live. It is well, for ever since Brian died and Leela went away to England, my life has been a cipher. I gave up my Bible lessons because I felt unworthy to proceed. I have been waiting for the end for some time now. I have decided that in these last few months left for me, I have to mend a few wrongs. And the wrong I did to you I must repay, although I am not sure if that will affect your writing in the future. You write beautiful books of children finding just rewards after facing tough challenges—inspiration to all children, especially to the ones of this country who face, not only the wrath of God in the form of droughts and tsunamis, but a dreadful war where trust between neighbours and loved ones has been destroyed forever.

Life with Brian was like the civil war that plagues this country, and Leela and you are like its displaced children. I have sold the tea estate and am slowly getting rid of my personal belongings. I still live in the crumbling remains of my once-proud home that will be bequeathed to a Home for the Aged once I die.

I have wanted to write to you all these years but every time my courage failed me. Death is a powerful motivator. I would love to see you. I hope you can visit me just once before I join Brian in the garden.
Yours affectionately,
Emma

That last line had caught my attention and spurred me into action. I had to get out from the trap that I had dug myself into—a writer for teens with a recurring theme that sold millions of copies but did not advance my soul one iota. I booked my first trip back to Sri Lanka since immigrating forty years ago, despite the civil war raging in the country, despite the bombs that were going off in random places. Emma was not going to outlive the war.

I look out into the garden and notice the addition that I have not seen while coming up the driveway: a marble tomb sits in the middle of the overgrown lawn, with two spikes, similar to the ones I have seen on the gates, sticking out of their centre, supporting a lion's crest. Oh, of course, the Sri Lankan lion, emblem of the country's national flag—that's what it must mean. For me, it also conjures Daniel in the lions' den, one of my early lessons with Emma. The tomb is surrounded by flower beds with a lush growth of hydrangea, roses and irises—so that's where the flowers had migrated to.

"Were the roadblocks tedious?" Emma brings me back to the present. "I'm told there is one at every junction, these days."

"A Canadian passport helps get me to the front of the line. But it added an extra hour to the trip up here."

A maid comes into the room bearing a tea tray—and chocolate cookies, the same brand from those many years ago. Leaving the tray conveniently placed on the bed, she silently withdraws.

"I thought you might like these," Emma says, winking at me impishly and then breaking out into a cough that wracks her frail body.

"Mustn't get too excited," she says resting back in the pillows. "Hand me those pills—the ones with the blue cap and the other with the red label. I have them all marked."

I reach for the side table by her bed with about a dozen vials of medicines on it and get her the ones she needs.

After she has taken her medication and is looking relaxed again, I settle back in my chair. "Well, Emma—we may as well begin, shall we?"

"Yes, we should." She takes a deep breath and hesitates. "But first, tell me about yourself."

"Nothing much to tell. The best parts of me are in the books I sent you."

"Yes, but your years in Canada? Your father. What happened over there?"

"Dad landed quickly on his feet, working for the Canadian National Railways. Only now, he was gone for days on end. Canada is a large country."

"And you?"

"Oh, the same—living with my uncle on and off. Boarding schools."

There was no use in bothering her with the pot smoking and the acting-out that accompanied me throughout my teen years in Canada. Or with the complete meltdown when I was 18, when Dad died in a rail accident while drunk on the job. Or the dead-end jobs that followed after dropping out of university that was funded by student loans I knew I could never repay. And then the retreat into my cocoon for survival, to write that first book about my alter ego, Allen Hamilton, an abandoned boy who triumphs over his adversaries and the unfair challenges in his life. Writing that book was my real therapy for the crummy life I had been leading up to that point.

"My first novel was a big hit. That's when my life became anything," I say, summarising those years. "Before that, I was like one of those sooty kitchens of the heathen we tried to convert."

"You fell off your horse on *your* road to Damascus," Emma's face is flushed with pride.

"Oh, I fell off that horse many times before that. One time—in this house."

Emma's face immediately clouds over. "Don't remind me. Brian was *my* husband, not Leela's. Did you know that?"

I sip my tea, digesting her words, wishing I had received this information many years ago—the final unanswered piece of the puzzle. "It helps explain a lot of things."

"Not everything. We met when I was a nurse in Colombo. He was a dashing young mercantile executive in a splashy sports car. I even mistook his bouts of anger for drive. He always dressed nattily and enjoyed the outdoor sports—rugby, golf. Soccer was considered a poor man's game by him. He had an opinion on everything. I guess he swept me off my feet. He was not the man you met. We married against my father's wishes. Daddy warned me against Brian after their first meeting. 'Too impulsive' he said, but I would not listen. 'I had him checked out,' my father pressed on, 'He's the bastard son of an Englishman who was here on a short overseas posting. He's got no family, no pedigree, and no money.' And still, I did not listen. All this information made Brian that more exotic, romantic and exciting.

"After our marriage in Colombo, *by registration*—because I found out that Brian had been married and divorced only after we applied for a church wedding and were refused—my father fell ill, and I decided to return to Bandarawala to care for him. Leela was too timid in these matters. Brian was vehemently opposed, but by this time, I was getting a little tired of his obsessive sexual demands on me and needed a break.

"I am not sure what happened to Brian during my absence, but he lost his job and the next thing I knew he landed on my father's doorstep, saying he was missing me. I think it was the sex that he was missing, for Brian was an insatiable animal in bed. Oh, yes—you probably saw plenty of that. He was also infertile, which he would not admit to. He said instead that he had divorced his first wife because she had not given him a baby. He even warned that we would end up the same, if I was barren. Unknown to him I had the matter checked out and found out that the problem was his."

I interrupt her. "How did you do that?"

She looks at me with her piercing eyes, devoid of any pretence. "Young man, a woman knows how to collect a sample of a man's seminal emissions for clinical investigation. Let's say that I had plenty of opportunity."

I sit back and realize that I am blushing.

"Looking after an ailing parent draining me with his demands, living with a frustrated husband who kept blaming the world for his misfortunes, and caring for a sister blossoming into womanhood and not knowing her raging hormones from her emotions, were deadly mixes in the cocktail I had chosen to drink.

"Not long after we buried my father, I came home early from an errand in town and discovered Brian and Leela *in flagrante* in her bedroom. I was devastated. I yelled and screamed at my sister but the poor girl was all mixed up and confused herself—Daddy's passing had thrown her into the arms of a man whose masculinity she was seeking, to replace the protection she had always enjoyed. I spent my days walking the streets of Bandarawala after that incident, asking for a sign for what I should do. And God answered: when Daddy's will was read out, I was left with his entire estate and Leela was made my ward. Brian had no access to any money, unless I gave it to him.

"I summoned both of them into a meeting. I knew I could not stop their affair. Leela was younger and more attractive than me and also more passive, which Brian fancied. But I now had a way to control them—how foolish was I to think that I could! I told them that I was selling up and moving to Nuwara Eliya where this smaller estate was available for purchase. They could come to live with me here. I felt indebted to them in a way, for having uprooted them from their lifestyle, and they had no means of their own. My only condition was that they pretend to act as husband and wife so that there would be no scurrilous talk in the new neighbourhood. There would be no domestic servants to help spread gossip either—Leela would have to manage the housework and cooking. And there would be no divorce— 'what God has joined together let no man, *or woman*, put asunder'—Brian and I had sworn on the Bible even at the Registry office.

"I began making secret arrangements to ship Leela off to England, unknown to Brian, so I knew that their affair would be short lived. I had a cousin in Kent who needed a nanny. In the interim, Leela would be safe under my watch because Brian could not get her pregnant. As for myself, I had decided to dedicate myself to God's work."

"But you were also having sex with Brian," I say. The words come gushing out, from the child inside me.

Calmly, she replies, "If having sex with Brian took the heat off Leela, whenever she was ill or indisposed, and if it kept my husband away from the whorehouses and the neighbourhood talk—yes, I would consent, even though it was the most repugnant act for me. Leela, though young and sexually flowered, was beginning to tire of his demands as well. And Brian would have ruined my work if he was seen screwing around with prostitutes or other men's wives. The hill country golf club was a hub of incestuous gossip in those days, and still is. That was my deal with him. When all else failed—screw me!" She exhales and lies back breathing shallowly. I think those words are strong, even for her.

After awhile, she stirs. "Bring me the red album on the book shelf. It's next to where your books were."

It's a bulky one. She opens the album and gestures for me to lean over. Pictures pour out.

"Leela's family—in England. She married a nice man, an engineer, and had four children, and now has eight grandchildren, and I am sure, there are more to come. I met the family five years ago when they visited Sri Lanka for the first time."

We pour through the pictures of Leela at different stages of her life in England: skinny, demure and wearing a sari, with an old Ford suitcase in hand at the airport in Heathrow, switching to slacks and jeans as she fills out in later years, in a wedding dress on the steps of an old church with a small party of guests, in maternity clothes, hanging onto the hand of a balding older Englishman with a kind face. There are more pictures of children on tri-cycles and on swings, in shaggy cuts and drainpipes and rap outfits and baseball caps; of suburban houses and cars and tiny narrow streets and church steeples and double-decker buses. Pictures at the seaside, in France, even a few taken back here in *Paradise* when Emma looked more agile but greyer than when I first knew her; and there were various children running about in the background.

"I gave her a new life, and the chance to bring all these other new lives into the world," Emma says, proudly caressing the pictures. "I tried to do that once with the poor heathen we visited while you were with me, remember? But they chose revolution over religion, death over spiritual growth. And so they fight a war that no one will win."

"When did Brian die?" I want to change the subject. Instead, my question unwittingly brings us to the central issue.

"He died a few months after you left for Canada. Oh, how I pined for not having said goodbye to you. But you were too young and these explanations would have only confused you. A lot of things happened the day Brian died. Do you see those spikes on the tomb?" She points into the garden.

"I saw similar ones on the front gates when I entered."

"Yes. Brian got this grand idea that we needed a crest for our property—his property—even though he did not own it; the grounds had become his obsession, next to sex. It was his separate state within the property I owned. It cost me more money to maintain his illusion but I allowed him this indulgence, if it would only make him quiet and happy. I had come to realize that as much as he had hurt me by defiling my sister, I had also robbed him by living in the estate where he had no hope of getting the type of job he was used to having in Colombo. This was a place only for planters and their kind, and Brian was a low-country boy, a city boy."

"He could have gone back to Colombo and got himself a job," I say.

"I suppose so. But after his own parents deserted him in his childhood, he felt that he was owed. I had the money, I had the power, and therefore, I owed him.

"Anyway, it was on the day that he had bought the spikes—all four of them. He planted them erect in a block of wood in the driveway and painted them black all around. The postman arrived and Brian stopped his work to pick up the mail. The postman's timing could not have been worse. Brian staggered into the house, trembling, brandishing an open letter in his hand that bore the crest of the British High Commission.

" 'What the fuck is this?' he glared. Leela came running in from the kitchen and hugged me from behind, trembling. 'Going on a holiday, hah?'

" 'I am sending Leela away for awhile,' I replied. I was partially relieved to unburden this secret, for we'd gone through a lot of cloak and dagger work to get her a passport and lodge the British visa application, without his knowledge. I even had to tell Brian that we were going to see a gynaecologist in Colombo regarding Leela's perceived lack of fertility when she and I went for her visa interview. I had lied repeatedly over this mission to get Leela away from him.

" 'And you did this behind my back?' He advanced towards us and for the first time I felt frightened. Leela screamed and held me so tight that I could not escape the blow he landed right in my stomach. I doubled over in pain. He grabbed Leela by the hair and dragged her into the master bedroom. I heard her screaming as he began beating her, demanding the passport. I dragged myself into their room only to see him waving the booklet in his hand. She must have revealed its hiding place during her beating. I charged at him, but not before he had ripped the document in two. We collided into each other and went down in a heap, but he was a strong man and he was up faster and started kicking me and tearing the passport further until it was reduced to scraps in his hands. I saw Leela's black eyes and swollen face and started to black out myself from the blows I was receiving. I heard him say triumphantly, 'No one leaves this place. You brought us here, now you are stuck with us.' "

Emma starts panting with her recollections and falls back into the pillows again. I rise and pour her a glass of water. "I think that is enough excitement for today," I say. "I have a room at the rest house in town. I'll come back tomorrow."

She shakes her head. "No…not tomorrow. I have waited too long to make my confession. It has to be today."

I resume my seat and wait for her to regain her breath.

Eventually, her voice gathers strength. "Brian got in the truck and took off in a blaze of gravel. I think he was heading to the club to get drunk. That's what he did every time he was upset with something—drink. I poured ointment over Leela's bruises and applied a compress to my stomach. There was no sense in calling a neighbour, or Mr. Hendricks, or our doctor. What would we tell them? All our secrets would be out in the open. Instead, I prayed for a sign. At about 6:30 in the evening, I fed Leela some soup, gave her two Panadols and she eventually fell into an exhausted sleep. I sat by this window and prayed some more. I collected the scraps of the torn passport, put them in an envelope and hid them under the piano lid. In his frenzy, Brian had crumpled the letter from the High Commission and dropped it on the floor, but had not torn it. I stored the letter with the remains of the passport. Any compassionate immigration officer would re-issue Leela a new set of documents, if I gave them a credible story and a suitable bribe. But I was worried about Brian and what he would do to us next. We had nearly pulled off this coup, but our failure at the last minute had only exposed his vulnerability, and now he was like a rabid dog. This was the first day he had resorted to physical violence against us."

Her voice takes on the dramatic quality of old. It transports me back to those many lessons from the Bible that I had sat through, enthralled with her delivery.

"And then the rain came down—in buckets. It was as if God had opened the heavens to wash the iniquity from this house. In the fading light, I saw fresh black paint drip off the spikes and overflow from the open can beside them, spreading around the earth, fanning our sins in wider circles, until the entire driveway was a pool of darkness.

"Thunder rolled in the heavens and lightening split the sky. I wanted to go out into the open and have one of those bolts strike me and deliver me from this mortal coil. Instead, I saw the lights of Brian's truck beam coming up the driveway.

"He staggered out of the cab, and he looked very drunk. He took two steps in the pool of black rainwater and slipped, falling heavily. I heard him yell and saw his flailing hands. I realized that he must have sprained or broken something because he could not rise from the mud.

"The next bolt of lightning gave me my sign. A deathly calm enveloped me, as if an angel had offered me her protective wings. I rose and looked in on Leela. She was fast asleep. Then I went out the front door."

Emma's jaw starts to shake and tears stream down her face. She is mumbling now and I have to lean forward to catch her jumbled words.

"He was defenceless, extending his hand for me to lift him up. He had always been weak, and here was my proof. But he was also erratic and dangerous. That is why I did not feel any emotion when I slung his arm over my shoulder and staggered to where the spikes stood—pointing accusingly at us."

She looks at me unflinchingly, those embers in her eyes blazing momentarily. "I threw him onto the spikes."

I gulp and remain silent. All I can do is nod.

She continues. "He sunk into the barbs like a punctured balloon, one spike through the heart, two others piercing his outstretched arms. Like a flipped-over Christ, his blood ran freely, colouring the black water, washing our dark sins away.

"I went inside, stripped off my wet clothes, got into my housecoat and telephoned the police. I said that there had been an accident..." Her voice trails away.

I have heard enough. I look out over the tomb again. She buried him there, and chose to stay in this house as a prisoner serving out her life sentence. *Till death us do part... or meet.*

Emma rings her tiny bell and the maid brings in more tea. After taking another set of pills from her assortment, Emma composes herself, sipping her tea.

"You know, it was wrong to do what I did. For my penance, I accepted this voluntary incarceration. I controlled both their lives—that was my sin. The best thing I did was letting Leela go free, but I had to kill Brian in order to do that. In a way, I set him free too. But, 'I am the giver and taker of life,' said the Lord. Even great men like Samuel Clemens failed to become God—who did I think I was?"

"You have set me free with your confession. That is a good thing."

She smiles despite the pain that now travels unfettered throughout her body, like Brian once did around this property. "A small compensation. But I'll take that as a blessing."

I take her hand in mine, grateful that she has finally let me into her truth and her pain. I am glad for having made this trip, even at this late hour.

I look outside. The sun has come out from behind a cloud, throwing a golden hue on the trees. Soon it will disappear over the hills and darkness will descend rapidly. "Are you able to go into the garden?"

"Only with the nurse who comes in three times a week. Today is her day off."

"Can I take you for a walk?"

Her eyes brighten. "Oh yes, I'd love that. Take me down to the pond. I haven't been back there in ages. We have to take my wheelchair."

She is animated as I wheel her down the pathway towards the pond, her bony long limbs jerking like ostrich legs, as she points to the things that need fixing around the property.

"And I used only two of the spikes on the gates. I thought that placing the other two on Brian's tomb would be appropriate…And he wanted a tiger motif on the gates, I chose the lion instead, after he died…How long are you staying…? Will you come by tomorrow too…?"

Inheritance

I had last seen Anil five years ago when Mother died, and, because of doctored photographs on Facebook posted around significant events in his life in LA, he looked older. He stepped out of the customs doors, dropped his bags and took a deep breath then looked curiously around him, the sweat streaming off his balding pate in the low air-conditioning of the terminal building.

"Welcome back to Sri Lanka," I said, nearing him, smelling the stale scents of after-shave, perspiration and that humid smell that adheres to all travellers getting off an aircraft after a long flight.

"Rohit!" His eyes bulged as he extended his hairy arms and grabbed me in a clammy bear hug. He was all soft flesh that rolled and jostled as our bodies met. "You are skin and bone, bro! The old man didn't feed you, or what?"

"Painters don't make enough money to feed themselves. Unlike software engineers."

"Bullshit! They are talking about you in LA, man!"

"That was Father's influence. Thank God it will not go on any more." I grabbed hold of his valise, determined to change the topic. "Shamila arrived yesterday from Sydney."

"Ah, how is she?" He hobbled after me, wheeling his suitcase and wielding the plastic Duty Free bag as if it was his passport to enter the country.

"Not much has changed. Still a spoilt brat."

"The divorce fucked her up."

"Divorces. This is her third, in case you forgot."

We stepped out into the heat and my breathing returned to normal. I did not do well in temperature controlled environments. Perhaps that's one of the reasons I hadn't settled abroad like my siblings had. Perhaps it was *because* of my siblings…

***

On the drive home in my father's Mercedes, driven by Jamis, whom we would now have to discharge, my mind went back to yesterday's arrival. It was an escape to blot out Anil's exuberant chattering which resembled John Cleese on steroids.

I had stood in the same spot in the terminal last evening and watched my kid sister emerge from the Australia flight. I'd heard of her recent divorce, the fights leading up to it, the beatings (something I think she should have received as a kid, perhaps then she wouldn't have been so spoiled), the car crash after an all-night binge, Father sending money for the legal proceedings and slumping into a deep depression, one he could never shake off until he died. There was always drama around my sister, just as there was braggadocio and emptiness around my older brother.

I was surprised to see her emerge, arm entangled in that of a tall blonde man in jeans and a tee shirt. She was laughing and swinging her free hand and he looked mildly embarrassed but intrigued by this bundle of nervous energy attached to him. A porter followed rolling four (Four? She was only staying for a week?) fuchsia suitcases on a cart that was also piled with duty free bags, shoulder bags and a handbag.

My sister was well endowed and curved and she had lush black hair that fell to her waist, and she loved sex. The last part I had known from the time she was in her teens and had taken on half my class on a dare during a house party when our parents were on an overseas trip. I wonder what would have happened if Father had found out. Or maybe he had, and had remained silent about it.

She paused looking around her, caught sight of me, dropped her companion's hand and rushed over, slobbering me with wet kisses, rubbing her large breasts all over me and making me glad that women did not excite me; besides, she was my sister with whom I had to remain chaste. "Rohit, so nice to see you, hon. How are you? I missed you all." More wet kisses.

She held me at arm's length and studied me and I caught sight of her cleavage though the undone buttons of her shirt, gold chains vanishing down soft depths. Her large dark eyes, the heart-shaped face on which the heavy make-up had slipped during the long flight, the hint of grey at her temples along with the beginnings of crow's feet around her eyes.

"Myee—you haven't changed one bit," she said.

I blushed and looked down at my sandled feet. "Who's the guy?" I asked. The guy in question was standing undecided from where she had left him along with the bewildered porter. She placed a finger across her lips and winked. "We met on the plane," she whispered, "Back in a jiffy." She returned to the man, gave him a card from the handbag reposing on the luggage cart, and followed up with a quick peck on his cheek. Then she pointed the porter in my direction, waved at the man, and headed over to me, beaming and winking some more.

As we loaded her bags into the Mercedes, she fanned herself with one of those delicate Japanese silk affairs that were more decorative than functional. Her hair was beginning to curl in the humidity and her skin was turning oily. Suddenly she gripped my hand.

"Oh, my God! Is the Bitch going to be there?"

I nodded. "Afraid so." The Bitch was our step-mother, five years younger than Shamila.

"Fuck!" Shamila's features darkened and I could see the tantrum-ridden teenager of not-so long ago. She stamped her foot down as if reluctant to get in the car. "Why does she have to be here?"

"She was his wife and is entitled to be at the reading of the will, even though they had a prenuptial agreement. Besides, she still lives at the *walauwa*."

"Then drive me to a hotel. I won't stay a day under the same roof with that …that slut."

"Which hotel?" I said without batting an eyelid.

We drove out of the airport in silence and Shamila busied herself freshening her make-up. She seemed to have temporarily, or permanently, forgotten her nemesis.

Anil's voice brought me back to the present. "Where did you drop Shamila off?"

"By the time we got home, she had changed her mind and asked for her old bedroom. She said she would only come out for meals and for the reading of the will."

Anil grinned. "Drama queen—nothing has changed."

"Then she was out all last night. The guy she met on the plane picked her up at eight."

"Hah!"

Anil reached into his shoulder bag and pulled out what looked like a brochure. "Here take a look at this."

It was some kind of a software application with a brand name Softer Logic. "One of your new inventions?" I asked. The fine print did not impress me although the glossy graphics and the picture of a young businesswoman, in dark-rimmed glasses and pulled-back hair tapping on a keyboard on a tropical island, were eye-catching.

Anil's chest puffed proudly and he tried unsuccessfully to curb his enthusiasm. "I've got six months of full VC funding. Silicon Valley's ecstatic about this one."

"What happened to the last venture? The one where you were going to be shooting applications to people from a cloud, like a god in the sky?"

"The fucking market crash of 2008—blame it on that."

"But the US is still not out of its woes."

"I need one decent break, bro. Look at Father. I never saw him fail at anything."

"He had powerful political backers—on both sides. They wouldn't let him fail."

"Maybe my inheritance will help me—help us all, I mean. My greatest wish would be never to have to ingratiate myself with those assholes in the Valley again."

I changed the subject for I saw his face clouding over and his breath sharpening. I did not want him getting another heart attack, so soon after the last one.

"How's the family?"

"Kids are killing me, man. Amal and Mano are always asking for money for college fees and tuition and all that. They are not even passing the bloody exams. Amal is a fifth year student—no degree yet."

"I thought Father had made some provisions…His only grandchildren and all."

Anil remained silent for once. I took it that the money had been spent on "other" things.

"Sakuntala bought a Lexus last month. Can you imagine? When I am struggling to get my company off the ground, she goes off buying luxury cars." He had met his wife Sakuntala while they were finishing their undergraduate degrees in Colombo, before they moved to the States for Anil's Masters at Stanford. She came from a modest middle class family and had always liked the good life, that's why she had latched onto my brother in the first place, I think.

I chuckled. "I remember her father ferrying her around in their old Toyota with its belching exhaust. The Lexus must be quite a step-up."

He gave me a startled half-look, undecided if I was commiserating or taunting. "Love was blind in those days, bro. I was like a bloody knight in shining armour. Rescued the wrong bloody woman, though."

Sakuntala worked occasionally for a women's journal and was a member of many social clubs in Los Angeles, I had heard. She was always experimenting with the latest diet, although it did not seem to have worked, at least for Anil. "Well, you have a family. Unlike the rest of us," I offered.

We drove in silence.

"What about you, bro?" he said suddenly. Then he bit his lip. "Oh, sorry…"

"Nimal and I are okay. I did not bring him out to visit Father after that first… 'incident,' but we have a contented life together. Nimal assists me at the art school."

"And is that all you want to do? Paint? I know you are very good at it. Your landscapes are a hit in my part of town. But it's hit and miss, isn't it?"

"Like software?"

I did not mean to be cruel but it was hard justifying my vocation to my siblings, over and over again. Even my father had understood it only in his last days.

I took a deep breath and gave it another shot. "The world has a lot of beauty, Anil. Unfortunately it is masked by fear. This gives way to greed and anger, and finally the cauldron boils over and we kill and destroy. There has been too much of it in this country over the last 25 years. I am trying to find the beauty and expose it. That's all I wanted to do since I can remember. I am glad the people in LA appreciate my work. I hope I can spread it around the world some more, but on my terms, not on my father's."

"Well, you won't have that problem anymore."

"But he cast a long shadow. There are still people who call me up and say, 'You are Cyril's son, the painter, right? Your dad told me about you.' "

"Well, he got you your first exhibition in America."

"And my education in England. And he threw out my life partner on our first visit together to the family home because it was 'disgraceful.' Yes, I suppose I have to be grateful."

"What was he like in the …last days?"

"Reflective. I went to see him in the hospital when You-Know-Who was not around. It was a week before he passed away. He told me that his life had been a big lie."

"What?"

"He said that he was tired of kissing politicians' asses to maintain his position. He said that he had been nothing but an arms dealer, a death merchant."

Anil's face blanched. "No! But that came later, no? He was an industrialist of a firm that diversified with the economy. What did he *not* have his hand in: textiles, call centres, construction, hotels. With his connections and his acumen, he was a logical choice to help the government procure the…the materials… to help win this war."

"He told me that what he made on those deals alone was more than what he made on all the others combined, in his entire working life."

Anil looked around him secretively, as if worried that half-deaf Jamis would overhear.

"You must not talk like that about him. After all, he was our father." He pointed out the window, at the new construction by the highway, construction that had started up again, furiously, the moment the guns had gone silent. "He did his part to bring about all this."

"He wasn't sure that this would be the end of hostilities. He said that we had not eradicated the fear in people's hearts. We had won the battle but lost the war. We had temporarily stunned the radicals with heavy sledgehammers. But even stomped ants recover after awhile."

"What else did he say?"

"Not much." I did not want to tell Anil everything, partly because it was none of his business and partly because he would never believe me. I remembered the old man on his deathbed, the gaunt, emaciated face, the distant stare, his ice-cold grip on my hand, and his words that chilled and would always stay with me, "You created the best work of all of us, *putha*. I was a fool not to see it. Now that you have done LA, London is next, then Milan, and Paris. You must atone for my sins."

We arrived at the large family home, the *walauwe*, as it was known, even if it was in the heart of Colombo 7, and I fondly took in the large gates with their spikes, the winding drive to the two-storey house partially covered by the giant jacaranda tree that periodically shed its purple flowers in the front yard as if to welcome guests. Now that I did not live here anymore and had a modest apartment in Dehiwala with Nimal, returning to the family home awakened nostalgia. I remembered playing hide-and-seek in the back garden as a child, dodging behind the traveller's palms and their fan-shaped leaves to hide from my pursuers. An innocent time, now lost.

When we pulled up under the porch, a foreign sight met us. Well, "foreign" is one way of putting it. My step-mother was sprawled on the wing-backed chair, indulging in her favourite pastime: tanning in a skimpy bikini in the sunlit part of the verandah that ran around the front of the house. Svetlana, or Lana as my father had called her, was Russian, 35, and a red-headed beauty. I could see her stirring my octogenarian father's loins in his last years. He had especially liked to parade her at the cocktail parties and VIP gatherings that he constantly attended up to the time of his last visit to the hospital from which he never returned. Her hazel eyes hid behind thick sun glasses; a glass of iced tea sat on a stool beside her. She was holding up a fashion magazine and did not shift her gaze from it, although I knew that she was studying us as we exited the car.

Anil dropped his suitcases on the front steps, expecting Jamis, or me, to take care of them, and ambled over to Svetlana. His eyes devoured her body as he extended a hand. "How are you, Lana?" He even embraced her clumsily as she remained sprawled on the lounge chair. I hoped he had rid himself of that aircraft smell by now.

As soon as she was free of his bear hug, she stood up, took off her glasses and tossed back her huge red tresses. She had an amused smile. I had not seen a sign of mourning or loss on that face in these two weeks since the cremation. My brother stood awkwardly, ogling her. "It's nice to meet in person, finally."

"The same," she replied in her heavy accent. It sounded like "Dha zame."

I noticed that there was no visible sign of my sister, even though it was nearly mid-day.

"Have you had lunch?" I asked Lana.

"Ze cook vill call when it is ready," she replied, picking up a wrap and throwing it around her svelte body, leaving the cloth loose around its only distended feature—her large silicone breasts—that Anil had hitched his eyes onto. "I vill not join you. Ze driver will be taking me to ze Taj. Now I need to take a shower. Nice to meet you," She smiled coquettishly at Anil and slipped back inside the house.

"Fuck, man! That's a real piece of goods. Father must have died having too much sex. No wonder Shamila is jealous!"

***

We did not have to wait long for the explosion. It came after lunch, which Nanda, our old cook, had put on for us, her former charges, with zest. The meal was sumptuous: rice, chicken curry, *brinjals theldala, seeni sambol, bandakka* in a white curry, devilled potatoes, and a mysterious *mallum* that I could not figure which leaf it had originated from, but which I ate with relish. Anil opened one of his bottles of duty-free scotch and drank half the contents during the meal. I had a tot of this single malt variety, new to my taste, to keep him company. Shamila would only drink red wine, which she had asked Jamis to stock up from Odell's store since her arrival yesterday. It was nice swapping small talk with my siblings, but I sensed unspoken tensions under the surface throughout the meal. Perhaps their heavy indulgence in alcohol was an attempt to dull the discomfort.

Nanda was clearing the plates away, complaining that we hadn't eaten enough, and Shamila had poured the remnants of the bottle of Merlot into her glass when an upstairs door opened and high heels clicked on the cement staircase.

185

Lana descended, dressed in a gold *shalwa khamees* which gripped her figure in the right places. She had chosen to go South Asian quite effectively. Her hair was blow-dried, lush and wavy, and her lips were artificially red.

Shamila took one look at Lana and burst out. "Some people think we are too cheap to eat with. They go out and eat at fancy hotels on my father's money."

Lana paused on the staircase and stared down at us disdainfully. "You are in *my* house, remember? This is your father's and *my* house. Mind your language."

"Mind my fucking language? Who do you think you are you…you money grabbing whore?" Shamila was up and charging Svetlana, wine glass in hand, before Anil or I could interfere. They met midway on the staircase, the wine glass splintered, crimson everywhere, mostly on Svetlana's elegant suit, and the two women went down in a huddle on the steps and rolled down, locked in mortal combat.

Anil and I sprang up from our rice and curry (and in his case, whiskey) induced lethargy and tried to pry the two roaring cats apart. I grabbed Shamila. Anil, very willingly, grabbed Lana under her breasts and hoisted her up and away from us, resulting in them falling again, she on top of him; the groan emanating from him sounded like she had crushed his balls.

When we had managed to restore a modicum of order, Lana wrenched herself out of Anil's grasp, took one look at her stained clothes, and let out a frustrated scream. She stormed up to her bedroom and slammed the door so hard that the house shook with the reverberations.

"Fucking bitch," Shamila straightened up, brushing pieces of glass from her bosom. "I should have stayed at the Meridien."

"I can always send Jamis around with the car," I said.

Without answering me, she bounded up the stairs, turned in the opposite direction to Lana and headed off to her bedroom at the far end. A door slammed, louder than Lana's, and Anil chuckled. "Women! I hope the will's left *nangi* enough money so that she *can* actually stay in expensive hotels." He rose from the floor, held his crotch and groaned again. "I'm going to get rid of my jet lag and give these old balls a rest. Maybe I'll get to actually use them on this trip." He ascended the stairs, slowly, to another room, between the women's, and the door clicked quietly this time.

***

I spent the afternoon in the garden, enjoying the majestic trees that had been a part of my boyhood. I remember my mother reading to me under the temple tree with its white flowers, and their fragrance, flowers which the servants gathered and took to the temple as offerings. Between the deep orange fruits on the king coconut trees ringing the back fence, the red of the flamboyant tree, the purple of the jacaranda, and the verdant leaves in all shapes and shades of green, I had enough colour to steep myself in and imagine the allure of the garden that had given me my impetus as a child to seek that same beauty in the world beyond these walls.

The garden brought back memories of Father. He always wore a tie with his white shirt and dark pants, even if the heat and humidity made it a suffocating accoutrement. He decked Mother with jewellery that made her stoop and hang her bangle-laden arms wearily whenever he took her out for formal events, himself dressed in either a full evening suit or a flowing white national costume, depending on which diplomatic or political party gathering they were attending. In his younger days he had sported an Errol Flynn moustache which had suited his tall athletic frame. Despite the many social gatherings he attended, and the copious amount of food and alcohol that was indulged, he managed to stay trim, and the shock of dark curls on his head only turned grey in his final years.

It was also in this garden that my father had upbraided me, at the age of 18, when he had caught me in the act of painting.

"Why do you spend such a lot of time on this silly pursuit?" he had asked me on that occasion. I remember he had just returned from a meeting with some visiting foreign dignitaries. His tie hung loose and limp below the open top button of his shirt.

"People do not see the real beauty of this country. It's only available on tawdry tourist brochures," I replied.

He was surprised at my rebuff. He was not used to retorts from his family members…well, except from Shamila. "Tourism makes money. This does not."

"Money is not everything. And this country has no money. How much aid did you fish out of those foreigners?"

He swore under his breath, spat, and instinctively raised his hand to strike me. I had pushed him over the edge this time and flinched in anticipation of the blow. But at the last second, he brought his hand down by his side. "I wish your sister would protest like you—with constructive words and arguments. And your elder brother is bloody useless—he never protests."

"I wasn't protesting. You were saying that my life was unlived. That's not true."

"We will have this debate another time. I think you should get yourself a business degree and come and work for me. We have built much during my time. But I have no one to follow after me."

I turned back to my painting and did not reply. Four years later he sent me to London, to complete my post-graduate studies in painting at the Royal College of Art. The four intervening years had seen many arguments between us, and pushed me to dig in, while he reluctantly retrenched towards accepting my true calling in life. Ten years later, he converted his companies into public corporations, retained leadership as Chairman and resigned himself to being a major shareholder, and to the fact that none of his children would ever take over the reins from him.

Father took a swipe at me years later, when I decided to come out of my private dungeon with Mother's passing and brought Nimal with me to the house. My father was sitting in his armchair on the veranda, sucking on his occasional pipe, sunk in thought—he looked the loneliest soul in the world, this man who made heads of state pay homage to him.

Seeing me and my partner walk up the driveway in the gathering dusk (we had taken the bus), he peered, then put his pipe aside and came running down the steps to embrace me. "Ah *putha*, you have come. Come in, come in. Bring your friend too."

He clapped his hands for Nanda to bring us some "refreshments," which was his usual bottle of Johnny Walker Black Label, ice and a bottle of soda.

"Nimal doesn't drink alcohol," I said. Father clapped again and Nanda came out wringing her hands "No soft drinks, *mahattaya*. Didn't go to the shop today. Jamis had gone to repair the car."

"What?" Father looked flustered. He had solved more important business and security questions in his time but this one seemed to flummox him.

"It's okay. Water will do," Nimal said.

"Break a king-coconut," I countered, to solve the problem. Nanda disappeared and I don't know how she climbed the tree in the back yard, but a freshly cut fruit with a straw sticking out of its belly appeared fifteen minutes later.

While we waited for the magic fruit, Father sat back in his chair, resumed his pipe, and a plaintive look descended upon him. "I miss your mother, you know. She was a quiet woman who went about keeping this house together. I only realize how much she did now that she is gone."

Then his face brightened up. "You must marry," he said. "You must not be alone like me."

"But—" I began, wondering why the hell he had picked this moment to come up with this strange idea. I saw Nimal blanch and look down nervously at his feet.

"Senator Pieris's daughter just graduated from London and has returned home. She will make you a wonderful wife."

I was glad for the king-coconut that arrived at that point. Nimal took the fruit in his hand but was too agitated to drink from it.

"Cheers," Father said, raising his scotch on the rocks. "To marriage! I am thinking of getting married too!"

"You are?" I thought this would be a nice way to change the subject from me. "Who to? I remember General Dissanayake's widow leaned on your shoulder rather heavily at her husband's funeral." Inwardly I felt betrayed because Mother was only dead three months and my father was already getting his gonads in a knot. However, I pretended to be amused and excited by his plans.

"No, no—Agnes Dissanayake is a good friend, that's all. I don't want to marry women who are going to die on me. I want a woman to be around to bury me."

I sipped my drink, put it down, and took a deep breath.

He took another gulp from his glass, his eyes dilating with the aggression that had been his hallmark whenever he was pursuing a new business deal. "No, someone younger this time, *putha*. I am an old man and I have worked my whole life. I want to have fun now. But here I am rambling about myself. Let's talk about you. Shall I put the word out to the Senator? Prepare the groundwork, as they say?"

I put my glass down. I had procrastinated enough— my entire life up to that point. I glanced at Nimal, who was looking increasingly ill at ease.

"Father, there is a matter that we came to discuss with you today." Again, I looked at Nimal, who was clearing his throat. For his sake I had to do this quickly.

"Tell me, *putha*." Father leaned forward eagerly, as if I was bringing him a new deal.

"Nimal and I are partners. Life partners."

Father's eyebrows narrowed as if he was confused, disoriented. "Partners? What do you mean—you fellows have some business deal that you did not tell me about? You want money?"

"No it's not a business deal. We are lovers. And we want to live our lives together."

He jerked back in his chair as if he had been shot. Then he jumped up, as if electrocuted.

"What? What nonsense? My son! A fag! What bloody nonsense is this? Did your mother know? My God, she will turn in her grave!"

"Mother knew. But she would never betray me. She said that I should reveal it when I was ready."

He had taken a few steps away from us and was staring at me with a mixture of wariness and disgust in his face.

"Get out! Get out from this house!" His voice was bottled, hoarse, and I felt he was going to have a heart attack.

Nimal rose to his feet and pulled me by the hand. "Let's go Rohit. Perhaps some other time. Your father is upset."

"Upset? You bloody fag! What have you done to my son?" Father advanced as if to hit Nimal but I stepped in the middle.

"There will be no fights here. I did the respectable duty of coming to tell you. If you can't handle it, we will leave."

I allowed Nimal to lead me down the driveway. His step was rushed and I was pulled along. When I looked back towards the veranda, I saw a hunched man scrambling for his drink. I thought I heard a heartrending sob.

A door slammed, bringing me back to the moment. A shock of red hair emerged from indoors, sailed over the tall plants surrounding the house, headed down the veranda and towards the mini SUV parked at the end of the driveway. When she came into full view, Lana had changed into a crème silk shirt and black pants with red heels to match her hair. She was carrying a suitcase. She threw the bag into the back seat, leapt into the SUV—a vehicle my father had bought her—and roared down the driveway. She stomped on the breaks just where I was seated, stuck her head out of the window and said, "I weel be staying at the Taj until your relatives leave."

"Will you be coming to the reading?"

"Yez. Bye for now!" And then she was off in a cloud of dust, horn blowing as she hit the main road. I had never really got to know Lana, and her monosyllabic conversations did not allow much room to figure her out either.

"Nice piece of ass, that." Anil had arrived beside me during that exchange. He was staring at the disappearing vehicle "I guess money talks. How did Father meet her?"

"She arrived with a trade mission. And stayed."

"He liked fair skinned women." Anil was referring to our mother who was a Burgher, very fair, some of which had rubbed off on us, particularly me. Father had liked parading Mother around when we were kids, I remember. Then she had tired of the facade, and as her looks aged, she retreated more into household matters.

Anil sat down beside me on the garden seat. "You know, I somehow feel that I failed my father. I should have stayed and helped him run his businesses."

"Did he ask you to?"

Anil looked askance at me. "Should he have? Isn't it a foregone conclusion in family-run businesses?"

"Nothing was assured with Father. He believed in picking the right person for the job."

"You mean—I did not fit the bill?"

I remained silent.

Anil sighed.

I remembered the hurried exit that Nimal and I had made down this driveway several years ago. "If it's any consolation, I think I also failed him."

For the first time I saw tears in my elder brother's eyes.

***

I decided that I would leave Anil and Shamila to their own devices to explore the city for the next few days. Now that

Lana was out of the house, no damage could ensue. Besides, I needed the healing company of Nimal, my paintings, and the creative energy of the art school to perk me up after this day of conflicting memories and conflicted people.

Therefore, as the shadows lengthened that evening on the day Anil arrived, I took my leave of him on the driveway and went indoors to do the same with Shamila. She was still holed up in her room. I tapped before entering. She was on her old bed, reading the faded hardcover of *Jane Eyre* that had always sat on the bookshelf in her room. The place was a mess of clothes from her four open suitcases, as if she had been undecided where to store them, had given up and taken to reading.

"These Bronte stories always make me feel better," she said, looking up when I entered.

"Lana has taken herself off to a hotel. You and Anil can have the house to yourselves. I am going to take my leave. You have my phone number if you need to call me."

"Must you go, Rohit?" There were tears in her eyes too. If not for her buxom size, she looked like my lost kid-sister again, crying every time Father would leave on one of his overseas trips. "I feel so alone."

"I thought you had made a friend on the plane."

"Bloody loser. All he wanted to do was fuck."

"I thought you liked that."

She gave me a steely look. "Yes, but at some point in your life you want more, no?"

"You won't find 'more' by chance on a plane."

"I wish I'd had kids."

"Well, Father had to pay for your abortions before you got married."

"Those bastard doctors must have cut off the wrong things. I think my exes left me because I was left barren."

I moved some panties and nighties aside, sat on the bed and embraced her. She was still my sister, even though she was more of a stranger now.

"I must be off," I said. "Perhaps we will meet for dinner at a restaurant in town. I will bring Nimal along."

"Why not bring him here? We'll get Nanda to put on another spread. And we can have an old style family meal, like in the old days."

"Nimal has bad memories of his last visit to this house. Let's meet in town. I'll arrange that before the reading."

I left her hugging her Bronte novel, as if the secrets for growing up and being a good woman were inside those pages, as the faded dust jacket claimed.

***

I sat at my easel mixing colours. Today's output was weak, too many grey's, even the sea was steely, the fishing boats were black smudges, and I had forgotten to introduce birds. I was painting from memory and I knew it was only for catharsis.

Nimal came in and brought me a cool drink. "Do you want anything to eat?" he asked.

"No thanks. Come back when the colours start to change." Despite his attentiveness to me, I wanted to be alone today.

I remembered the day Father visited me at our apartment. We hadn't talked for nearly a year after the Nimal incident. In between I had heard that he had remarried.

Approaching sirens accompanied the roar of motorcycles that day. Another politician going shopping, I thought. We had got accustomed to our fear-riddled politicos moving about the city under armed guard, understandably, for many had been assassinated by roadside shooting or bombs the moment they had let their guard down. This time the sirens did not move past but came to rest outside my window.

I looked out and spotted Jamis opening the rear door of the parked Mercedes, across the street from my studio window. Our old driver bowed and scraped as his lord and master alighted. The road, normally busy with pedestrians, was deserted. Then I saw the military motorcycles parked in front and behind my father's car, poised like hounds to protect their master at the first sign of danger.

"This is a surprise. Why the escort?" I asked, opening the front door before he even knocked. I was shocked to see a stooped figure. My father had lost 20 pounds and looked ten years older than when I had last seen him. Perhaps his young Russian wife was making him feel his age.

He coughed. "It's standard procedure now. I've come to see your gallery. See what you do."

I was glad that Nimal had gone to buy the groceries and wouldn't be back for at least an hour. "Let me show you around then."

We started in the reality room and I showed him my "hope" series: a woman cradling her infant while reading a letter from the military advising her of her husband's death in the civil war; there is light everywhere around her and she is looking towards the sun with the letter crumpled in her hand. Father stopped and observed the portrait of the men building a tsunami ravaged dwelling using thatch and castoffs to reinforce the roof. "I like this one—it shows resilience, they are not waiting for government handouts."

"They are the smart ones," I replied. "They know that there will be none."

We skipped through the abstract section, as I had surmised—Father was a practical man and wanted to see things in concrete form.

He took his time in the portrait gallery where I had kept prints of the originals. There were some pretty famous names in there, many of his political connections who had paid me well to have their portraits done. He stopped for a long time by the original of my mother.

"I did not know you had done her portrait," he said. He looked crestfallen.

"I painted her when you were on one of your extended overseas trips."

"You have captured her inner beauty, the way she turned her cheek, the luminous pools in her eyes. Now I realize why I could always talk to her about my business problems. She could absorb and neutralize my troubles."

"Mother wanted to have her portrait adorn the *sala* in the *walauwe*. But after she got the cancer, she cried every time she saw the portrait. So I brought it here with me."

He scanned the room, noting the other paintings, committing them to memory. "I am sorry that I reacted that way with you and Nimal."

"You had better apologize to him."

"I will write to him. I can't trust myself to speak again."

I was surprised at this revelation from a man who had always been cocksure of himself. Then I realized that his emaciated state must mean something else.

"Are you all right? Married life seems to have taken a lot out of you."

He stirred, remembering something then started to make for the exit. "Come with me. There is a place I want to show you."

Father dismissed his escort before we got into his car. The lead military officer protested at first and spoke anxiously into his walkie-talkie before shrugging and signalling his men to leave.

"You are not afraid of a 'stray' bullet?" I asked.

"What we are about to see is worth taking that risk," he replied.

We remained silent as the car sped out of the city, along the coastal road to Bentota. He never answered me about the health-related question. A few miles south of the tourist strip of the former fishing village, we cut inland and drove over a potholed road which ended at a large white-washed building that looked like a school. There was no signage to indicate its purpose or function. Compared to the other crumbling structures we had passed along this rutted road, this construction could not have been more than a year old. Children were playing in the yard.

"Don't get out. Just watch," Father said, winding down the window on his side. The children looked happy in their routine. One kid fell down while running and started crying. An older woman quickly came to his rescue and took the child indoors.

Father nodded. "Good, I hired the right people to look after them."

"What is this place?" I asked.

"An orphanage for the children of war and tsunami victims." There was a look of excitement in his face. "I set it up last year. When I die, it will be named the Cyril Gunasekera Orphanage. This is the best thing I have done with my life."

"Why is it such a well guarded secret?"

"Because I am savouring the art of giving. The moment people find out, it will become a circus. They'll call it the act of a guilty conscience. First I maim them with my arms dealing, then I comfort them with an orphanage, they'll say."

"Why are you showing it to me?"

"Because I am trying to do what you have done and yet I have such a long way to go."

"Well, at least you have the money to spare."

"But I don't have time."

He let his words hang inside the car.

Then he wound up the window, instructed Jamis to drive back, and settled in his seat. "I discovered a prostate problem soon after I married Lana. Not good."

"There are treatments. You could go abroad."

"I was scared of losing my erection with a nubile wife. Now I have left it a bit late. I have to go in for major surgery. It's spread."

I took his hand. It was bony and gnarled. He let me stroke it.

"*Putha*. I am going to write to my contacts in LA—you have to take your paintings there. I can only do small bits from here. You must take our story across the world."

Now as I sat here in my studio, I realized that that day had been the turning point in my appreciation of my father.

***

We had dinner at the Galle Face Hotel. Nimal had politely declined attending as he knew that this would be a rare opportunity for the three offspring of the late Cyril Gunasekera to reconnect. I liked the old-world charm of this colonial hotel that held the many triumphs and tragedies of the nation in its bosom. It was relaxing to sit on the patio with a smorgasbord of seafood and cocktails, watching the sun set on the Indian Ocean. When we were children, Father had brought us to this hotel on many an occasion, and we had flown kites on the Galle Face Green, when it had still been a green.

Anil, Shamila and I were quiet during the meal, helping ourselves to delicious mouthfuls of crab, shrimp, cuttle fish and king fish while settling back into our memories. I had also brought them here because I knew we would not bump into Lana—the GFH was too staid for her.

Shamila drained her pina colada and sighed in contentment, then settled back in her rattan lounge chair. "I hope I can afford to come back to Sri Lanka like this more often. I hope Father considered that when writing his will."

"Oh, I think you will be well off," Anil squeezed out, just before he slid a shrimp off a long skewer into his mouth. He munched, spittle hovering on the edges of his mouth, then swallowed, and said, "You were his pet."

"I wish I could have understood him in his last years. Especially after he married his whore."

I recalled my trip with our father to the orphanage. I hadn't told my siblings about it because it would have confused them. My father had never been a charitable sort.

"Our stay-at-home-boy Rohit knew him best," Anil said, signalling the waiter for a refill of his whiskey sour. I did not elaborate on Father's last months. I sipped my glass of white wine and gazed at a solitary steamer crossing the horizon like a worm moving across the window sill.

"I wished I hadn't screamed at him the last time I was here," Shamila said, "when I came for his wedding."

Anil's eyes narrowed. "What happened?"

"I told him that he was making a mistake with Lana, a woman younger than his daughter. I told him it made me think of him as a pedophile."

Anil coughed. "That wouldn't have gone down well at all!"

Anil's drink arrived and we sat in silence. I decided to paint that ship moving across the skyline when I got home. The hues of vermillion and grey interspersing over a dimming indigo sky were marking their presence in my imagination.

Shamila opened up again. "He didn't speak to me after that. He just had Jamis drive me to the airport two days later."

"Did you at least write to him?" Anil asked. "Afterwards?"

"I wrote many times but he wouldn't reply."

"He talked about you afterwards," I said. "He was angry that his pride was preventing him from reaching out to you."

"Poor Father," Shamila said, sniffling. "I hope he realized that we loved him, even if we…I…screamed at him occasionally."

"He knew," I lied.

Anil drained his glass. "This is all getting very sad. I vote we go to the Cave. It's a new night spot I discovered a few days ago, not far from here. Great disco music. Nice guys and gals. Shamila , you might even get lucky!"

Shamila's face brightened. "That sounds great. I'm all for it." She was already rising and grabbing her handbag. "Let me freshen up."

I signalled the waiter for the bill.

***

The Cave made me tense, although I tried to participate by grabbing a corner at the bar and nursing an iced tea. The place was dim, packed, and full of young people throwing money around. A strobe light in the centre of the small dancing space made the room wobble and flicker, and the music was too loud to allow for conversation. The economic hardship facing the rest of our war-ravaged country was not evident here. This was another world, a world that people like my father had helped create with their industry, and thereby ensured that the rewards only went to a few.

Anil recognized two heavily made-up local women as soon as we entered and was dragged onto the floor by them. Shamila sat with me for a few minutes, sighing, waiting like a bitch in heat for any stray dog to oblige. I bought her a double scotch which she gulped down gratefully, and then she decided to go and freshen up (again?). On her way back, I saw her talking to a couple of guys by the entrance, and in no time she had dragged them onto the crowded dance floor, hands over her head, gyrating and rubbing hips with one of the men who looked ten years younger.

Looking at my brother and sister, both fast approaching middle age, if not there already, cavorting like teenagers, I began to understand my father's disappointment in them. I began to dread what tomorrow would bring when the will was to be read.

A commotion broke out on the dance floor and I saw two burly guys, bouncers, rush from the bar area to the scene of the action. The dancers on the floor had parted to reveal two women locked in combat under the strobe.

Anil staggered over, his shirt dishevelled and drenched in sweat. "Rohit—come! We need to separate them!"

The bouncers had got to the two brawling women, and when they were pulled apart, I was not surprised to see my sister and Lana screaming invective at each other; they had been finishing the unfinished business from their last entanglement, it seemed. I had misjudged Lana showing up in a dive like this.

Anil hissed into my ear. "That hussy was here with a guy half our father's age."

I shrugged. "Perhaps that's the type of guy she should have gone for all along."

I saw Shamila wrestle free from her captor for a brief moment to land a kick on Lana's shin. Lana screamed and spat but did not reach her adversary. This time the bouncers pulled the women completely away from each other's reach to either end of the dance floor.

I grabbed Anil and we went over to the bouncer holding onto Shamila, whose blouse was now ripped; finger nail scratches ran down her exposed neck and half-naked breasts, the latter threatening to spill out of a perilously teetering bra.

I peeled off a couple of thousand rupees; my hard earned savings that I had known were going to be needed for this family visit. "Sorry for the trouble. We will take her home," I said.

The man pocketed the money quickly. "She bites like a snake. Yes, get her out of here. If they hadn't been women, we would have called the police."

As we herded the sobbing Shamila out of a side door, I caught a glance of Lana being embraced by a tall blonde man in a jacket, and being walked over to a table on the edge of the dance floor.

In the taxi, Shamila wailed and held onto me, her tears wetting my cheek and collar. "I'm such a failure, Rohit. I should have clawed her eyes out."

"At least you landed her a good kick," Anil piped up from the front passenger seat. "I think you won the fight just with that blow."

I shook my head and held her closer to me for the rest of the ride home. I was going to have to paint that picture of the ship on the horizon tonight; it was the only form of therapy open to me.

***

Horace Pieris, LL.B, QC (London) JD (USA) was one of my father's oldest friends. They had been in university together, and Horace still practiced law in his crumbling office, a renovated colonial bungalow behind the law courts in Panchikawatta. Passed up for judge several times due to his irascible and incorruptible stances, he was a pariah in the political establishment but the darling of clients wanting to know that their secrets would go to the grave with him.

Anil, Shamila and I were assembled in Horace's outer office, which had rattan chairs, a water cooler with no drinking cups, a row of metal filing cabinets, and dusty papers in bundles piled in corners. A military looking secretary in her sixties, worked a typewriter and a clunky old desktop computer outside Horace's door, looking up from her reading lenses from time to time to make sure that we had not run away or were not going to spy upon the many client secrets strewn about the room. I was grateful for the major domo's presence, for it kept us in check when Lana and her boyfriend waltzed into the room.

"Ah, you are the wife?" the secretary asked, rising. "Wait, I will get a chair."

She went out into a side room and emerged with another rattan chair. She placed it down for Lana and then looked up at her blonde companion. "And who are you?"

The man's accent was heavily Russian. "I vit Lana."

"Relative?" The major domo's eyes narrowed like a hawk's as she surveyed the man from head to foot.

"No. Friend."

"Stay outside, please. Only family are needed here. There is a chair in the veranda." She shooed the man outside. Lana sighed, carried her chair to the extreme end of the room, away from the three of us, and sat down. She buried her nose in a magazine from the pile of faded literature on a side table. Given that it was a Reader's Digest issue from several years ago, I doubted it had anything of interest to her other than for being a safe barrier from her three step children.

The secretary returned, surveyed us in our respective corners, grunted in satisfaction, went back to her desk and busied herself with her work. I noticed that she seemed most adept at using the typewriter, and swore under her breath regularly whenever she had to switch to the computer.

Our strained silence, punctuated only by anxious glances between us siblings, was relieved after about ten minutes when the door to Horace's office opened and the old man himself, dressed in his signature bow tie, white shirt and black pants, stood in the doorway and crooked his index finger at us several times. I guess he was saving his strength for later. We followed him in, like meek but hungry lambs.

I carried my chair and Anil's into the musty office as I knew we were going to be short of sitting accommodation, and I was right. Only two visitor armchairs stood in front of a teak table littered with paper. There were more piles of paper on the floor and all around the table. Horace's pipe lay in an overflowing ashtray, the quietly smouldering flame threatening to ignite the old parchments within range and burn the whole place down. Behind his desk, a wall cabinet held many hardbound tomes of legalese behind glass panelled doors. A world globe balanced on a bronze stand by the window and creaked on its hinges every time a gust of wind blew in. I was willing to bet that none of the new countries that had emerged since the break-up of the British Empire were located on it.

Horace was an anachronism. He stood just over five feet, reed-thin with a stentorian voice. He was bald except for a fringe around his pate that fell over his collar. His glasses magnified his eyes out of proportion to his narrow face. Attempts at growing a moustache had resulted in two drooping fangs of grey hair that licked at the corners of his thin-lipped mouth. I made a note to return one day and sketch this scene and its inhabitant: a vanishing and priceless portrait of our colonial legacy.

Horace stepped behind his desk, picked up a bulky manila file and cleared his throat. He looked like a hybrid between an actor about to deliver his lines and a politician warming up to make a speech.

He focussed his enlarged eyes on Lana who had pulled one of the rattan chairs and placed it out of kicking range, for Shamila's foot was cocked and rocking to a nervous beat.

"Ah, you are the new wife?" Horace looked inside the file. "Svetlana…is that right?"

"Yez."

"I knew the first Mrs. Gunasekera, these children's mother. A capital lady," he said, and let the compliment hang heavy in the room.

Lana bit her lip and remained silent.

"Ah yes," Horace began, in earnest this time. "Cyril Gunasekera, my client and my long- time friend, entrusted me with a sacred duty which I am about to carry out to the best of my ability. He was a very wealthy man with assets both at home and overseas. And yet he was a very troubled man and he did not die happy. All we can do is ensure that at least his last wishes are complied with. I take it that you do not know that he changed his will a week before he…he passed away?"

"He did?" Lana sat up in her chair.

"Yes, I saw him in hospital outside of visiting hours per his request. It was also his wish that I keep this new will secret until he passed away. That is why I have summoned you here today."

I glanced at my brother and sister and saw that their faces had taken on a pale pallor. Sweat beaded Anil's brow and Shamila's leg was kicking faster.

"So let me deal with each of you in turn. First you, Mrs. Gunesekera, if you don't mind me calling you Mrs. Gunesekera. I understand…rather, I *know*, because I actually drafted it…that you had a pre-nuptial agreement with your husband. You were to receive a sum equivalent to ten million rupees, about a hundred thousand dollars, on his death. Nothing more, is that right?"

I heard the exhalation of breath on the part of Shamila. Anil whispered in my ear, "A bloody expensive screw!"

"Yez," said a downcast Lana.

Horace cleared his throat again. "In his latest will, Cyril…er, your husband, modified that to add another five hundred thousand dollars to your inheritance."

Lana's eyes widened in amazement and Shamila screamed, "The fucking idiot was out of his head!"

Horace swivelled on my sister, his tone cutting. "Shamila, I ask you to keep your mouth shut. I will not have any disrespect displayed in my office, and especially, not towards your dear departed father."

He returned to his manila folder. Something suggested to me that Horace was enjoying his theatrical performance. His voice took on a silken note.

"But Mrs. Gunesekera, there is a caveat to you earning this bonus."

Lana shrugged. "But I will always obey my husband's wishes." A look of humility had arrived from somewhere and settled itself uncomfortably on her countenance. A painful mouth fart squeezed out from Shamila's side and was extinguished only when Horace swung back in her direction.

After everyone had settled down once again, Horace continued. "Mrs. Gunesekera, you will receive the extra money in tranches of one hundred thousand dollars a year for five continuous years providing you work as a volunteer in the Savitri Home for Incurables. If you stop for any reason, even for illness or a vacation, the money will be withdrawn."

Lana had gone ghostly white. "But…but I don't understand. What is this place? What must I do?"

"Your husband notes here that you have a high degree of intolerance towards those who have fallen by the way, he writes of your distaste for getting your hands dirty and of your desire to indulge in frivolous pursuits, like shopping and night-clubbing. He says that he believes this experience at Savitri will broaden and deepen you as a human being. The Savitri Home is a place where the absolutely crippled and the living dead are dumped. They shit and vomit on themselves and their wards stink if not kept clean. The only clean things in that place are the souls of the incurables, many who have never lived a normal life in this world from the day they were born. Your job will be to clean their bodies and their beds to better reflect the purity of their souls."

"But…but I have not the training. How could Cyril expect this of me?" Lana's manicured fingers were gripping the edges of Horace's untidy table.

"Serve her bloody right," Shamila murmured under her breath.

"You will receive all the training you need at the Home, Mrs. Gunesekera," Horace continued. "They are always grateful to have volunteers. Of course, you can take your originally promised one hundred grand and scram and forego this generous top-up."

Lana collapsed back into her chair. Five hundred thousand dollars was too much of an incentive for her to run away from.

Leaving my step mother to wallow in her dilemma, Horace turned on my brother.

"Anil, my boy, it's good to see you after all these years. I remember your father was so looking forward to you playing for the First Eleven cricket team in your old school, our old school. What happened there?"

Anils's face flushed. "That was a long time ago. I think the competition was stiff and the coaches had their favourites."

"Your father says here that you always had a way of blaming others for your lack of accomplishment."

Anil flushed again and I feared he was going to have another coronary. He coughed and said nothing. Horace looked into the folder. "Your father also says that you like to start up companies but they usually fizzle out. Well, he is giving you a chance to be in a decision making role in an organization that will last a bit longer than the ones you have dabbled in. Your father has entrusted me and his accountants to sell his house and property, the shares in his corporations around the world, all his assets in fact, and set up a foundation that will look after certain charities, the Savitri Home being one. The other is the newly opened Cyril Gunesekera Orphanage. The Foundation, also aptly named after your father, will have an executive board comprised of some of the best minds and influence in the country. You have been reserved a board seat and will represent the Gunasekera family. Oh, and by the way, it is a non-paying position although expenses will be covered. Everyone on this board is doing their job on a volunteer basis—it's their way, like it was your father's—of paying back."

"That's all?" was all Anil managed to croak in response. "That's all my father left me?"

"That's all he has left *you*, but he has made provision for his two grandchildren—your children—to finish their college education. He has decreed that the Foundation, upon receipt of *authenticated transcripts* from both your children's institutions of tertiary education, reimburse them the cost of their tuition spent to earn those degrees. There will be no advance payments to them like before."

This time it was Anil's turn to collapse. He let out a loud groan and did not make any attempt to suppress it.

Horace turned to Shamila, who promptly rose. "I can't stand this," she threw back at him. "What does my father think he can do? Torture us from his grave?"

"Sit down, young lady," Horace said, twirling his straggly moustache. "You will find this very interesting."

I rose and put my hand on Shamila's shoulder and she wilted into me. I helped her regain her seat.

Launching into his throat-clearing preamble, Horace said, "Shamila, your father realized that you were a half-person without a child of your own. All the tantrums, the yelling, the divorces. He has a provision for the Foundation to fund a child picked by you for adoption."

"How can I adopt a child and live like a single mum in a bloody expensive place like Sydney, with a crippling mortgage? Does he want me to be poorer than I already am?"

"Ah, yes, as for the mortgage, that will be fully paid up by the Foundation. You will be debt free to adopt your child."

"And what do we—me and this child—live on?"

"Your father says that everyone has to live by the sweat of their brow. In exchange for you paying a faceless bank two thousand dollars a month in mortgage fees you can spend that on your adopted son or daughter. And yes, you will still have to work for your living."

I patted Shamila's hand as she burst into tears.

"I guess it's my turn," I said. "I never expected much from my father, so make it quick. And if there is any money, with conditions attached, you can forget about it. If there is just money and no conditions, then you can divide the cash between my brother and sister here. I never cared for my father's ill gotten gains, however much he has tried to atone for his actions now by diverting his money to worthy causes which need other people's sweat equity."

"Ah the stubborn one—good speech, by the way." Horace's giant eyes threatened to swallow me up. His chin was pointing up defiantly, for I had risen from my chair during this exchange. "Well, your father was right about you. You will be happy to note that he wanted me to thank you for being his conscience and for reminding him of the better man that he could have become. No, he has not left you any money, with or without conditions. But he has left you these letters, which I will mail, upon your approval." He extended a handful of letters to me.

I opened the first one.

My father's crisp cursive writing stared back at me. The letter was addressed to the curator of the National Gallery in London, introducing me and my work. The other letters were similar: to the principal of the Musee D'Orsay in Paris, the director of the Civico Museo in Milan and so on. By the tone of each of the letters, my father seemed to have known the head of the respective institution personally; he hadn't just been an arms dealer, as he had classified himself in his last days, but also a man of culture who had cultivated a rich roster of personal contacts. Perhaps he had set out to make these connections for my benefit, and now I was seeing the fruits of his efforts. Much as I wanted to fling the letters back at Horace, the sheer audacity of my father's reach into the art world, something I could never have dreamed of achieving, took the wind out of me and it was my turn to fall back in my chair.

Horace placed the manila folder back on his cluttered desk. "This has been a hard day for you all, for me too. I suggest we adjourn now. No doubt, some of you will be leaving the country soon, maybe sooner than expected. You have a month to deliberate on these provisions and get back to me on how you would like your components executed. In thirty days, if I have no response from you, all proceeds on the sale of Cyril's assets go to the Foundation, all offers of financial assistance to you and your loved ones will be null and void, Anil, your board seat offer will be withdrawn, and Rohit, I am advised to destroy these letters of introduction. I will now bid you all a good day as I have to be in court in half an hour."

***

"He manipulated us," Shamila said, sucking on the straw of her iced tea. "Just like he manipulated everyone in his life."

We were at the airport, three days after the meeting with Horace. Anil and Shamila had advanced their departure plans, both were flying on Air Lanka to Singapore and from there dispersing to their respective homes on either side of the Pacific.

Anil interjected. "But we have to assume good intent here. I don't mind the idea of flying in once a quarter for a board meeting of the Foundation, all expenses paid." He was already into a beer and it was only ten o'clock in the morning. Perhaps he was acclimatizing to Pacific Time.

"Rumour has it that Lana was seen at the Savitri Home yesterday, meeting with the matron in charge," I contributed, sipping my ice coffee.

"She'll quit after the first day when her delicate finger nails are caked with shit." Shamila said.

"Or she will walk away with an extra half a million dollars and a purer soul in five years," I said.

"I didn't know the old bugger had so much money. More than us beggars in the so called First World," Anil said.

"Commissions on arms sales are priced in US dollars. Payable anywhere." I reminded him.

Anil nodded. Then he asked me. "Are you going to use those letters of introduction?"

"I don't know."

"It's all about connections, Rohit. Don't let your pride get in the way. I wish I had connections in the Valley—it would make my hunt for venture funds that much easier. It's a pity that Father had no connections there."

"He did not invest in invention, only in destruction." Shamila said. Anil downed his glass and contemplated another. Then he put the empty glass down and looked at his watch. "Time to go through customs and immigration. And what is our sweet *nangi* going to do?"

Shamila stood up, her iced tea unfinished. She slung her several hand bags over her shoulders. "Accompany you to Singapore for starters. Then I'll also think about it."

"Don't take too long," I reminded her. "We do not have much time.

I hugged and kissed them, and felt a pang of regret at their parting. I wished we could have all been living in Colombo like we had done years ago, I wished that my father had not accumulated all this money, and that we were not strangers who had just had our private lives wrenched open for a few days, making us resent what we had seen under our sarongs, so to speak.

As I left the airport terminal I couldn't help but feel still tied to my siblings, not by mere blood but by the strings of a master puppeteer, who even in death was trying to lead us on his Enlightened Path.

Another painting was starting take shape in my head, Dali-esque, and yet the still-to-be-produced *Puppet Master* would be the only thing of beauty about my father's life. I would stand it next to Mother's portrait in my studio and let him live forever in her shadow.

Uphill or Down?

The old man watched the four-wheel drive heading up the hill, raising a trail of dust, just like it had come to him in his dream. This was an off-schedule transport; not the one that brought weekly groceries to the monastery and then continued on to him, nor one of the farm vehicles belonging to the cloister.

The vehicle would arrive in ten minutes. It had to pass the Benedictine monastery at the highest point overlooking the valley and wind down over two smaller hills to end at his residence.

Time to get ready. He pulled his cardigan tighter around him and headed indoors, passing the roses, the hydrangea and the anthuriams; he would miss them the most. When he was not writing or healing, he had spent his days pruning, fertilizing, and watering; infusing love into the plants, a love that had outlived family and friends. He had returned home after the final goodbye to his dear wife Gwen at the hospice last year. Today, the flowers looked like they needed water, but he did not have time. *Perhaps later, if this is a false alarm.*

He entered the house. It had once been an estate manor, converted to a guest house in the '70s, then abandoned when the tourists stopped coming in the aftermath of the civil war. He had rented it cheap; the owner was relieved to have at least one long-stay guest paying in valued foreign currency.

He walked through the cavernous entrance hall, past the wide mahogany staircase that led to the upstairs rooms that were now closed and filling with dust. He entered the study to the left. Just this room, and the one at the other end of the hall, his en-suite bedroom, were in use. A woman from the village used the outdoor kitchen when she came in three times a week to cook and clean for him.

The study, lined with bookcases, contained withered volumes of imperial war history, featuring personages from the now-defunct British, Dutch and Portuguese empires, captured in all their privilege, inscrutability and obnoxiousness. *Their legacy of selfishness still flows in the veins of this country.* He had read the fragile tomes on solitary evenings by the fireplace, looking for clues in the past that would explain the present. He kept the fire lit despite the tropical latitude, as nights in this mountain retreat were cold and clammy.

He switched on his laptop computer, the only sign of modernity around; even the telephone was a rotary device, more ornamental than functional; he rarely used the telephone. His lawyer and the custodian of his estate sent him occasional e-mails from New York, until the Internet service cut out two weeks ago and no-one at the local service provider seemed to know how to restore it.

Eight minutes to go. The vehicle had passed the monastery; it wasn't stopping, but continuing towards the guest house. It went around the first bend and grew ominous with its temporary absence. He felt a sinking feeling in his stomach and his palms began to sweat. *Even Christ sweated blood in the garden of Gethsemane.* Then he saw another vehicle start up the hill, regurgitating the dust raised by the four-wheel drive. This vehicle had not been in his dream.

***

"You'll incur everyone's wrath," Father Michael had told him two months ago. They had been having a quiet meal at the monastery on a rare evening when Fr. Michael had the free time to entertain. A newspaper was spread out before them.

"Do you believe in taking sides, then?" the old man asked.

"This is not about taking sides, Ben. It is about survival. We run the farm, employ the local people, do not get involved in politics, and survive."

The old man looked out across acres of fruit trees running downhill from the monastery: neat rows of orange, wood apple, peaches. In the abattoir, a pig squealed an unearthly yell that faded into life-ebbing grunts.

"I came back to be unbiased," he replied. "I've spent my whole life taking sides of the rich and powerful, because it was safe."

"They will have you killed."

The old man nodded gravely. "I have considered that possibility. After Gwen died last year, I wonder if death will be a release."

"Is that why you came back?"

"There was nothing more for me in America, except dodder into old age, alone, end up in a nursing home and be kept ridiculously alive with a multitude of drugs that my estate could well afford. Returning to the land of my birth, the place I left unresolved in youthful anger was a better proposition."

"And now you get everyone angry with your writing."

"'If the suit matches, put it on'—isn't that the saying?"

The man-servant cleared the table and Fr. Michael took out his pipe, puffing clouds of smoke that wafted through the open window, colliding with the incoming mist. The old man shivered. The thought of death bothered him, despite seeing much of it in his profession.

"You were an important man in America," Fr. Michael continued. "Don't tell me you did not exercise discretion?"

"I did, until it hurt me to look in the mirror."

"Very well, if anything... untoward... were to happen." Fr. Michael's face remained impassive. "We will request that you have a Christian burial in our cemetery."

Amid fruit trees, deceased labourers and animal carcases. The old man looked downhill towards the boundary of the monastery where the graveyard lay.

He slid a sealed envelope towards Fr. Michael. "These are instructions for the disposal of my body. Promise to read them only when you have to."

The priest looked at the white rectangle, reluctant to touch it, sensing the challenge it must contain.

"Even Christ picked up his cross when asked," the old man said.

"Humph…" Fr. Michael tucked the envelope inside the folds of his cassock.

The old man rose to leave. Fr. Michael placed his pipe on a saucer; it tipped and spilled smouldering ashes onto the porcelain. "I envy you, Ben. If it happens, I hope there is no 'three hours agony' involved."

"I think their technology has improved, since."

***

He reviewed the documents quickly—they had taken a long time to compose, percolating in his mind for months, finally spilling out in a frenzy of words these last two weeks. The loss of access to the outside world via the Internet had prompted him to hurry. He saved them on a memory stick—*how small these things are getting these days and yet how much more data they stored.*

He lingered over the first file—the letter to the editor of the independent newspaper across the border that had started the riot in the local media which had, to that point, loved him for bashing the rebels and their terror tactics. This letter began a shift in position: hinting of complicity by the ruling government to keep the war going, for many were making fat commissions on arms sales—who cared if a few village youth got killed in the north?

That letter had prompted Fr. Michael's urgent invitation to dinner. That letter had caused the curtain of military protection around him to be withdrawn. That letter had led to the sudden disconnection of his Internet service, he believed.

Two minutes. He pulled the memory stick out of the laptop and covered it with its smooth cylindrical cap. It looked like a harmless container of Blistick. It may not stop the war but it had enough incriminating material to embarrass both sides internationally; even to cut off foreign aid for awhile; aid that went for the procurement of arms, not for rehabilitating innocent victims of the conflict. *My contribution to the war effort.*

Now for the messy part. He pulled out a tube of haemorrhoid crème and squeezed a liberal coating onto his fingers. He dropped his pants and applied the crème into his anus, fingers reaching deep. He had practised this routine frequently and was used to the sloppiness, discomfort and soiling that ensued. He tossed the remnant tube out of the window into the dense flower bed. Squatting, he inserted the memory stick into his arse and pushed until it could go no further. He pulled up his pants and took a few steps to manoeuvre the device into a comfortable position. He now understood and sympathized with anyone walking around with foreign objects stuck in their bodies—hearing aids, breathing tubes, pacemakers, tampons. He hoped Fr. Michael would not be squeamish when he followed the letter of instructions, if he did.

He returned to his laptop, deleted all its documents and powered the machine down. The four-wheel drive had pulled into his driveway. On the hill, the second vehicle, a nondescript truck, passed the monastery—another unscheduled transport.

He walked out of the front door. Four wiry men in civilian clothes lounged around the vehicle; two carried automatic rifles. The leader, wearing sunglasses, a baseball cap and a thick chain around his neck with the undisguised cyanide capsule dangling from it, spoke. "You are Ben Alfonso?"

"Yes," the old man replied.

"Show us your files." Northern accented English, the voice of an educated man, one who seemed to have been left out on the margins of society. The old man knew this type; he was one himself.

"You don't waste time," he said, trying to sound casual.

"Normally, we just shoot. Come."

The leader followed him as he turned back towards the house. Out of the corner of his eye he looked up towards the monastery. A white cassocked figure was walking its sloping grounds—Fr. Michael. The priest would be at vespers at this hour, even he suspected something unnatural taking place.

The old man looked for signs of the second vehicle, but it must have gone behind one of the smaller hills. The sound of its engine would be audible only by the last turn in the road. He saw the leader pause and follow his gaze. Then a solid piece of metal nudged his back and his captor said, "Hurry up."

They entered the hall and the leader paused opposite a row of faded colonial paintings depicting the country when it was just a collection of trading posts for foreign conquerors.

"Is this your house?" the man asked.

"No, I just rent here. This house reflects the decline of our country."

"You call yourself a countryman? Then why do you attack us so much in your writing?"

"Because I don't subscribe to your methods. Strapping bombs around orphans to kill innocent people, or using kids as human shields is not my idea of a just war. Remember, I volunteered in the military hospital up north until recently."

"Do you know what the other side has done to us?"

"I saw that too. That is why I have not spared them in my writing either."

They reached the study. The old man pointed towards the laptop. "All I have is in there."

The old man turned towards the leader and saw the pistol in the man's hand. The leader scanned the rows of books. "Foreign literature. Nothing about our own country."

"The colonizers were not interested in us."

"Neither is the present government," the leader said.

"True."

The leader opened and closed drawers, rifled through papers, not finding what he was looking for. Finally, he grabbed a newspaper file press, hanging from a leather strap on the wall.

"Your writings?" he asked, thumbing the loose sheets trapped between the hinged wooden bars of the file.

"Guilty."

The leader ripped the newspapers into pieces, arranged them in a pile on the floor and held a match to it.

"You will set the house on fire," the old man said, the sinking feeling taking hold again.

"Why do you care? You are just renting, no?"

The leader ripped the laptop off its connections. "Let's go outside, before it gets too hot in here."

They walked outdoors with the smell of smoke following them.

The other men had not moved from their positions around the vehicle; they stood indolent in the peaceful sunny surroundings. The old man looked at his flowers—he will miss them—if he'd only watered them today. Across the way, Fr. Michael was standing by the fence, staring. There was an implied plea in his posture. Was he pleading silently with the rebels, or with God?

"Is your cyanide pill quicker than a bullet?" the old man asked.

The leader grinned. "It depends where the bullet is applied."

"I am old enough to be your grandfather. I hope you will be kind when you pull the trigger."

The leader laughed again. "You are not as strong as the writer of those articles."

"We are all cowards in the face of death."

"Why did you come back here?"

"I was a doctor in a private hospital in America. I cared for people who had never known what real conflict was. The well heeled ones—people who would complain if they suffered a heart attack and had to cut down on caviar. People who alternated between diets and gorging, or overdosed on drugs and alcohol because they were bored. They were their own enemy and I couldn't do much for them. Still, they did not hurt others."

"So you came here to die?"

"I came here to expose the greed in people's hearts that cause innocents to die. You are all greedy, you know. Your big chief is hungry for power. He knows how to wage a guerrilla war, but he does not know how to run a country."

The leaders' brows furrowed. The old man looked around. There was still no sign of that second vehicle.

"Did you bring reinforcements with you?" he asked the leader.

"What do you mean?"

"There was a truck following you, about a mile down the road."

The leader leaped into life and yelled a command to his men who started to bestir. Just then the air erupted in a cacophony of gun fire.

The old man dove on his face and felt sand in his mouth as his world filled with the sounds of dying men. *Why did I open my big mouth?* He saw the three rebels by the four-wheel drive rupture into minor explosions of blood and body parts. The vehicle's windows shattered instantly and its chassis shook with pinging bullets.

Almost as soon as it started, the firing stopped; echoes of gunshots ricocheted across the valley like the diminishing strains of a grandfather clock that had lost its spring.

He rose painfully and remained kneeling until his legs regained strength. The rebel leader lay bullet-riddled, inches away; his face contorted. The laptop, bent out of shape, was in the dirt beside the dead man. Flames leaped out of the open windows of the house.

A hand reached out and he took it gratefully. Uniformed soldiers ran into the yard. The truck made its appearance around the bend, a soldier at the wheel.

The old man looked at the owner of the extended hand: dark complexion, brush moustache, beret, combat gear and the insignia of a captain; and eyes like diamonds in lustre.

"Thank you," the old man said, glad his sphincter had not given way in the excitement—it would have been hard to explain the contents of his stools. "I didn't think I warranted rescuing. Not after I insulted your president."

The captain nodded. "We got here just in time." He pointed at the dead rebel leader. "This guy is pretty high up in their hierarchy. You must be important."

"I'm grateful that you came," the old man, said dusting himself. The captain shouted orders. The shattered bodies of the three subordinate rebels were tossed into the rear of the truck. The four-wheel drive was secured to the military vehicle with a tow rope. The captain picked up the twisted laptop and tossed it into the truck.

"Where does that road lead?" The captain pointed to the roadway leading down from the monastery along which everyone had arrived.

"It dead-ends in a grove of trees behind this house. We pile our garbage there for burning."

The captain issued more commands; two soldiers picked up the rebel leader's body and took him downhill towards the garbage heap. The old man could not understand this.

"Can you save the house?" he asked, knowing the futility of his question even as he asked it. Flames were licking at the roof.

The captain shook his head. "I am afraid not."

"Then I'd better get to the monastery. Can you give me a ride up there?"

The truck started and moved slowly, tugging the battered four-wheel drive behind it. The soldiers walked alongside the departing vehicles.

The captain's flinty eyes were back on the old man. "We have to take a little walk. You and I."

That's when it all became clear to him. The sinking feeling returned, and stayed this time. *Ah, yes. I really cannot shit in my pants now.*

"And you don't have a choice of cyanide vis-a-vis a bullet do you?"

The flinty look sharpened. "No."

The old man looked up the hill. Fr. Michael was walking back towards the monastery. The priest was probably reassured now that he had seen the troops arrive and watched the gunfight. *Not so fast Father, turn around, a witness may deter them.* Fr. Michael continued his walk. The old man wanted to scream—*Fr. Michael, will you truly pick up your cross? The one I have given you?* The aging priest stepped indoors and closed the large wooden doors of the sacristy.

The old man walked to the road with the captain. On his left, the vehicles clattered along, raising dust in his face; the soldiers with their backs turned, followed wearily up the hill. Further up, lay the monastery: a safe haven just out of reach. To his right, the path zigzagged around a bend, where he visualized the dirt heap with its putrefying vegetables, fruit and the leftovers of the cook's meal from two days ago, a magnet for stray dogs and scavengers. The dump will add a new flavour into its mix today—the dead rebel leader, and who else? All dressed up to point the accusing finger at the rebels.

The old man sighed. He had not imagined it ending this way. His life's achievements, the ones he could be proud of, were in those smouldering newspapers in the study of the burning house, and nestling in a layer of shit and haemorrhoid crème between his legs. Still, his situation beat the vacant faces of patients he had cared for in distant America; people who had lived and died and found no purpose for their suffering. He thought he heard Gwen calling to him.

He turned towards his captor. "Well, Captain, in which direction shall we walk—uphill, or down?"

Glossary

ammi	mother
aney	expression of sadness or pity
araliya	Frangipani flowers
ayah	servant, nanny
ayyo	exclamation of disappointment
baba	baby
balli	bitch
bandakka	okra
beedi	small hand-rolled cigarette
bhikkhu	Buddhist monk
bo tree	sacred fig tree
brinjals	eggplant
brinjals theldala	eggplant cooked in oil and spices
Budhu Ammo!	Mother of God!
Burghers	minority ethnic group of European heritage
chappatis	unleavened flat bread
hartals	civil riots
jaggery	dark solid sugar from palm sap
karapincha	curry leaves
kassippu	bootleg alcoholic drink
kavums	traditional oil cakes
lafais	poor Burghers
leg before wicket (LBW)	unexpected pregnancy before marriage
loku nona	the lady of highest rank in a household
lunu miris	a savoury sambol mix
maama	maternal uncle
mahattaya	Mister or gentleman
mallum	local dish of shredded leaf vegetables
massala vaddes	a South Indian/Tamil snack
missie	miss
nangi	younger sister
nombera eka	number one
pottu	decorative dot worn on forehead by women
pukka sahib	a true gentleman
putha	son
rampe	Pandan leaf used to flavour cooking
rastiadu	layabout
rotties	flatbread

sala	drawing room
santhosam	bribe
seeni sambol	sweet onion sambol
shalwar khamees	traditional dress in South Asia
Sinhalese	majority ethnic group in Sri Lanka
Sinhala	language spoken by the Sinhalese, sometimes also used to describe the ethnic group: i.e. Sinhala people
sinnathurai	estate superintendent
stuthi	thank you
sudu mahattaya	fair-skinned gentleman
Tamils	minority ethnic group of South Indian origin
thathi	father
thosai kades	restaurants that serve South Indian food
Vesak	festival commemorating the birth, enlightenment and death of the Buddha
walauwa	family manor house

Author Bio

Shane Joseph began writing as a teenager living in Sri Lanka and has never stopped. From an early surge of short stories and radio play scripts, to humorous corporate skits, travelogues, case studies and technical papers, then novels, more short stories and essays, he continues to pursue the three pages-a-day maxim and keeps writer's block at bay.

His career stints include: stage and radio actor, pop musician, encyclopaedia salesman, lathe machine operator, airline executive, travel agency manager, vice president of a global financial services company, software services salesperson, project manager and management consultant.

Self-taught, with four degrees under his belt obtained through distance education, Shane is an avid traveller and has visited one country for every year of his life. He fondly recalls incidents during his travels as real lessons he could never have learned in school: husky driving in Finland with no training, trekking the Inca Trail in Peru through an unending rainstorm, hitch-hiking in Australia without a map, escaping a wild elephant in Zambia, and being stranded without money in Denmark, are some of his memories.

Shane is a graduate of the Humber School for Writers in Toronto and studied under the mentorship of Giller Prize and Canadian Governor General's Award winning author David Adams Richards. His published works include the novels *Redemption in Paradise* (2004), *After the Flood* (2009) and *The Ulysses Man* (2011). His previously published short story collection is *Fringe Dwellers* (2008). His short fiction has appeared in literary journals and anthologies internationally. His blog at www.shanejoseph.com/blog is widely syndicated.

After immigrating (twice), raising a family, building a career, and experiencing life's many highs and lows, Shane has carved out a niche in Cobourg, Ontario with his wife, Sarah, where he continues to work, write stories, and sing and play guitar in a dance band.

More details on Shane's work can be found on his website at www.shanejoseph.com

Acknowledgements

I wish to thank the many readers who have read these stories and given me valuable feedback, in particular: Brian Mullally, Patricia Calder, George Boycott, Felicity Sidnell Reid, Stephanie Wickramanayake and Waheed Rabbani.

To Jake Hogeterp, whose critical eye went beyond the page into structure and style.

And to Blue Denim Press, for publishing what could have been an orphaned collection, as marooned as the characters that populate its stories.

Shane Joseph
2013

www.ingramcontent.com/pod-product-compliance
Lightning Source LLC
Chambersburg PA
CBHW020627110726
47899CB00002B/678